Also by Anna Priemaza

Kat and Meg Conquer the World

FAN THE FAME

ANNA PRIEMAZA

HARPER TEEN
An Imprint of HarperCollins Publishers

To my parents,
who taught me to work hard.
And to Lorne, who helps keep me from
working myself to death.

HarperTeen is an imprint of HarperCollins Publishers.

Fan the Fame
Copyright © 2019 by Anna Priemaza
All rights reserved. Printed in Germany.
No part of this book may be used or reproduced in any manner
whatsoever without written permission except in the case of brief
quotations embodied in critical articles and reviews. For information
address HarperCollins Children's Books, a division of HarperCollins
Publishers, 195 Broadway, New York, NY 10007.
www.epicreads.com

ISBN 978-0-06-256084-1

Typography by Torborg Davern
19 20 21 22 23   CPIG   10 9 8 7 6 5 4 3 2 1
❖
First Edition

@LumberLegs: Heading to LOTSCON! NERD
CONVENTION WOOOOOO! About to board the plane!
TO THE RIFT! Oops I mean, TO THE CON!
[2.3K likes]

ONE

Lainey

THEY'RE CALLING THE GIRL MY BROTHER, CODY, UNCEREMONIOUSLY DUMPED a slut. It's all over social media. I'm not even friends with her, and still it makes it onto my feed. I scroll through the posts on my phone as Cody and I hover in the Boston airport near our gate, travelers rushing past as he flirts with yet another girl who's asked for his autograph. Not that there are that many girls who ask; Cody has several million YouTube subscribers on his gaming channel, but the majority of those fans are male.

I skip past another post about Janessa, my seventeen-year-old classmate who allegedly slept with my situationally famous twenty-one-year-old brother. Apparently someone overheard her talking about it in the bathroom. That's the way they phrase it: she slept with him, which makes her a slut. Never mind that Cody is the one who started it all, asking me about "that hot girl with the boobs" one day when he picked me up after school. And never mind that one of the posts says she was crying about losing her virginity, while when I asked Cody about her, he called her "just another hookup."

At least it's only my classmates who are talking about her. Judging by the way Cody flirted with every pretty, made-up girl he crossed paths with at the Boston gaming convention we were just at, his fans don't even know Janessa exists.

"Lainey! Stickers!" Cody barks at me now, and I hit the power button on my phone and shove it back in my pocket, returning to the job I'm supposed to be doing.

The Asian teen girl Cody's talking to is younger than I had registered out of the corner of my eye, maybe fourteen or so. She looked older at a glance because even in a winter coat, she actually has a figure. Lucky. My boobs didn't start growing until I was fifteen, and they grew for maybe six weeks, then decided that was enough and called it quits, the lazy jerks.

Cody must not have been flirting with her after all; she's only a kid.

As she grins at him, I want to tell her that she needs a new hero, but instead I sigh, pull a Codemeister sticker out of my pocket, and hand it to her, making her squeal before she goes running excitedly back to her parents. That's what I do as Cody's gaming convention roadie: hand out swag, carry his stuff, keep my mouth shut. In return Cody's paying me two hundred dollars in cash, room, food, and flights, and the chance to get out of our tiny prison of a town for my entire March break. We've just finished at PAX East in Boston and are headed to Toronto for LotSCON, the convention for the video game Legends of the Stone.

When Cody invited me along, I jumped at the chance to get away from home. In my defense, since Cody moved out a few years ago, I'd forgotten that spending large amounts of time with my brother sometimes makes me want to strangle him.

Cody has wandered back to our seats at the gate to rejoin Noogmeister, another of the six guys in the famous YouTube gaming group Team Meister. "If Lainey wasn't here," Cody tells him, "I'd totally have boned that."

I whirl around, cutting off Noog's laugh with my glare. Until this trip, I hadn't realized how often Cody makes jokes like that to his friends—or how often they egg him on just by laughing. "Cody!" I whisper-shout. "That girl's like fourteen!"

"So?"

I march toward them. "So you're twenty-one. That's illegal!" And gross. And so inappropriate. I thought it was bad enough that he apparently charmed a seventeen-year-old into sleeping with him.

Cody rolls his eyes. "Lainey, don't be a buzzkill."

"A buzzkill? I'm not trying to kill your buzz, I'm trying to stop you from being such a dickhead." I regret the words as soon as they escape my mouth. If there's a way to get through to Cody, it's not by calling him a dickhead.

"A dickhead? Really, Lainey? Am I going to have to tell Mom to have a bar of soap ready when you get home?" He's joking, but there's an edge of anger under his words.

Simply the mention of Mom's soap bar makes my own anger stretch tight inside me, like an elastic band. When we were kids, Mom'd wash my mouth out for failing to "talk like a lady," while Cody could say the exact same thing as me and Mom wouldn't bat an eye. But I've learned from experience that getting angry at Cody only makes him shut down, so I ignore the anger and back-track instead. "No, sorry, I'm just a bit wound up because people are calling Janessa a slut."

"Who?" Cody asks.

I throw my hands up. "Are you serious? Janessa! From my school! Blond hair, big eyebrows, quiet as a mouse. You apparently slept with her. Ringing any bells?" I barely know the girl, since she only moved to our school a year or two ago, but I'm not about to identify her to Cody by her boob size.

Cody puts his own hands up in surrender. "I'm joking! Of course I remember who Janessa is."

I glare at him. "Did you really sleep with her? She's *my* age! People are calling her a slut because of it."

Cody shrugs. "It's not my fault people are jerks."

Noog stands and steps up to us. "She slept with *this guy*?" he asks with a sneer, pointing his thumb toward my brother. "Then she *is* a slut for stooping that low."

"Hey!" Cody smacks him in the arm, and then Noog smacks him back, and then they're both laughing.

Dickheads.

Cody and I have fought for years about the obnoxious things he says, but I hadn't realized how bad things have gotten. Or maybe they've always been this bad, and I never realized it.

After seven days of listening to Cody joking crassly about girls to his friends, a sick feeling has built up in my stomach along with the usual rage that bubbles there. Because I'm fairly certain that if Cody doesn't change his ways, his jokes are going to turn into his reality, and he's going to end up the headline of some big new #metoo scandal.

Or, I realize, thinking of that fourteen-year-old he joked about banging, even end up in jail.

And though sometimes I want to knee my brother in the gut, I don't want him to end up in jail.

I should talk to him. Or get someone else to talk to him. Or something.

Right now, though, he and Noog are still grinning from their abhorrent jokes and all I can picture is how their heads are basically hamster dicks. Tiny, hairy hamster dickheads. Which, uh, is maybe not the best way to start off a heart-to-heart with my brother.

So instead, for now, I simply give them both the finger and then stalk away.

■　■　■

I'm on the plane and about to buckle my seat belt with a satisfying click when LumberLegs appears beside me in the aisle. He's not on Team Meister—though he's just as famous—but he spent most of the time at PAX East with us. I knew he was headed to LotSCON, too, but I hadn't realized he was on our flight. Most of the guys left last night.

"Would you mind switching?" he asks the woman to my right. "I was hoping to sit with my sister." He gestures toward me and holds his ticket out to her, his dark-brown hair flopping charmingly over the edges of his rectangular face.

She agrees, and then we're all standing and doing an awkward dance around each other as LumberLegs stumbles into his new seat beside me.

"Sister?" I echo as Legs fumbles for his seat belt.

"Friend," he corrects. His knee bumps mine as he pulls one of the seat belt buckles out from under his butt. "Didn't want her to say no."

My cheeks flush hot, even though he'd just as likely have switched to sit with one of the guys if they were in coach. Anything to keep from sitting alone. The sadness that he won't talk about oozes out of his pores like garlic, though none of the guys have seemed to notice so far. "You just took the middle seat and gave her the aisle," I point out. His knee is still touching mine, and I feel an urgent need to establish that I am most definitely not his sister. "She wasn't going to say no."

He stretches out his legs in the tiny space—or at least tries to—and the release of pressure on my leg is an absence I wasn't expecting to feel. He shrugs. "Couldn't risk it." He lets all his limbs relax, taking up so much more space than the petite woman who was there before him, not that I mind. We've been texting a lot since I helped Cody out for a single day of a convention in Columbus six months ago, and I spent more time with him at PAX East than with anyone else.

"You don't fly first class like Cody?" I ask. My brother is settled into his comfy, spacious seat a couple dozen rows up. Legs might have a million or so fewer YouTube subscribers than Cody, aka the high and mighty Codemeister, but a million less than several million is still several million.

Legs shakes his head. "Waste of money." His knees almost touch the seat in front of him.

Cody has been a YouTube gamer since I was a preteen, and absurdly famous for almost as long, and I grew up assuming that other big-name YouTube gamers would be just as pretentious as him. But then I started getting to know Legs and Z and some of the other guys, and it turns out that not every famous person is a douche. Some famous people actually make pretty good friends.

"Code didn't buy you a first-class ticket?" Legs asks.

I shake my head. "No, thank goodness. I don't think I could handle sitting with him and Noog after they were just joking about sleeping with a fourteen-year-old." These trips make me feel like an elastic—sometimes stretched to my limit and ready to snap, other times relaxed and at ease. It all depends on who's around.

Legs's dark eyebrows furrow together. "I'm sure they didn't mean it like that."

I frown. I like Legs a lot, but he's too quick to assume people didn't mean to cross a line. Too quick to see the good in people and ignore the bad.

"Maybe" is all I say. But now I'm thinking about how easily Cody steps over those lines, and that sick feeling in my stomach is back. I pull out my phone and stare again at those posts about Janessa. What if Cody's already stepped over lines, and not just the small, sleazy ones, like dating some girl four years younger than him who's still in high school? What if he's already stepped over the big, red, flashing lines without even realizing it? What if Janessa was crying in the bathroom about losing more than her virginity?

I pull up Janessa's profile and hit the link to send her a private message. The flight attendant is probably about to tell us to put our phones on airplane mode, so there's no time for careful wording and subtlety.

I type: Hey Janessa, I'm probably the second-last person you want to talk to, but I need to know: Did my brother cross any lines with you or pressure you to do anything you didn't want to? I . . . just needed to check.

I hit Send before I can change my mind, and then I stare at the screen until the flight attendant does indeed come on the loudspeaker and tell us to put our phones away. There's no response from Janessa, no sign that she's even read it. I shove my phone into my backpack as the plane starts to roll slowly away from the gate and the stewardess starts to tell us all how to survive in the event of certain death.

Why do I feel so sick to my stomach?

Oh, right, because I just messaged another girl to check whether my brother raped her. Because over the past week, that's something I've come to fear my own brother might be capable of doing.

I sink back into my seat, into my fear. Beside me, Legs sinks into his sadness, his whole body slouching with a sigh. We're quite the pair.

I'm not sure what Legs is sad about, but his sadness follows him everywhere. One late night at PAX, I was waiting for Cody, sitting on a bench outside the hotel bar where Cody and Noog and Ben were getting the level of drunk where the latter two would joke right in front of me about how screwable I was, just so they could laugh when Cody tripped over his feet as he threatened to punch their faces in. Which is probably only my third-least favorite level of drunk.

Anyways, I was sitting there trying to read a book on my phone over the ruckus coming from the bar when Legs slipped onto the bench beside me, mumbling something about how I shouldn't be sitting out there alone so late. He was trying to be a hero by keeping me company, I think, but even heroes can have broken bones and broken hearts, and as we leaned into each other's shoulders, I had the distinct feeling we were holding each other up.

I bump Legs's shoulder now. "Hey, did you hear about the bill that was proposed this morning?" Sometimes the best way to take your mind off your own problems is to think about the world's problems. And does it ever have problems.

Legs shakes his head, and I tell him all about the newest idiotic bill that was introduced in Congress this morning, and Legs listens, because that's one good thing I've learned on this trip: some places, people listen. Back home, no one listens to anyone or anything except that stupid news station. Oh, and their pastor. And while Dad's pastor's all right, Mom's is a prick. Maybe if I lived with Dad instead of Mom, I'd actually like going to church.

"Will you call your senators about it next week?" I ask Legs. I'm still two months away from being old enough to vote, while Legs has been able to vote for over a year.

"If you tell me what to say again."

"I'll find another script online."

At that moment, the wheels of the plane lift off the ground, and Legs and I both turn to watch out the window as the city below becomes smaller and the clouds become larger, as we head north to Toronto. And I tell myself that the sick feeling in my stomach is simply motion sickness.

I can't check my phone again until we land, which is going to make this flight feel long, but at least I'm sitting not with Cody but with Legs, whose actual leg has settled against mine again. He plugs his headphones into the armrest between us and holds out one earbud to me. "Want to watch something with me?"

I have my own TV screen, my own controls, my own

headphones in my pack at my feet. I ignore all that and accept his earbud with a smile, and together we relax and watch a stupid comedy for the rest of the two-hour flight.

I check my phone as soon as we land, but there's still no response from Janessa. She's probably avoiding social media altogether, but I can't shake the fear that she's seen my message and doesn't want to tell me the terrible truth. "Everything okay?" Legs asks, and I force myself to smile and nod.

When we find our way through customs to the baggage carousels, Cody is waiting for us. He's still wearing his blue knit beanie and gray hoodie, and he's already pulled on the bulky coat he brought specifically "for the Canadian cold," even though the temperature here's not going to be much different than home.

"Legs, my man!" He holds out a fist for Legs to bump, as if we didn't all just spend the last six days together.

Once they've bumped fists, Cody turns to me. "You'll get the luggage?"

I cross my arms. "Obviously."

"Great! Noog's gone ahead to hail a cab. I'll hit the pooper!" And with that, he ambles off in the direction of the bathroom, free of having to worry about getting his own luggage, because he's a world-famous YouTuber—sorry, "content creator"—and he's got his roadie sister to worry about things like that.

Legs and I head off in the other direction, toward a couple of elderly women wearing bulky scarves so bright that it's like they've magically rerouted all the color from their white hair and pale skin into the yarn. Their elbows are linked, and they lean on each other as they wait for the baggage carousel to start doing its job and delivering up some luggage instead of going around and around and accomplishing nothing. We settle in right behind them, because we're both tall and have a perfect view of the conveyor belt over their heads, but also because we're probably thinking the same thing—if these brilliant women need help with their bags, we'll be here to give it.

I check my phone for a response from Janessa about five more times before the carousel finally blares with an obnoxiously loud horn and starts vomiting up luggage from its depths. "What does yours look like?" I ask Legs, thankful for the distraction.

"Hmm?" He's staring off toward the back wall.

"Your luggage. What does it look like?"

He snaps back to the present day. "Oh! That's mine. The very first one. Lucky day!" He slips into the crowd and returns moments later with a simple black rolly suitcase.

"You up for tonight's FAQ panel?" I ask him as he leans against his suitcase with his hip. Legs is the opening act of the entire convention—a fact that I'm sure makes Cody seethe inwardly with rage. But I doubt Cody could handle a whole FAQ session all on his own. He needs a video game or his Team Meister bros to riff off of.

"The FAQ's tonight?" Legs asks, and my throat constricts. Maybe Legs can't handle a panel on his own, either—at least, not in his current state. But then he laughs. "I'm kidding. It'll be fine. All I have to do is . . . stop thinking."

"Right. Stop thinking. Easy."

"Easy-peasy," he says.

"You're right. Just use dorky words like easy-peasy the whole time, and you'll have all of LotSCON eating out of the palm of your hand!"

He laughs, and then Cody's suitcases start showing up on the carousel, and then so do the badass old ladies' bags (and they don't need our help at all), and then we're heading back to Cody, his bags of clothes and electronics and swag all piled on a luggage cart. All I've got with me is my carry-on, which I balance on top.

Cody's black marshmallow coat is so big and fluffy that for a moment I don't notice the ball of fluff in his arms—until it reaches its snout up and licks him right on the mouth, making him laugh and snuggle its black shape closer.

"Cody, why do you have a dog?" I ask.

He grins and scratches the puppy behind the ear, fingers disappearing into soft black curls of fur. "Offered to watch her while her mama used the bathroom. Isn't she beautiful? Here, hold her." And then he's reaching out and settling her gently into my arms and we're four and eight again and holding our brand-new gray and white schnoodle, Terra, for the first time, together. When she died last year, Cody cried more than when our grandmother died the year before, and when I reached out to take his hand as Dad buried her body, he let me.

Cody releases his grip on the wriggling bundle, and I bury my face in the soft fur of her back to hide the tears that suddenly prick my eyes. I want Cody to be this Cody always—the one who is kind and gentle and compassionate.

"Maybe I should get a dog," Cody says, and for a moment I picture a saggy-tongued bundle of energy racing around his apartment and tagging along when he visits Mom's place or Dad's place. Cody might be a substandard human in a lot of ways, but he'd be an excellent doggy daddy.

Except: "You probably travel too much," I point out.

His thoughtful smile falls. "You're right." He reaches out and takes the puppy back from me, gently. "I could never put you through that kind of stress," he says to her, scrunching his face into hers. Proof that Cody's not entirely unreachable; he does listen to reason sometimes. Just not when it matters most.

"Well, good," Legs jumps in, "because I'm pretty sure her owner's going to want her back."

Cody laughs and looks over his shoulder at the girl in her twenties who's walking toward us carrying a dog kennel. A girl with skintight jeans, red hair, and flawless makeup, who Cody most definitely flirted with. I step back and put a hand on our luggage cart while Cody hands the dog back to her, saying something I can't hear that makes her laugh.

My phone pings then, and I whip it out. There's a reply from Janessa. Finally.

No, he didn't. Are people saying he did?

My shoulders sag with relief. There's still time to save Cody from himself.

I slip my phone away and step forward to where Cody's talking to the girl. "Hey, we've got to go," I tell him.

He smiles at the girl. "It was nice to meet you. Take care of this cutie." He gives the dog a last scratch behind the ear and then turns to join Legs and me at our luggage cart. And that's it. Not a single crude joke or flirtation or final turnaround to give the girl a lewd wink.

My heart pulses with hope as we start to push the cart forward. Maybe Cody's not as far gone as I thought. Maybe I can still stop him from making big mistakes.

"Hey, Cody, can I talk to you about something?"

"Sure!" He's so chipper. In the past, when I've tried to call him out on things, I've been angry, and then he gets angry, and then we both end up yelling at each other. But this time, I've chosen the perfect moment. This time, maybe he'll actually listen.

I find the words carefully. "Earlier, when you said that thing about that girl . . . well, that crossed a pretty big line. I mean, she was just a kid." I can see Cody's face starting to cloud over at my accusation, so I quickly change tack. "I mean, I know you wouldn't actually do anything inappropriate," I add, desperately wishing I could fully believe that. "But even just laughing about things like that can encourage sexual harassment and rape culture, you know? It's harmful to women. Harmful to *me*." Legs's shoulder bumps into mine then, and I can tell by the way it doesn't draw away that it's intentional. A little bump of support.

The cart slows as we near the exit. Cody turns, puts his hand on my shoulder, and looks me in the eye. For one long, hopeful moment, I think he gets it. I think that this is it, I've finally gotten through, and he's going to apologize and start his growth into a better person. His growth into the hero his viewers deserve.

Instead, his round face grows even rounder as his expression unfolds into the grin of someone choosing to dismiss the seriousness of the moment. And then he says, "Lainey, one of these days, you're going to have to learn what a joke is."

Yeah, and one of these days, I'm going to punch my own brother in the nose.

TWO

SamTheBrave

IT'S FRIDAY NIGHT, AND HERE'S HOW I'M SPENDING IT: DOING HOMEWORK AT Opa's dining room table, same as every other Friday evening when Mom works the long shift. The seconds tick loudly by on the intricate wooden cuckoo clock on the wall. There's still a full hour before Mom comes to pick me up, assuming the thing's set to the right time. I can't check it against my phone because my phone's sitting by the front door in the basket I have to put it in every time I come over.

I look up from my science textbook as Opa enters the room. His hatred of technology makes him seem a million years old, but he doesn't look it. He walks with shoulders tall and broad and chin jutting out like always, and though his hair and goatee might be going gray, it doesn't show amid the blond streaked with the odd strand of red.

"No plans tonight?" he asks as he settles into the chair across from me.

I do have plans—I'm streaming Legends of the Stone at eight—but that's not the sort of plan Opa means. I tried to explain streaming to him once—how I'm not just sitting alone at my computer playing a video game, and instead have viewers watching me, interacting with me—but he still thought it was an antisocial waste of time. I wonder if he'd feel different if I had thousands of viewers instead of only a dozen or two at a time. Probably not.

If Mom wasn't working tonight, she could have driven me to LotSCON now instead of waiting until tomorrow, and then I would have had even better plans. Though I don't know that Opa would consider going to a video game convention— alone—to be any better. And besides, if I had gone to LotSCON tonight, I'd have missed my stream, and the internet advises small streamers trying to grow their channels to choose a regular streaming schedule and stick with it. That and get a really high-quality microphone, which Mom gave me for my birthday over a year ago.

Just the thought of trying to explain all this to Opa is exhausting, so instead I simply shake my head in answer to his question. No plans.

He taps his fingers on the table, each tap thudding heavily against the thick, dark wood, out of sync with the cuckoo clock. He narrows his eyes as he studies me, as if my lack of plans personally offends him. "Sam, you're a likeable young man," he says. "You're smart, and you can tell a mean joke. If you just put your phone away, got your head out of those video games, and cleared up your face and maybe muscled up by joining the hockey team, you should have no problem making friends."

I duck my head toward my science textbook, focusing my gaze on electrons and protons instead of on Opa's face.

Right, if I freed myself from the apparent ugliness of my body, I'd have absolutely no problem making friends. No problem except one: everyone at school knows I'm Opa's—aka Mr. Dietrich's—grandson, and everyone has had their phone confiscated by Mr. Dietrich at some point or another. And since they can't take their anger out on Opa, I get to enjoy the threats, name-calling, and body checks into lockers instead. Once, when Opa confiscated Brad Hemsworth's phone for a full week, the guy tried to dickpunch me. He missed, barely. I had a big purple bruise the shape of a hamburger on my thigh for weeks.

"Don't do that. It's a disgusting habit," Opa says, and I realize my fingers have found their way to a pimple on my chin.

My mottled skin flushes hot as my hand drops into my lap. There's a dot of blood on my finger from the pimple. Already, my fingers are itching to find their way to a tiny bump of skin on my wrist and scrape it off.

Disgusting.

Habit.

I can free myself from the latter word, at least. I close my eyes and conjure up my psychologist's words. "It's not just a habit, Sam. It's a mental disorder related to OCD." When I started meeting with her a few months ago to start cognitive behavioral therapy, her words were a relief. There was a reason, suddenly, why my fingers roam my body searching for imperfections to tear from my skin, why I can't control it even when I try. And it's not just because I'm weak, either, but because something is wrong in my brain in a diagnosable way: I have dermatillomania, aka excoriation disorder, aka skin-picking disorder.

Her words don't give me relief now, though, because they might take away the second word, but they don't take away the first: disgusting. My disorder is disgusting.

Before either Opa or I can say anything further, Oma glides into the room, carrying with her the scents of schnitzel, apple, cinnamon, and dish soap all at once. "Apfelkuchen?" she asks in her soft, raspy voice, and I look up as she holds out a slice of her melt-in-your-mouth apple cake.

"Thank you." I take the plate of pale cake topped with apple slices and baked to perfection and my mouth instantly waters.

"I took this to our seniors' potluck yesterday, but your opa made me save you a slice."

I look at Opa, who smiles. "I know it's your favorite," he says.

That's the thing about people: they're complicated. Opa would be easy to hate if all he ever did was take away my phone and call me a fat slob. But then he does something like this.

Opa stands to his feet. "Well, we'd better get out of here, Inge, and let the boy finish his homework. His teachers tell me he's on track to be on the honor roll this year." He beams at me.

I smile back, first at Opa, then at Oma. "Thank you," I tell them both. Then I take a bite of sweet, sweet apple cake and bury my head back in my textbook as they leave the room. Admittedly, that's the one good thing about my time at Opa and Oma's: finishing my homework early means stress-free weekend plans. And Opa might not consider them worthwhile, but this weekend I have big, big plans. And with this apple cake, surviving the forty-five minutes until my weekend starts for real just became a lot easier.

When Mom picks me up, she lets me spend the first few minutes checking messages on my phone, as always. There aren't many. A couple of YouTube comments and a message from Jones confirming that we're playing Legends of the Stone tonight at eight p.m. EST. She's in Atlanta, so we're both in EST, but we always throw the EST on there for Dereck, who's in Australia. It's Saturday morning for him, and he's got a cousin's wedding to go to, so tonight it'll just be me and Jones and the nefarious plot I've been working on all week.

Yep. And I'm getting you back this time, I type.

Her reply pops up right away: We'll see.

I ignore the little surge of electricity that pulses through me and make sure to send back the tongue-sticking-out emoji without the wink. Jones is one of my only friends. I can't risk losing her because she thinks I'm flirting with her, especially when I know she has a boyfriend. She sends the same one right back, which for some reason makes me laugh.

"Are you excited for this weekend?" Mom asks as I slip my phone back into my backpack. She's still in her nursing scrubs—well, the turquoise pants anyway, plus a plain white T-shirt—with her brown hair pulled up in a simple ponytail. She looks the way she always does at the end of her twelve-hour shifts—a little more rounded at the edges, like every muscle in her body is giving in to exhaustion.

My stomach lurches with nerves. "I'm not sure excited is the right word at the moment," I admit. I catch my fingers before they quite make it to the scab on my wrist, and instead pick up the fidget ball we keep in the cupholder. This one is tennis-ball-sized, forest green, textured with small bumps, and squishy like a stress ball.

"Oh, come on, Sammy boy. Code is going to love you. And your videos." She reaches over and pats my knee.

"If I can even get him to talk to me." I let the bumps of the fidget ball find their way between my fingers as I wrap my hand around it.

"Well, you'll have lots of chances to try."

I squeeze the fidget ball as tightly as the knot of nerves in my stomach. "Only two. The panel and the autograph session."

Mom puts her blinker on to turn left. "And maybe you'll just see him around at the convention."

"Yeah, I mean, trying to talk to him when he's standing two urinals down from me in the bathroom sounds like a great idea."

She laughs. "I'm sure you wouldn't be the first one."

I laugh too, then stop abruptly and squeeze the fidget ball even tighter. "Oh man, what if I actually do something as stupid as that?"

Her own laugh dies off naturally, but her voice stays happy and encouraging. "You won't. You'll charm him immediately, Sammy love. He'll be itching to watch your videos."

This has been my plan—our plan, really, since Mom was fully on board from the beginning—ever since Codemeister was announced as a LotSCON guest months ago and I watched one of his streams for the first time, my stomach knotting with envy as his chat log buzzed with the energy of thousands of simultaneous viewers joking, spamming, and asking questions.

It's not that I'd never seen a stream like that before. I watch LumberLegs sometimes, and his are like that, and I've watched Wolfmeister once or twice, but they both only stream live once in a blue moon, and it's a big event. Codemeister streams multiple times a week and still manages to bring out the big crowds every single time.

And since I also happen to stream multiple times a week but on opposite days from Code, his viewers would be the perfect audience for me.

"Imagine if it works, and he shouts out your channel to his YouTube followers," Mom says now.

"Twitch followers," I correct her.

"Right," Mom says. She doesn't use Twitch, which is for livestreaming, while YouTube is for posting videos that can be watched anytime. Our deal is that Mom's allowed to watch the carefully edited highlights videos, which I post on YouTube afterward, but not my livestream itself. I get too self-conscious and jittery if I know she might be watching, even though she's my biggest fan and would never say anything negative.

Twitch is where I most want to build up followers, though. I like posting videos to YouTube; I *love* streaming to Twitch.

Maybe, just maybe, I'll gain a few new biggest fans this weekend, though. Convincing Code to give me a shout-out to his viewers is a long shot, maybe—probably—but since I can't seem to break three hundred followers on Twitch, I have very little to lose and a practically infinite amount to gain.

Mom crosses the bridge over our small lake that's more like a river and passes the side road leading to the high school. You can't quite see the weirdly shaped brown building from here, but I can feel the weight of its presence like the Dark Lord of Mordor in *Lord of the Rings*. In fact, I feel a lot like Frodo when I'm there—trudging alone through swampland with Sauron's eye ever searching for me—except I have no Samwise at my side. No Gollum either, since even Gollum hates getting his phone taken away, apparently.

Thanks, Opa.

I break the silence that's settled over the car. "Can't I just stay home when you're working the long shift? I can make my own supper. I can make both of us supper and have it ready for you when you get home."

"Oh, Sammy. I know it's not exactly fun going to Opa and Oma's." She sighs. "And heaven knows my dad isn't the easiest to get along with." She and Opa *are* always arguing about one thing or another; maybe she's going to let me do it. But then she says, "But they're family," and I know I've lost. Family trumps everything. It's the reason she and Opa spend so much time together even though they fight all the time. It's the reason she's been driving me the two hours to see my dad once a month for my entire life, even though he and I have nothing in common and don't think about each other at all between visits and scheduled phone calls. And now it's the reason I'm probably going to be stuck having supper with Opa and Oma when Mom works the long shift for the rest of my life.

Oh well. I don't have to worry about them for the rest of the weekend. And in just half an hour, I'll be streaming. I pull out my phone again and post a reminder on all my social media sites.

I get one reply right away, from BlastaMasta742: Yessssss! It's going to be epic!!! Can't wait!!!!

I guess I could call BlastaMasta742 a regular, since he or she hasn't missed a single stream the past two weeks, even the secret one that I didn't post about on social media so Jones wouldn't see it and find out what I have planned for our Legends of the Stone battle tonight.

Legends of the Stone took the sandbox concept that Minecraft made so popular and brought it to another level, with incredible graphics, finely tuned fighting mechanics, and high stakes; if the players on a server don't work together to fight their way through, defeat, and close up the rifts that spawn randomly throughout the world, the world becomes more and more unstable, making buildings slowly fall apart and items disappear.

Most people set their servers on cooperative, so they can't accidentally hit each other during a rift run, but as in any sandbox game, the variations you can make to how you play are practically endless. And tonight, we're turning on PvP and fighting each other to the death!

A grin slips across my face.

BlastaMasta742 is right: it's going to be epic.

Three hours later, I'm cornered.

In game, I huddle in the back storage room of my castle, hidden behind some shelves. The only way out: through the long front hallway guarded by my mortal enemy, Jones. Her username, MarthaJones, paces back and forth—the only part of her visible through the wall.

"Come on out, Sammy boy." Her voice thunders through my headset. She overheard my mom call me that once, and it's stuck ever since. "I'll let you surrender."

"No way. I'm not falling for that one again, Jones," I say. Her name isn't actually Jones, or even Martha, but that's what happens when you get to know someone by username first.

I press myself against the shelf full of my redwood and coral supplies—great for building, but no good to me now. "I'm good where I am. My castle's a maze. You'll never find me." I breathe slowly in and out. In and out. The scab on my left arm, just above the wrist, screams at me to pick at its edges, but I scream back that I am much too busy—in my head, anyway. Outside, I say nothing at all, just keep breathing.

And then it happens. My finger slides forward on the mouse wheel, and for a moment, I'm out of hiding. SamTheBrave username fully visible.

I switch right back into hiding, then hold my breath. Did she see it?

"Riiiiight," she says. "So true. Such a maze." Her username glides toward me, visible through the redwood wall.

She definitely saw me. My heart pounds as I glance at the livestream chat.

> This gonna be good
>
> LMAO
>
> perfect
>
> My body is ready
>
> Lolololololol
>
> die Jones die Clara is better
>
> yesssssssssssssssssssssssssssssssssssssssssss

I grin. Because the chat knows what Jones doesn't:

1. That last week, a rift spawned maybe ten feet from my castle. I could have closed it up. I should have closed it up. I

*definitely shouldn't have built my castle around it like it didn't
exist.*

*2. That last night, when Jones thought I was studying
history, I instead ran a top-secret livestream from eight p.m. to
one a.m. to prepare for today's PvP face-off.*

*3. That five hours is a long time. Long enough that even
if you die thirty times in the process, you can probably manage
to wrangle a good fifteen or so shadowwolves, three venomous
wereboars, and a mutant rabbit into a tiny built-over-a-rift
closet.*

4. That I slipped out of hiding on purpose.

Jones opens the closet door. The door she thinks is my door.
"What the—"

MarthaJones was slain by a mutant rabbit

I laugh so hard as her death message comes up in the game
log that I can barely make out her murderous swearing in the
background. I glance at the chat again. It's so full of LOLs and
ROFLs and memes and emoji that you'd never guess there were
only twenty people in there. Not that I'm complaining. It's the
most viewers I've ever had at one time!

"I'm going to kill you, Sammy boy," Jones says once I stop
snorting. Her voice is heavy with amusement, though. She's
impressed.

"Told you I'd get you back," I say to her, the words bouncing
with my leftover laughter.

"And you did indeed get me back." She pauses while we both catch our breath from all the laughing and swearing. "So . . . your base is full of shadowwolves now, right? What're you going to do about that?"

My grin falls off my face. "Oh. Uh . . ." I glance at the shelves behind me full of redwood and flowers and building supplies. My sword is on the lawn outside, where I dropped it to make her think I'm helpless. The only way out of this room is the hallway now full of the monsters I trapped there. Oops. Maybe I didn't think this through.

I glance at the clock. Almost eleven p.m., the end of my regularly scheduled stream time. Often I stream longer than that, but tonight I want to turn this stream and last night's stream into a highlights video so I have something great to show to Code, and the editing for that will probably take a couple of hours.

"A problem for another day!" I shout, like it's a victory cry. "Eat my balls, shadowwolves!" And then I hit the Log Off button, exiting the server, but not the stream quite yet.

Jones laughs. The chat is full of laughter. It could be at my brilliant victory, or at the fact that I've trapped myself in my own base, but it doesn't matter to me which it is. It's all of it, probably. I'm laughing at all of it myself. That's the thing about being a video game streamer—you don't have to be good at the game, you just have to be entertaining.

Right before shutting off the stream, I catch one more comment in the chat: Best stream everrrrrrrrrrrrrrrrrrrrr

It *was* good, wasn't it, BlastaMasta742? I might never have more than twenty viewers at one time, but at least—I think, I hope—I do entertain them.

As I open my editing software, the giddy warmth of the whole night flushes through me. Maybe I don't belong at school, but I belong here, in the Legends of the Stone gaming world. And I'm going to be at LotSCON all weekend long.

Maybe it's a long shot trying to get Code to look at my videos, but still, as I start combing through my stream for highlights, I can't stop smiling. This is my world, and maybe that makes it not such a long shot after all.

@LumberLegs: LotSCON FAQ session in an hour!
Looking through your supremely awesome questions
now! So excited!
[1.7K likes]

THREE

ShadowWillow

A GUY IN LINE IS DRESSED AS A DRAGONLORD, AND IT'S ONE OF THE MOST impressive cosplays I've ever seen. His wings spread out behind him, black piping strong enough to support an expanse of sheer red fabric glimmering with gold, and yet somehow kinked and engineered to fold in on itself at the press of a button in his vest. It's not just the engineering that's impressive, though. He's put so much attention into every detail. His skin is painted gold, with scales sketched meticulously into the paint. And the armor is spot-on, from the black shadowdragon that stretches around his chestplate—head breathing fire down the front of one arm, tail curving down the back of the other—to the gold edging, made to look worn from years of battling in the rift.

I'm about as awkward as a baby skunk in a box of kittens when I talk to strangers, but I'm desperate for a picture, and taking pictures at a con without asking first is a huge no-no. So I take a deep breath, pull out my phone, and approach him. "That dragon is stunning," I say when I reach him. "I mean, absolute perfection. Just really, really incredible. Like out-of-this-world incredible. Could I—could I get a selfie with you?"

I'm pretty sure he blushes beneath his gold paint as he stammers out his agreement. *Why hello, fellow baby skunk.*

It ends up being impossible to fit the wings or any of the best parts of the cosplay in the picture when I hold the camera out for a selfie, but the sweetheart of a girl just ahead of the dragonlord in line offers to take a picture for us. Her hair is shaved on one side and streaked with blue on the other, which looks epic but also chilly out here in the windy line that's stretched along the side of the convention center. The dragonlord has her take one on his camera, too, which is cute. He must be doing that thing where he takes pictures with everyone who asks to take pictures with him.

When the girl hands my phone back, I check the picture. The wings are cut off a bit and the lighting's kind of dark, but it'll have to do. "Thanks," I say to her. "That's perfect."

I turn back to the dragonlord. "And thank you!"

He gives a slow, shallow bow, then says, "And, uh, could I get your, uh, autograph?"

"My . . . autograph?"

He nods. "You're Willow, right?"

"ShadowWillow." I correct him on reflex. He must be a Code-meister fan. The hundreds of thousands of them that have been flocking to my channel again lately keep calling me Willow, like I'm the kind of player who spends endless hours in game collecting outfits to fill my closet. I'm supposed to be ShadowWillow or just Shadow, the kind of player who's only interested in collecting dragon heads for my wall. Not that I'm complaining. I'm definitely not complaining.

The girl who took the picture for us whirls around. "Wait, you're Willow? I mean, of course you are. Holy crap. I thought you looked familiar, especially with that purple hair, but everyone's got purple hair these days, you know?" She runs a hand through her own half head of blue-streaked hair, then leans in. "So is it true? Are you and Code dating?"

I'm thankful for the shadowy evening lighting and the high-collared coat that hides my neck and chest, which tend to flare much brighter red than my cheeks ever do. Here it is, the question that's been dominating the comments section of my videos ever since I did that tournament with Code.

Are you dating Codemeister?

I SHIP THEM SOOOOOOOOOOOOOOOOOO

BAAAAAAAAAAAAAAAAAAAAAAAAAD

CodeWillow <3 <3 <3 <3 <3 <3 <3

You + Code = HOTTTTTTT

"I, um, well—" I wasn't prepared to be asked this so quickly. And by strangers. Random strangers who recognized me and want my autograph. Holy shadowdragons, this is so cool! I take a breath, metaphorically straighten my little skunk tail, and smile at them both as I reach into my purse for the Sharpie that Claire made me pack despite my protestations that I wouldn't need it. "No comment, sorry. But you said you wanted my autograph?"

And they do; they do want my autograph! The photographer girl has me sign her program. The dragonlord has me sign his armor—his armor!—right below the dragon's head. It feels almost sacrilegious to mar his work of perfection with my Sharpie scribble, but if it's what he wants, I'm not saying no. And then I'm telling them it was nice to meet them and marching off like I've got somewhere to be.

Somewhere to be, apparently, is the washroom, where I lock myself in a stall, lean against the graffitied wall, and message Claire.

I just used the Sharpie!!!!!!!!

While I wait for her response, I pull up my phone camera and start to use it as a mirror—then decide that's stupid, since there are full-size mirrors just outside my locked stall door. I'm about to head out there when my phone pings, and then pings again.

DOES THAT MEAN WHAT I THINK IT MEANS?!?!?

YOU JUST GOT THERE!!!!

I grin stupidly as I tap out my response.

It does. It does mean that. Someone in line asked

for my autograph. Two someones, actually.

ZLIFJELAIFJSMCVNPQOW!!!!!1!1!!!!!!!!!

Ha ha

You're the one who made me take the Sharpie

I know, but I didn't really think you'd need it

Gee thanks

Well, did you think so?

No! Not aside from at my actual signing

Dude, you're totally famous!!!!!

I mean, outside of this convention, no one knows who
I am. I could walk one street over and I'd just be some
weird girl with purple hair and a bow-legged walk

No one notices your walk except you

And you're NOT one street over. You're here! And here,
you are famous!

What's it like finally being out in the real world, btw?

How's the sun?

I shoot her back a tongue-stuck-out emoji, then unzip my
coat and smooth out my extra-long gray shirt and black leggings.
Claire knows I've spent the past ten months working twelve-hour
days in my parents' basement, trying to build up my YouTube
channel. And I'm not actually famous—I don't have millions
of subscribers like Codemeister or LumberLegs—but things are
finally starting to happen. All my hours spent in front of a computer while my friends moved away for university or spent their
gap year traveling the world; all the hours and hours of video that

I recorded and edited and threw away and recorded all over again because the first version wasn't good enough; all the time I spent reminding my dad that he and I had a deal, and my year wasn't up yet—all of it has brought me here.

And by "here," I apparently mean hidden away in a bathroom stall at a convention center, texting my best friend. I unlock the stall and head over to the bathroom mirrors as another message comes in from Claire.

Have you met Codemeister yet?!? Or Wolfmeister? Noogmeister? Deadmeister? Zzzzzzzzzzzzzzzzzzmeister? How many Zs are in Z's name anyway? Is Wolf as stunningly gorgeous in real life as in his videos? Don't forget: I neeeeeed a photo. Preferably one that I can photoshop myself into licking Wolf's face.

Ew, that's gross!

You don't want to lick Code's face?

Dude, no! And I haven't met any of them yet. I've got that LumberLegs panel first; then I'm meeting his sister to take me to the rental.

I can't believe you're staying with them!!!

I can't believe it either. Three months ago I was gradually building my channel, finally seeing a bit of traction and making a few good connections, but for the most part still a nobody. But then Team Meister was short a player for that tournament, and I'd been chatting with Pyro, who's friends with Etho, who was in the tournament, and then suddenly I was recruited and paired with Code and we were so close to winning the whole thing, and my subscriber count doubled that first week and tripled the second and I thought I had finally made it—until the subscribers started leveling off and the comments shipping me and Code together became more and more infrequent. It's hard to keep up viewers' excitement for it when I was nothing more to Code than a blip on his radar. Rumors need fuel and I had none to give them.

Until recently, when Code's sister needed a roommate for LotSCON, and Code messaged me out of the blue and asked me. And obviously I said sure, not even realizing that it'd be in the house Team Meister was renting for the Con instead of some hotel room.

> I know. It's going to be weird
> I think you mean awesome
> Awesome AND weird

When it got out that I'd be staying with the Meisters for LotSCON, the dying embers of fans' Codemeister + ShadowWillow excitement burst into flame again, and more important, my subscriber count also caught fire—in the good way. This time, though, I can't let the momentum die off. I need to make an impression—on Code's viewers and on Code himself. Something that means I'm going to stick in their consciousness for a long, long time. This is my one chance. No pressure or anything.

> I wish you were here
> Say hi to your textbooks for me

I will lick their covers hello for you

You're gross

<3

<3

I shake my head and slide my phone back into my purse. I wish Claire was here instead of halfway across the country study-ing history at Dalhousie University in Nova Scotia. Though even if she wasn't halfway across the country, she'd still probably be buried in textbooks instead of joining me—despite the lure of Wolf's apparently lickable face. She's trying to get top marks all through undergrad so she can get a scholarship to law school and achieve her life goal of becoming a Bay Street lawyer.

She has a life goal. I have a subscriber count.

I spend a couple of minutes in front of the mirror before I head back out—touching up my makeup, trying to smooth out that one strand of hair that always tries to be curly when the rest of my hair is stick straight. It's hard to be mad at it when I feel like it's a metaphor for my life.

A Filipina girl in jeans and a LotS shirt under her unzipped coat and a white girl with thick rectangular eyebrows and a long black winter coat zipped up to her chin enter the bathroom. I glance up at them, half expecting to catch some recognition in their eyes, because apparently the number of autographs I need to sign to take me from feeling like a nobody to expecting to be recognized as a somebody is two. But their eyes barely pause on me before they disappear into their respective stalls. Which isn't a shock. I'm still not even halfway to a million subscribers.

And getting there is going to be either really hard or really easy, depending on why, exactly, Code invited me here. If it's only to make friends with his sister and I barely see heads or tails of him all weekend, I'm going to have to get creative. If, on the other hand, it's for *reasons*, well, let's just say that being one-half of a YouTube gaming power couple would keep me in viewers' minds for longer than whatever they had for breakfast, even if their breakfast was a delicious cinnamon roll with cream cheese icing. Plus Code's not bad to look at, with those round, baby-face cheeks and his infectious grin.

Admittedly, I didn't think of him that way until *after* the tournament, when people started shipping us together, but that means nothing. I went on two different "dates" with my last boyfriend before I realized that he was thinking of them as dates and not just as friends, and we ended up being together for eight months. Plus, during the tournament, I was much too busy trying to win to think about things like flirting. And we managed to come in second overall, which was disappointing at the time but was actually pretty darn good considering that we'd never played together before and that Code is not exactly skilled at PvP. So at least I know we work well together.

I don't normally have time for dating or even meeting new people—not in the real world, at least. I reserve all my socialization energy for networking with other content creators online. Though I'd make an exception for Code.

I check my messages from him. The last one from two days ago says simply: *Great! See you there!* Not exactly strong evidence of incoming power-couple status, but I've got all weekend to change that. And there's no sense in worrying about that right now, because now I get to see LumberLegs, the kindest, smartest, most hilarious YouTuber in the entire universe! (Perhaps let's not tell Code I said that.)

I give my mulberry lip gloss a quick refresh, then head back out to line up on the chilly street. The line was long before I went in the bathroom, and it's only grown. I pull my coat tight around me to block out the almost-spring wind as I head toward the back of the line—then stop. I've been to a couple of conventions before—last year, Claire and I even made the same four-hour drive I made today to come all the way up from Windsor for FAN EXPO Canada—but always as an attendee. Never as a panelist or an invited guest.

Until now. I'm still not sure whether it's my shiny new subscriber count or Code himself that got me invited as a guest and panelist.

I pull out the VIP pass that hangs around my neck and read the fine print on the back. It doesn't say what it gets me. I head back inside the building, where the line starts just outside the auditorium and winds up and down both sides of the long hallway before the outside portion even begins. There are LotSCON signs everywhere, and tables set up for tomorrow morning's registration, and an enormous black shadowdragon that I somehow completely missed when I went to the washroom. Its black hide shimmers as it stretches over its fleshless skeleton, the white bones visible through a gaping hole in its chest.

Fighting the shadowdragon is my favorite part of playing Legends of the Stone, though he spawns so rarely. The bigger the rift, the harder it is to defeat, and the greater the chance that a shadowdragon will spawn in it. Some people who really love building or other nonfighting stuff in LotS use mods to keep the rifts small or entirely nonexistent. I, on the other hand, use mods to make them spawn plentifully, and in their biggest size, so my friends and I can search out the shadowdragon to kill.

I realize I'm staring, mouth open, at the extremely lifelike shadowdragon, so I snap my mouth closed and glance toward the guy with the LotSCON shirt who's standing at the nearby auditorium entry doors. Surely there's no harm in asking. Worst-case scenario, I have to walk back outside to find a place at the back of the line.

I square my shoulders and head toward him, holding my baby skunk tail tall, trying to look like I belong. It'd be pretty badass to get a seat in the very front row, with LumberLegs almost close enough to touch.

As I near the door guy, I pull out my pass and hold it out to him, and before I can even say anything, he opens the door he's blocking, steps aside, and ushers me in. And just like that, I'm inside the auditorium. At LotSCON. Staring right at the stage where Legs is shortly going to be.

I turn back to say thank you, but he must think I'm going to ask something, because he says, "Panelist VIP room is over there, through the door to the right. Where Lorne is." He waves at a guy on the other side of the auditorium, who waves back.

"Thanks!" I say. And then before anyone realizes I'm an impostor who most definitely shouldn't have been given a VIP pass that apparently grants all sorts of magic powers, I stride across the hall, toss my coat on a chair in the front row, then march right up to Lorne. I flash him my VIP pass and he flashes me back a grin that shines through his goatee, then opens the door to the panelist VIP room.

Which, it turns out, is empty other than me and a shoulder-length-brown-haired girl with an athletic build who's in the corner getting a coffee.

Oh, and just a few feet away, slouched in a chair, staring off into space: LumberLegs.

This is officially the coolest thing that has happened to me in my entire life. If this is what the Codemeister + ShadowWillow excitement gets me, I can't let that momentum die, no matter what.

No matter what.

FOUR

Lainey

WHEN CODY TOLD ME MY ROOMMATE WOULD BE "JUST SOME GIRL I WAS partnered with for some competition a few months ago," I thought it was weird. Why would he invite some girl he barely knows to stay with us?

But the minute I see her, I get it. All week, I've seen the types of girls Cody flirts with—the ones with perfected faces and hour-glass figures—and this Willow girl fits that archetype perfectly. She's gorgeous. (Or as Cody would probably say, Hott with a capi-tal *H* and a double *t*. Ick.)

Standing in the VIP room entrance, she's all pink-cheeked

and fresh-faced, with hair dyed purple in the same way girls bleach their hair blond—she's going for fantasy dream girl, not punk rebel. She's the kind of girl who wears leggings as pants and doesn't once wonder whether they make her butt look too big or too small. Even her slightly off-kilter way of standing only makes her stand out.

Cody is clearly trying to get in her pants. Or rather, her leggings.

Legs is talking to her already, having yanked himself out of his funk and plastered on a friendly face almost as soon as she wandered into the VIP room. I'd be jealous, except that his friendly face is like his gamer persona—not quite his real self. And besides, I could look just as pretty if I was willing to spend an hour or two in front of the mirror every morning, which I'm not. Who wants to spend a twelfth of their life just staring at their own face?

I stick a lid on my coffee cup and wander over. "Hi, I'm Lainey."

"Marissa." She smiles in a genuine way that makes it obnoxiously impossible to hate her. "You must be Code's sister."

I shrug. "That's what our parents tell us."

"That's perfect! I'm staying with you." She points to herself. "I'm ShadowWillow. Code told me to meet you after the panel."

"Yeah, I heard you introduce yourself to Legs."

"Right. Because I'm standing here talking to Legs. Legs! Like he's a person." She turns to him. "I mean, I know you're a person. It's the talking to you part that—I don't know. Gah, sorry, I'm going full baby skunk. I'm just excited! Aren't you excited?"

I'm saved from answering by the fact that the LotSCON volunteer with the goatee pops his head in and tells us that they're about to open the doors to the auditorium.

"Oh!" Willow says. "I'm going to grab my seat before someone steals it. Are you heading out there? I've got a nice spot saved right in the front."

I glance at Legs, who's nodding along with everything but barely saying a word. "I'm going to hang back."

"Sure. I'll save you a seat then."

"Oh, I—um, thanks."

And with a swoosh of her purple hair, she's gone back out of the room.

"I think you made her day just by standing there," I say to Legs.

"I bet you say that to all the boys."

"Only the sad ones." The words slip out of my mouth before I have time to think about them, but it's just as well. It's about time he talked about why it's like he's been walking around with a backpack full of rocks.

Legs only slumps down into his chair. "Is it that obvious?"

I shrug. "None of the guys seem to have noticed." Which isn't saying much; they didn't even think to come to their friend's event tonight. Not that I'm complaining. When it's just me and Legs and the idiots aren't around, I actually almost enjoy myself.

"Well, that's good," Legs says, which is sad. What is it about guys not wanting to show each other weakness? "You did, though?" he adds.

I slip into the seat beside him. "Yeah." For a moment, we both sit there in silence as the sound of bottled chatter grows and grows outside the door. I hand my coffee to Legs and he takes a sip, then hands it back, and as I take a sip, I try not to think about the fact that my lips are where his lips were.

As the coffee settles comfortably into my stomach, I wrap my fingers around the warm cup. "Want to talk about it?"

His jaw tightens, rounding out the corners of his square jaw. "It's silly."

"Whatever it is, it's okay to be sad."

He slumps farther into his seat, apparently taking me at my word. Which would be great, except I've just remembered that there's a whole auditorium of people outside that door who are expecting Legs's happy gamer persona.

"Though, uh, maybe shove the sadness aside for a bit," I say. "Because I think that crowd's expecting to laugh." I gesture toward the door.

"Right." Legs straightens in his seat and holds his hand out for my coffee, which I pass over.

I hate that I've had to push the topic away just when it seemed like he might finally talk about it. "Hey, you want to meet for breakfast tomorrow morning?" I suggest. "There's a coffee shop near Meister Manor."

"I'm not great with early," Legs says.

"Oh, okay." My cheeks flush hot, which is stupid, because it's not like I asked him on a date or something. It was just coffee, just a chance to talk. "Never mind, then."

"No, I mean—" He breaks off awkwardly and rubs at the dark stubble on his jawline. I bet he could have grown a full beard at twelve. "I meant, could we make it more like brunch?"

"Oh, um, yeah, probably. Cody's panel's not until after lunch, so that should work." Ugh, I hate that Cody's impacting things even when he's not here. Though I guess if it weren't for him, I wouldn't be here at all.

The realization that I really do want to be here makes my cheeks flush even hotter.

Legs and I agree to meet midmorning, and then I quickly change the topic before I say something stupid. "You going to manage okay out there?" I gesture toward the door.

"Once I get going, I'll be fine. I've got my starting joke, I'll get some laughs, and then I'll be In. The. Zone!" He throws on his gamer voice for the last bit.

"Give me that." I snatch my coffee back as I shake my head. "You're not allowed any more juice if it's going to make you all corny."

"What?! I thought corny was a good thing."

"Corny is definitely not a good thing."

"There are five million people who disagree with you," he says, referring to his ever-growing subscriber count.

"And there are close to seven million people who think my brother is God's gift to the earth."

"An excellent point. Maybe we'd both better just—" He

stands, grabs my coffee, takes two steps, and drops it into the garbage with a thunk.

"Hey!" I say, but we're both grinning.

The LotSCON bouncer guy sticks his head into the room. "We're ready for you, LumberLegs, sir."

Legs nods, and his face falls. Whatever sadness he's feeling can't be chased away by a few silly jokes. Legs pauses by the door, ready-but-not-ready to go out and face a crowd expecting forty-five minutes of laughter.

I point my hand into a gun at him. "Starting joke," I say. "You've got this."

"Starting joke," he says, finger gunning back at me, then striding out the door.

As the crowd starts to roar with excitement, I hurry after him to the seat Willow saved for me, not at all worried. Legs is an entertainer, used to putting out regular videos no matter how he's feeling, and he's got this.

Except it turns out I should have been worried after all, because Legs says his joke, but the mic isn't working. Willow beside me must have supersonic hearing, because she laughs, but the rest of us can't make out the words.

As a LotSCON guy rushes forward, and they fiddle with the mic, I watch Legs's face, which is red and crinkled with the concentration of trying to hold on to his gamer comedian persona. By the time they sort it out with a screech from the sound system, Legs has lost his grasp on the joke; he stammers out an introduction, and then there's nothing. Silence.

And for a moment, LumberLegs is gone, and onstage is my good friend Caleb Hanna, who's wearing his sadness like a big, fluffy beard that can't be shaved.

But then some girl shouts Legs's catchphrase, "To the rift!" and then the whole auditorium erupts with the cry, and Lumber-Legs is back with a quick shake of the head and a crooked grin, and I could kiss that girl who started the shout.

Everything else goes smoothly; Legs is charming, the crowd laughs, the applause is thunderous, and then it's over and Legs is heading out to do autographs, and I'm left with Cody's new fairy princess, who is beaming and still clapping, even though Legs has practically disappeared.

"How old are you?" I ask her once she finally stops clapping.

"Eighteen. Why?"

At least she's legal. "Just wondering."

"He was great, wasn't he? It's so cool being here. He's got to be my favorite YouTuber of all time." She bites her lip. "Well, one of my favorites, I mean. I have lots."

"I almost had a heart attack near the beginning," I say, not sure why I'm admitting that to her. "When he lost his . . ." I want to say persona, but that feels like divulging a secret, so instead I say simply, "words."

"Nah! It just made him seem human," Willow says as she fidgets with her purse strap. "Takes the pressure off, knowing that even Legs is human."

At that moment, a couple of pimply guys tap her on the shoulder and ask if she's Willow and if they can have her autograph, and she grins and pulls an at-the-ready Sharpie out of her purse. Which means apparently she's big-name enough for face recognition. The way she's been fawning over Legs and the convention, I'd have pegged her as having about a hundred subscribers.

Those couple of autographs lead to more autographs, but eventually she's done and ready to head out. Since there's no parking at the rental, she'll have to leave her car here and walk back to the house with me.

On our way out to her car to grab her stuff, we swing by the autograph table, but the crowd is huge and the line is long, and I don't want to interrupt, so we just head toward the door. Before I make it there, though, my phone pings, and when I check it, the message is from Legs.

Thanks for today. See you tomorrow.

I turn to look at him through the crowd, and he's looking at me with his phone in one hand and his signing pen in another.

He waves and smiles, and I wave and smile, and yeah, I'll admit it, my heart maybe kinda sorta flips over once or twice in my chest.

Then he goes back to signing and I go back to following Willow out to her car to grab her stuff.

Willow lugs a huge, bright-pink wheeled suitcase out of the trunk of her beat-up old car, then pulls out a bulging tote bag and starts to slip it over her shoulder.

"Here, I can—" I take the plain blue bag from her and sling it onto my own shoulder. As I do, I spot a bright-yellow novel with a white daisy on the cover. "You're reading *The Hundred Lies of Lizzie Lovett*?"

She slams her trunk closed. "Yeah, I'm about halfway through."

"What do you think?"

I brace myself for some kind of dismissive comment, because there's no way she loves the same books as me. But instead, she says, "It's brilliant. Chelsea Sedoti is a literary genius."

I can't help but grin. "Right?! She's my favorite author."

"Well, she's fast becoming one of my favorites, too, so good choice," she says, and I could say the same thing to her. Perhaps I judged her too quickly.

We talk books for a while, pulling her luggage down the dark Toronto streets. In another time or place, it might be creepy, but the sidewalks are busy with people, and a scraggly-looking guy asking for change is the only interruption of our discussion. When I give him a quarter I find buried in my pocket, he demands I give him more but then saunters off when I give him the finger.

Willow raises an eyebrow at me.

"A quarter's all I've got," I say.

"It wasn't the quarter I was reacting to," she says.

I laugh. "Look, at least I gave him something. Unlike you. Cheapskate."

Her face falls. "Oh!" She glances over her shoulder. I grab her arm so she doesn't go running after him, but all she does is say, "Well, apparently he wouldn't have appreciated it anyway."

"Truth," I agree.

We're silent for a bit after that. Then Willow says, "So, Code didn't go to the Con this evening?"

Ick. I forgot she was here because of Cody. "Nah," I say. "Cody's not into watching people other than himself get attention."

She laughs like I'm joking.

I wish I was joking. Maybe if Cody thought about someone—anyone—other than himself sometimes, he'd realize how broken the world is and how much power he has to help fix it. Millions of subscribers hanging on his every word, and all he does is joke about dumb blondes while he screams his way through video games. He could easily do more. Like Legs, who takes time to answer viewers' real-life questions, giving advice and encouragement to them in videos and livestreams.

A memory comes back to me then, of paddling down the Little Miami River with our church group, when we were maybe thirteen and nine. Cody and I were in a canoe together, me in the front, Cody in the back. There was no question in my mind that he'd steer us in the right direction as we sang dorky songs together and paddled in unison on the beat, totally in sync. He didn't make a single crude joke, didn't try to flirt with the girls in the other canoes, didn't care that we looked ridiculous. We were in it together.

I miss that Cody. I trusted that Cody. I want that Cody back.

"Do you think people can change?" The question slips out of me. For the better, I mean, since the opposite has already happened.

"Of course," she says immediately, which says a lot about her and nothing about Cody. "Why do you ask?"

I'm saved from having to answer by the arrival at our street. I guide her down it, glad I took the time to remember which townhouse we've rented so I don't have to whip out my phone and use up any of the scant international data I purchased.

The front door of the townhouse has a white piece of paper taped to it with "BE QUIET STREAMING" scrawled on it in pen. We stop talking as we quietly maneuver Willow's luggage through the front door, trying not to bang the door against the luggage or the luggage against the door or the door against the wall. Down the hall in the living room, the guys are all piled onto a couch, hands full of controllers, shouting and laughing. If it was just Cody, I wouldn't bother being quiet, but I like Z and Wolf, and even Ben's not so bad most of the time, even if he is a million years old.

"Upstairs," I whisper at Willow, but I'm not sure if she catches it, because she's staring at the guys.

I move toward the stairs, looking back just in time to see Cody wink at Willow. The same way he winked at Janessa when he picked me up at school a few months ago. I was right. He wants in Shadow's leggings. Gross.

When I glance back at Willow, her cheeks are flushed pink and her eyes are twinkling like something exciting just happened. Double gross.

"He's a misogynistic jerk who's not worth your time," I want to tell her, but I doubt she'll believe me.

"Don't be silly. He wouldn't be so popular if that was the

case," she'd probably say. Which is too bad, because I was actually starting to like her, but I don't have time for people who live their lives with blinders on. I dart up the stairs ahead of her, leaving her to trail after me. Or not. I couldn't care less which.

Up in the bedroom, I collapse onto my bed and pull out my phone. Thinking of Janessa has reminded me that I never responded to her earlier question. I pull up my private chat with her. There's her original reply of No, he didn't. Are people saying he did? followed by another message from her that I hadn't noticed until now:

Why did you ask?

It's way too complicated to explain to her, so I simply type:

No reason. Just making sure.

Then it occurs to me to ask:

You okay, by the way?

It's got to suck to have the school calling her a slut. I hope she owns it and goes the whole scarlet-letter route.

Her response comes right away:

I'm fine. I can take it.

If she means that as a *Hamilton* reference, she's cooler than I realized. Stupid Cody.

I'm about to slip my phone away when Willow backs into the room, pulling her suitcase behind her. She must be a ninja to have gotten that thing up the stairs without making any noise.

She releases the suitcase and pulls out her own phone. "This is so great," she says, holding up her phone to snap a picture of the room. "Do you mind if you're in the picture I post?"

"I'd really rather I wasn't," I snap.

"Okay, no problem," she says pleasantly, then adjusts her angle so I'm not in the oh-so-exciting shot of our small bedroom with two single beds, a closet, and that's pretty much it.

I roll my eyes. This is the annoying thing—well, one of the many annoying things—about traveling with content creators; everything you do could end up on the internet. All week long, the guys have been posting public pictures and vlogs of everything we've been doing.

Which is when it occurs to me: judging by the way Cody and Willow were ogling each other, there will probably be video up of them sucking face by tomorrow. Triple gross.

I need to warn Janessa. I barely know her, but that doesn't matter; women should support other women. I open my chat with her again and type a new message.

By the way, do yourself a favor and stay away from Cody's social media, okay? Nothing to worry about. Just a tip.

And with that good deed done, I grab my pajamas out of my suitcase to change, head into our en suite bathroom, and firmly lock the door between Willow and me.

FIVE

SamTheBrave

WHEN I WAKE SATURDAY MORNING, THE GIDDY FEELING FROM MY STREAM THE
night before is replaced with drool caked onto my cheek, a newly
sprouted patch of achy pimples—not on my face, but on my butt
of all places—and my sheets turned into a drastically lopsided
tent.

I am going to LotSCON today.

I am going to LotSCON.

I repeat it to myself to try to amp myself up, but I can't shake
the desire to lie here forever and wait for my brain to transcend
and leave my stupid body behind. The fact is that I am going to

LotSCON by myself, to wander around all by my stupid lone-some, because that's what I do when I have to exist in the real world, where people think of me as a thing to shove into lockers instead of as a human.

My phone buzzes with a notification, and I roll over and stare at it on my side table. Reaching for it feels like a gargantuan task, but it could be Jones or Dereck, or a YouTube comment, or another streamer wanting to do a co-op—and the thought of any of those is enough to propel my arm out to snatch it.

It's a YouTube comment. There are five of them, actually—four on the streaming highlights video I stayed up way too late editing, and one on an older video.

One of the comments, of course, is "FIRST!!1!" I used to roll my eyes at those comments until Jones shot down my whining one day and said, "Dude, I think the sign of having made it as a YouTuber is if people excitedly try to be the first to comment on your videos."

Which is bogus, because I definitely haven't "made it" as a YouTuber, but she's right that those "first!" comments are a good thing. Gone are the days when I'd stream or post videos and get only crickets and maybe ten views, which I'm pretty sure was just Mom playing my video on repeat. After a year of streaming regu-larly, polishing my editing skills, connecting with other streamers, building up my social media, playing niche games regularly to stand out in a saturated market, and following every other bit of advice I can find online, at least I finally get comments now. And views. And people in chat. But I'm doing everything I can think to do, and I'm still a nobody. Which is why I need Code.

I glance at the "FIRST!!1!" comment again. It's from Mortal-Wombat, who's claimed first on other videos, I'm pretty sure. I scan through the comments on my other videos. On the last one, the "First!!!" is from Chickennuggetzzz, but the one before that is from MortalWombat. I used to assume the "first!" comments were from randos trolling the internet, but I've started to notice regulars. Which gives me an idea.

I scroll through my last fifteen or so videos and count them up, then return to MortalWombat's latest comment and type out my reply:

> MortalWombat, you're currently winning the "First Comment" competition.
> MortalWombat: 7
> asfdeLOL: 5
> Chickennuggetzzz: 2
> Who will be victorious?

I giggle to myself in a way that the guys at school would definitely make fun of me for, then return to the other comments. A "nice vid" and a "lololol" and then an "OMG THIS IS AMAZING I LOVE YOU SO MUCH!"

From a girl. A hot one, with red hair and bright-green eyes.

Instead of going to LotSCON, maybe I should stay in bed all day and let my mind go places that turn my sheets back into a tent.

But then the sound of Mom's clomping around the kitchen just down the hall reaches me and the fear that she might poke her head in and check on me is enough to force me out of bed and into the shower to clear away the evidence of my body's constant desire to betray me. My dick should never play poker.

In the shower, I come up with a million different brilliant ways I could respond to the girl's comment, but when I finally get out, instead of picking up my phone, I wipe away the steam from the mirror and just stand there and stare at myself. I've been told in health classes over the years how hair would fill in down there and how dealing with both hair and pimples would be a new fun game for my face. What no one ever mentioned was that those same pimples can pilgrimage their way down your neck and back to settle on your big mound of a butt. Or how hair can grow not just on the normal places of your face and your chest and around your junk, but also in inconsistent patches on your shoulders and butt and toes—like you're a tree battling an invasion of toxic moss.

Some guys wax, don't they? In real life, I mean, not just the movies. The movies make it look like torture. I guess that's one good thing about probably being a virgin until I'm eleventy-one: no one's going to care if I'm a sasquatch. No one but me.

I sigh. I wish there was a virtual LotSCON that I could show up to in my LotS skin. It'd be easy to walk up to Code as a shadowlord, wings spread wide, sword glinting in the sunlight. Instead, I've got to do it in this crappy body.

I turn backward and peer over my shoulder to try to check

out my shiny new butt pimples in the mirror, which is a terrible idea, because the next thing I know, it's ten minutes later, and there's skin and blood under my fingernails, and the two pimples on my butt, a scab on my back, and a pimple right smack-dab in the middle of my forehead have all been reduced to bloody holes.

I hate my skin. I hate my hairy butt. I hate my stupid compulsions to tear off any bump on my body—compulsions that are apparently like OCD, but not enough like OCD that OCD medication will make them go away. If I had a prescription instead of just prickly fidget balls and cognitive behavioral therapy, maybe Opa would stop calling it my "disgusting habit" and telling me to "get over it."

In the morning after I shower is always the worst time for my picking. Knowing that should make it easier to control, but instead it makes me feel like a complete failure, because no matter what I do, I can't ever seem to stop. I give up on trying to stop the bleeding, ignore my phone, which blinks with a new message, and trudge into my room to get dressed. I ignore the clothes I set out for myself last night and instead throw on black sweatpants and a long-sleeved black shirt, because black hides the bleeding and long sleeves hide the scarring. And besides, it's comfortable.

In the kitchen, Mom stares at me like she wants to say something.

"What?" I snap.

"Nothing. Eat your breakfast first." She hands me a plate of scrambled eggs, bacon, peanut butter French toast, and an orange cut into thin, fancy slices like at a restaurant. The smell alone is almost enough to distract me from the call of the scab on my wrist, and the entire time I'm eating, I don't pick at it once. When I finish, I check my phone, and there's another new comment on my video: "Hahaha, this is hilarious! Nicely done."

I respond with a "thanks, man!" then scroll back to the other comments and reply with a smiley face, another thank-you, and on the comment from the girl, a simple *blushes*.

By the time I'm done, I feel a whole lot lighter, so when Mom says, "Now go get changed—you look like an emo couch potato," I listen.

I throw on jeans and the T-shirt I bought specifically for this weekend: a light-blue shirt that says "CODESTER" (what Code calls his fans) in electric green, with Code's logo underneath. It's one of about seven million pieces of merchandise on his site. Then I wrap Band-Aids around my two main picking fingers and slip a tiny orange fidget ball into my jeans pocket, and Mom and I head out.

An hour and a half later, we're pulling into a parking lot full of people with LotS shirts and LotS swords and full LotS cosplay who are all exiting their cars and heading toward the convention center doors, like they're all pulled in by some homing beacon.

LotS lovers. Gamers. Geeks.

The giddy thrill I felt last night comes thrumming back. This is my place. These are my people.

A girl with mutant-rabbit ears and a short white skirt passes us, and the last of the self-loathing that was keeping me in bed this morning completely disappears.

"Okay, Mom. Thanks, Mom. See you later, Mom."

"Wait a minute, Sammy boy," she says, clearly not understanding the gravitational pull of the homing beacon. I sigh as she makes me go through all the normal mom checks.

Do I have my phone, debit card, and some cash? Check.

Do I remember what time to meet her back at the car? Yes.

Have I jotted down anywhere what section—B7—of the parking lot our car is in? Um, no, but—yes, now it's in my phone, see?

Then she releases me, and the homing beacon pulls me in—though I've only gone a few steps when I turn back. "Thanks, Mom. You're the best."

"You can do it, Sammy boy," Mom says. "Just be yourself."

And at this moment, surrounded by fellow Legends of the Stone fans, gamers, and nerds, that feels like enough.

My plan is to rush through registration so I can get to the vendors hall and find the perfect conversation starter for Code to autograph, but the moment I step inside the convention center, I halt, letting my jaw drop. Beyond the registration area, just before the escalators, is a shadowdragon the size of my entire bedroom. Its eyes glitter silver as it glares over the crowd, and its black skin gapes open at its chest to reveal the bare white bones inside. Chills run through me.

I never dreamed I'd get to go to a LotSCON; since Legends of the Stone chooses a different international location each year—last year's was Finland—and considering how many countries there are in the world, the odds of them choosing Canada were low. But then they did, and here I am.

I stare up at the shimmering shadowdragon for a moment longer, then realize I'm blocking the flow of people coming in the door. I hurry out of the way, toward the nearby registration tables as planned, and soon I'm exchanging my printed ticket for a wristband, program, and Legends of the Stone tote bag emblazoned with the LotS logo—a red shield, *Legends of the Stone* in yellow block lettering, and a diamond.

Then it's off to the vendors hall—except before I can go two feet, a grinning Asian guy taps me on the shoulder and asks me if I'll snap a picture of him and his friends below the shadowdragon's menacing glare. The group of five all squishes together. Two of them are cosplaying as an elf archer and some kind of dwarf, while the other three are in various nerdy shirts. They all smile cheerfully as I move back as far as I can without knocking anything over and take the shot.

Of course, I have to ask the guy to return the favor. I hand him my phone and hurry to position myself right by the dragon's reaching claw before someone else nabs the spot. Then I freeze my body into a run and my face into a scream, and the elf archer girl laughs, and for a moment, I wonder if this convention is so magical that I might have a chance with her. But by the time the guy hands my phone back, all four of his friends—including the girl—are almost at the top of the escalator that leads to the vendors hall, having already forgotten about me and my hilarious pantomime.

Which is fine. I have things to see and places to go. My fingers slip to the re-formed scab above my wrist, but the Band-Aids snap me back to attention, and I stop myself and head past the shadowdragon and up the escalator into the vendors hall, which takes up the entire top floor of the convention center.

As soon as I step off the escalator, I'm surrounded by booths of nerd gear, Noar the Boar shirts, fan art, handmade purses and baby clothes, and knit dragon hats. The booth two down looks like it's selling handcrafted chain mail and other armor. The hall isn't too busy yet, though the pathways between the booths still flow with people in nerdy shirts and cosplay. My people.

I try to keep one eye out for Code or any of Team Meister, though I'm not expecting them to be here. Seeing them here would be an added bonus—one extra opportunity—but I've got certain chances later today: the Team Meister panel after lunch, and the signing late this afternoon.

Until then, I've got my morning planned. The vendors hall now, then the girl gamer panel, followed by the mutant rabbit versus wereboars debate.

When I mentioned the girl gamer panel, Dereck called it hot (and then Jones reamed him out for a long time), but my main reason for going is ShadowWillow. I started watching her channel after she and Code completely destroyed in the PvP tournament a couple of months ago. And yeah, she's hot, and I'm not going to pretend that purple hair hasn't made it into my dreams a couple of times, but mostly I watch her channel because she's the most badass sharpshooter I've ever seen.

I mean, in that tournament, she single-handedly wiped out about half the opposition, and her channel's full of videos of her completely whooping butts at CS: GO or Rainbow Six.

There's this one video I've watched approximately a dozen times where her entire team's wiped out immediately, and she's the last one standing, so the other team's all cocky—until she snipes one of them from a rooftop, then drops in through a hole in the ceiling and takes out the other four in this stunning bam-bam-bam-bam whirlwind of a circle. It blows my mind. I'm stoked to see her in person, because I'm not sure I believe she's not actually a robot.

At a nearby stall, I pick up a magnet that says, "Ask me about my kill:death ratio," then realize I'm thinking of ShadowWillow, not Codemeister. Code's known for his hilarity, not for his gaming prowess; in that tournament, Shadow totally carried him. Fortunately for me, the entertainment factor is what people care about most.

I glance around the stall, which is mostly full of factory-manufactured knickknacks that fifty different people here could buy and ask Code to sign. Not a good way to stand out. I put down the magnet and move back into the aisle.

"Nice shirt!" I say to a guy passing by whose black shirt features a cartoon of three LotS shadowwolves howling at the moon.

"Thanks, man!" he says with a grin before moving farther down the aisle with his girlfriend.

I've gotten distracted again, but it doesn't matter, I realize. I've got plenty of time, and I know I'll find something epic. Here, the universe is on my side. Here, the universe is mine.

Sure enough, in a booth of artisan-crafted nerd stuff less than fifteen minutes later, I find it: a LotS diamond, about the size of my fist, made of some sort of foamy clay. It's the "stone" in Legends of the Stone that you never actually see in game, only in the logo; Code did a whole ridiculous video series searching for it. The perfect thing for him to sign.

"I'm pretty sure I just beat Legends of the Stone by finding this," I say to the girl running the booth as I hand over my money, and she actually laughs.

This is my place. These are my people.

It's going to be a good day.

SIX

ShadowWillow

CODE ISN'T IN THE KITCHEN WHEN I WANDER DOWNSTAIRS, WHICH IS DISAP-
pointing. After that wink from last night, hope tingles over every inch of my skin; maybe this will all be even easier than I thought. Maybe great things are ahead, and for once, I won't have to work so hard for them.

This morning, though, the whole place is empty except for Zzzzzmeister, who's staring into the toaster like it's an entrance to a rift, his reddish-brown hair pointing straight up in fear of the shadowdragon within. He's all arms and legs, as if on his latest birthday, his family each grabbed a limb and stretched and stretched until he aged up a year or ten. At eighteen or so, he's the youngest member of Team Meister, though in his wrinkly shirt and shorts, he looks like he's about twelve.

"I think it's like boiling water," I say.

He glances up at me, then back down at the toaster, then back at me. "Oh, hi. Yes, um, no one was supposed to see this." He tries to hold my gaze, but his eyes keep sliding back to his toasting bread.

"Supposed to see what?"

"My epic toaster battle. It—aha!" he shouts, and I jump as he leaps at the toaster, jabs the eject button, and yanks the two lightly browned pieces out onto his plate. "Take that, you jerk!" He picks up a spoon and points it at me. "The toaster, not you, obviously."

I laugh. "Toaster troubles?"

"Burned yesterday morning's to a crisp. Last night's too, even though Noog's turned out perfectly. Can't help but take that personally, you know." He side-eyes the toaster as he spoons a wad of grape jelly onto his toast.

I shake my head but can't help grinning. My disappointment is gone. After all, Code might not be here, and Z might not have as many subs as he does, but he's got more than me, and he's on Team Meister, and here I am hanging out in the same house as him while he jokes about toaster battles. Maybe it's just because prioritizing my channel means I turn down most party invites and don't get out much, but at this moment, it feels like life doesn't get much cooler than this.

"So, how does this work?" I ask. "I paid for my share of groceries, so can I just sort of eat whatever?"

"Oh, yeah, have at it." He waves his spoon around, and a little ball of purple goo drops onto the floor. "I wouldn't touch Wolf's energy drinks, and don't eat that packet of dried bugs on the counter, but otherwise, help yourself."

"Um . . ." I wander to where he gestured while he wipes jelly off the floor with his finger, and sure enough, there's a packet of enormous dried beetles on the counter. I pick up the corner of it with two fingers and hold it up. ". . . why?"

He looks about to lick the floor jelly off his finger, but at the last minute, he thinks better of it and washes it off in the sink. "Noog's planning to challenge VintageBeef to a bug-eating contest."

"Right." I set the package down, wondering how many subscribers I could earn if I ate that one as big as my thumb, with long pointy bits sticking out the front like ears or claws. "Is there yogurt?"

"Yeah, in the fridge. Orange juice and fruit and stuff, too. It's a good thing Ben does all the shopping, or we'd probably just live on bacon and hot dogs." He bites into his toast and jam.

I don't actually watch a whole lot of Team Meister, but I watch enough to know that Ben—Deadmeister—is kind of like the dad of the group. At around thirty, he's almost a decade older than most of them.

I grab a yogurt and a kiwi from the fridge, and Z points out the cutlery drawer. "Why do you guys call him Ben instead of Dead?" I ask as I grab a knife and cutting board. My dad thinks it's so weird that I call my gamer friends by their usernames when I talk about them at the dinner table, but I find the opposite strange. How, exactly, do you go from calling someone by one name for hours or days or years online, then at some point switch to something else?

And how, exactly, do I get Code and his followers to stop calling me Willow? I'm ShadowWillow, or just Shadow! Isn't it standard to shorten names to the first half, not the second? Apparently not.

Despite his username being Deadmeister, Ben is Ben to everyone—his followers, too. Not that he's got that many followers compared to the rest of the team. *I've* almost surpassed him—which is a completely bizarre and giddy-making thought.

"I don't know," Z says. He opens the garbage so I can toss my kiwi's peel in. "He's always been Ben to me. Maybe it's because it's weird calling someone Dead. 'Who's your friend?' 'He's Dead.' 'You're Dead, right?' 'Hey, Dead, did you grab some toilet paper at the store?' Actually, I take it back. That all sounds pretty great."

I laugh again. I haven't watched many of Z's videos, but I think I'm going to have to start. "So, where are the guys?" I ask, trying to sound casual.

"Does that mean I'm a girl?"

My face burns. Foot, meet mouth. Baby skunk, meet box of baby kittens. "Sorry, I didn't mean—"

"No, that's great. That means I get to wear girl clothes, right? I've been dying for a pink Team Meister shirt. Did you know that you can't get men's shirts in pink? Like, on the site we use, it's not even an option to offer that. I mean, maybe it's for the best, because Code and Noog would probably veto it, and some fights just aren't worth it, but still.

"Anyway, the guys are still sleeping," he says, moving on before I can find the words to ask why Code would veto it. "We were up excessively late streaming. Well, they were. I sorta fell asleep on the couch partway through." He grins sheepishly. "At college—it's my first year—I've discovered I can sleep absolutely anywhere, even right through my professors' lectures. I mean, not all of them, but my philosophy prof has this voice that could hypnotize a squirrel on speed, so it's really not my fault. So yeah, I fell asleep and they did not, so now they're asleep and I'm not."

"Right," I say. I'm fully aware how late they were up streaming, because I was up late watching, wondering if Code would mention anything about me, and just marveling in the fact that everything I was seeing on my screen was happening right downstairs. Bananas. Triple bananas. Triple banana split with whipped cream and chocolate sauce and seven maraschino cherries on top.

I wore headphones so I wouldn't disturb Lainey in the bed next to mine, who got all quiet when we got to the house, and then conked out almost immediately. She disappeared this morning while I was in the bathroom erasing the bags from under my eyes. Thank goodness I'm way too keyed up about everything to be tired.

Code didn't end up saying a thing about me, annoyingly. I glance at the time on my phone. I can't hang around much longer before I head up to the center. "Do you think they'll be up soon?"

"Nah. Our first thing isn't until after lunch. Your panel's this morning, though, right? Mind if I come with you? I'll just, uh, change out of this mess first." He looks down at the wrinkled clothes that he's probably been wearing since yesterday, then heads toward the door. "Hey," he says, turning back, "do you have anything pink I could borrow to wear? No? Too bad." He grins, then rushes down the hallway to get ready.

I finish my breakfast in the quiet, empty kitchen while I wait. If Code's wink meant what I want it to mean, I guess I won't find out until later. Which is fine, because in the meantime, I have my first ever panel to keep me busy!

It takes longer to get to the convention center than I remember from last night, so by the time we find the right hall, the rest of the panelists are already there, hanging around by the make-shift stage that's set up with a podium, a long table, and a series of mics. It's a smaller room than last night, but if all these chairs fill up, that's still a decent crowd.

Z walks right in with me, then rushes ahead to one of the girls—GrayscaleRainbow, I think—and basically smothers her in a hug. She squeals, and once he releases her, she reaches up and tousles his unruly hair, which he did absolutely nothing to when he got dressed. She's as short as he is tall, with dyed black hair in a pixie cut that highlights her prominent cheekbones, a black shirt with a colorless rainbow on it, and gray sweatpants that gather into thick elastic at her ankles.

Not too far away, the two other panelists, IsabelPlaysGames and Emmaleie, chat with our moderator, Aureylian. They're all in their thirties, though they don't feel a million years older like Meister Ben does, probably because they aren't going gray early like he is.

All of us—the panelists, the moderator, even our friends in this room, actually—are white. Did the organizers not think to try to get a woman of color on the panel? It feels isolating, sometimes, to be a girl gamer in a world where the big names—PewDiePie, Markiplier, even second-tier big names like Codemeister and the rest of his team—are almost all guys; I can't imagine how much harder it must be to be a person of color on top of that.

Beside GrayscaleRainbow, a girl I don't recognize with long burnt-orange hair and big eyes turns around. She's in impressive elf archer cosplay, complete with brown leather vest, pointy ears, and a shimmering gold bow. "Z," she says, emphasizing his nickname with a nobleness that makes it feel like she's calling him King George Henry Percival the Fifth, instead of a letter of the alphabet. "Hello!" And then the hug smothering happens all over again.

How many conventions have they all been to together? How many video collabs have they done together?

I slip my hand into my purse and run my fingers over the Sharpie that I've already used over a dozen times. And I haven't even had my autograph session yet.

This little skunk belongs here, folks!

I march toward them, trying to exude confidence (as opposed to exuding skunk stink).

Just before I reach them, Z spots me. "Willow! Have you met Gray?"

(See? GrayscaleRainbow shortened to Gray? That's the proper way to do things.)

"Hi!" I stick my hand out. "I'm ShadowWillow. You can call me Shadow."

Gray smiles brightly and shakes my hand. Her skin is absurdly soft. "Hey, Shadow."

If Z notices the change in my nickname, he doesn't say anything, just gestures toward the other girl—who, I've just noticed, has the elven crest, a circle of woven vines, stamped into her leather vest. Perfection. "And this is Marley," Z says.

"My girlfriend," Gray clarifies, slipping her baby-soft hand into Marley's. Marley scrunches her nose at Gray, who scrunches hers back, like some kind of adorable mating sign they've learned from fluffy bunnies.

Marley turns to Z. "So, Z, are you on this panel with Gray?"

Z shakes his head sadly. "No. I tried really hard to get on it. I mean, I told them, 'A panel about girl gaming with only girls on it? That's just not fair. You've got to give us white dudes a chance.

Equal opportunity!' But they said no, those bigots."

We all laugh. I have really got to start watching Z's channel.

"Nah," he clarifies, "I'm just here to support Gray and Shadow." He twists his wrists out to point his thumbs at the two of us.

Just then, the LotSCON volunteer from last night—Lorne, I think his name was—pops into our little circle. "We're going to start letting people in, if you want to take your places up on the stage."

"Thanks, Lorne," I say, and his grin tells me I got it right.

"Let's find a seat," Z says, threading his scrawny arm through Marley's.

"Don't go stealing my girlfriend!" Gray calls over her shoulder at them as we head up the stairs to the stage with IsabelPlaysGames and Emmaleie, as well as our moderator, Aureylian.

"I'm pretty sure I'm not her type," Z calls back.

It's not until we're settled onstage and the crowd is in their seats that I realize: Z called me Shadow.

I don't have time to dwell on it, though, because Aureylian dives right in, introducing us with her usual entertainer's charisma. If I were to ask for her autograph after this, would I seem like a hack who doesn't belong on this stage? I've watched a lot of panels on YouTube, and I've never seen anyone moderate with as much poise and charm as she does.

I've watched a lot of panels, but I've never *been* on one before. Until now! Dear brain, please stop ogling Aurey's talent and take in the fact that YOU ARE ON A STAGE AS PART OF A

PANEL! Triple banana split with a dozen maraschino cherries!

I grin out at the crowd with a broad smile that's hopefully friendly, not creepy, because there's no way I can reel it in.

It's a smaller hall, but almost all the seats are filled. People are holding up their cameras, taking pictures or video, and some guy with a LotSCON shirt is operating a very fancy camera, which I'm pretty sure is streaming this to Twitch.

I run my fingers quickly through my hair, glad I spent the extra time covering up my eye bags this morning.

"You'd think, what with my being an openly lesbian gamer," Gray is saying in response to a question from Aurey, "that I wouldn't have to worry about things like guys sending me pictures of their dicks, but apparently guys think they can 'fix' me." She makes air quotes with her fingers around the word "fix." "But guys, let me tell you a secret." She leans in close to the mic. "If there *was* a way to 'fix' me"—air quotes again—"it wouldn't be by sending me a picture of your floppy, hairy junk."

The laughter is thunderous. It's the right crowd for that kind of joke, apparently, which makes sense; it's the kind of crowd who'd get up early on a Saturday morning for a panel on girl gamers.

"What about you, ShadowWillow?" Aurey asks. "What's one of your pet peeves as a female gamer?"

We got the questions ahead of time, thankfully, because my brain is still nomming on that triple banana split and would never be able to answer that from scratch.

I lean toward the mic. "There's this moment that happens sometimes in Battlegrounds, when I'm playing pairs with strangers. You can hear it in a guy's voice just after the audio clicks in, when he says hi, and then you say hi, and then you can just tell: he's super bummed he got paired with a girl. I mean, being a girl means I obviously must be a noob."

"How can you tell that's what he's thinking?" Aurey asks, in a "please carry on with this fascinating story" way, not in an "I don't believe you" way.

"Because he'll usually say something right away like 'So do you even know how to play this game?'"

"Oh, brother!" Emmaleie says.

"I hope you utterly destroy in the game when that happens," Gray says.

"Uh, no," I admit. "I, um, usually crash our vehicle into a tree or set off a frag grenade and get both of us blown to smithereens, then say, 'Oops.'" I say the "oops" in the girliest, singsongiest voice I can manage, and the place erupts in laughter.

It's official. I adore this crowd.

I adore this panel.

I adore my life.

I want this to be my life forever. I have to make this happen.

We answer a couple more preplanned questions, and then the floor is opened to the audience.

"Please please please," I silently wish into the universe as people line up at the microphone in the middle of the aisle, "let one of these questions be for me. Just one." With Aureylian and Gray, long-term powerhouses with devoted fans, beside me on the stage, it seems unlikely that the questions will go to anyone but them, but I can hope. Maybe, just maybe, I could have a few fans of my own here.

A fourteen-or-so-year-old South Asian girl with perfectly straight hair rocks back and forth from her toes to her heels as she says, "My question's for Willow."

"*Shadow*," I want to correct her, but my annoyance is replaced with sudden joy as it sinks in: her question's for me. The very first question is for *me*! Thank you, universe. You're pretty badass, sometimes.

"So, are you and Code dating?"

"Are Code and I dating?" I parrot back, and the girl giggles. Her Codester T-shirt, which has a cartoon of Code's avatar standing atop an enormous diamond, jumps out at me. She's a Code fan. Of course.

I refuse to be disappointed. After all, this is why I'm here: to turn Code fans into ShadowWillow fans. And she still rushed to the front of the line, just to ask me—*me!*—her question.

The answer, of course, is "No," or at least "Not yet," but she doesn't need to know that, so instead, I put on the most "I don't know what to say; I'm so awkward and frazzled" voice I can muster and say, "Uh . . . I can't answer that, sorry."

Which sets the girl off on another small fit of giggles and sends a wave of whispering through the crowd. If questions about

Code send excited chattering about me through an entire crowd, then I'll happily answer those questions all day long.

Gray rolls her eyes at me, and I shrug in a hopefully-can-be-interpreted-fifty-different-ways kind of way. I want Gray to like me—I want everyone to like me—but I've got a lot more to gain from Code's millions of subscribers than from her half a million. And he *did* wink at me last night.

The next question is for Isabel and then two for Gray.

Then a sixteenish-year-old guy steps up to the mic. He's got a bit of a potbelly and he's clearly entrenched in an ongoing battle with acne that, judging by the spattering of scabs amid the pink dots, he's losing, but his eyes shine bright from under his mop of naturally blond hair, as though he's a kid at Disney World. This time, I spot the Codester shirt right away, so when he looks at me, my heart leaps with anticipation. It's going to be another question for me!

And I'm right. He opens his mouth and says, "Shadow, I have watched your video where you drop through the roof and slaughter the entire opposing team with a single 360-degree turn probably . . . a couple dozen times. It's badass. So my question is: how did you become so brilliant at first-person shooters?"

It's not a question about Code or about shipping. But it's still for me. I blink at him a few times as I play back the question in my head, then my stomach twists in knots as I realize that he's looking at me—like, really looking at me. He's not just Code's fan, he's mine.

As I find my voice and start to tell him about how I've been playing video games practically since I was in the womb, and how my earliest memory is of the whole family gathered around the TV playing Smash Bros. or Mario Kart, the words spilling out of me without planning or forethought, for a moment I let myself imagine a world where these are the types of questions I get from fans. A world where every tenth comment on my videos isn't about my boobs. A world where I have hundreds of thousands of fans of my own who don't care what my relationship to Codemeister is. A world where I'm on a big main panel and not just on the girl gamer panel that's first thing in the morning in what suddenly seems like such a small side room.

And then I push all those thoughts away, because that world is not this world.

I'm working with what I've got, and what I've got are a bunch of Codemeister fans that ship us together. And this one kid.

So I answer his question and smile.

SEVEN

Lainey

IF MOM KNEW I WAS OUT BY MYSELF ON THE STREETS OF TORONTO, SHE'D flip and probably never let me go along with Cody to one of these things again.

Mom has zero opinions about anything, except when it comes to me. Seriously, when I try to push her on anything—same-sex marriage, immigration, whether chocolate or vanilla is better—she says, "Well, I just don't know, Lainey." I don't think she even voted in the last election, despite me constantly hounding her. And when I asked her if she regretted it, she just said, "We'll see," as if nothing at all had happened yet that she could base an opinion on.

She has lots to say about me, though. I need to wear padded bras, I should try a Christian dating site, I'm not allowed to go with Cody to LotSCON unless I have a female roommate because "it's a house of boys, Lainey, and boys will be boys." Ugh.

Like last night, though, Saturday morning in Toronto isn't the slightest bit scary—at least, the couple of blocks I walk from the Meister Manor to the coffee shop aren't. There are already so many people around that the city feels awake and alive, despite the fact that not-alive brick and concrete stretch up all around us. The buildings are tall but handsome, with brown and tan brick and countless windows, giving the street a historic feel. I can't tell whether they really are old or whether they were built to look that way.

A morning away from Cody is just what I needed. I didn't bother asking him, just texted him that I'd be there in time for his early-afternoon panel. He probably won't be up until noon anyways.

When I make it to the coffee shop on the corner, the whole place is packed, but Legs has somehow managed to secure us a coffee table and two armchairs. I weave my way through the busy shop and slip into the armchair across from him. On the table are two coffees, a croissant, and a chocolate chip muffin. "You know, it's pretty antiquated for a guy to presume he knows what a girl wants to order," I tease, then feel my cheeks flush warm. I didn't mean to imply that this is a date. It's not a date, it's two friends meeting up for breakfast, same as a week ago at PAX, when a bunch of us were supposed to meet for breakfast, but

Team Meister all slept in and it ended up just being me and Legs. The fact that this time we planned for it to be just the two of us is irrelevant. You know, aside from the fact that, if I'm honest with myself, I do actually wish it was a date.

"These are both for me," Legs says, picking up both coffees with a grin.

"Give me that." I snatch one of them from him and swallow a mouthful of rich warmth. It's perfectly sweetened, which is no surprise; we discovered at PAX that we like our coffee the same way—sugar only, and not too much of it.

When I set the coffee down, Legs is grinning at me. I narrow my eyes at him. "What?!"

"Nothing." He takes a sip of his own coffee.

"Nothing what?!"

"You drink coffee like you've been in a desert for a week and it's the first liquid that's passed your lips since you ran out of water four days ago."

I lean back in my chair. "That is the perfect analogy," I say. "That's exactly what coffee is like. Except it's about sleep, not water. I feel like I haven't slept in a week." I take another sip of coffee. "Willow snores."

Legs snort-laughs. "She doesn't!"

"What, you think girls don't snore?"

"No, of course—I . . ." He fiddles with the lid of his cup as he trails off, then starts up again. "I mean that you don't look tired. You look nice."

My face burns hot again. He means it as a joke, probably,

to distract from his 'girls don't snore' comment, but he said it so sincerely that it's hard to take it that way.

"Shut up." I look down to hide the red in my cheeks.

"Hey, so you weren't interested in that girl gamer panel that's on now?" Legs asks. "Seems like your type of thing."

I didn't even know it was on right now. I haven't looked at the program at all. "Why, because I'm a girl and only girls are interested in hearing other girls talk?" I raise an eyebrow at him. "No, wait," I joke, "I already called you out on one sexist comment just now. You're probably maxed out for the day."

If I said that to Cody, he'd probably yell at me, but Legs only laughs. "You can call me out on my stupidity anytime. In fact, please do."

"Okay, good, because I've got another thing to call you out on."

"Oh?" Legs looks nervous.

I point at the table between us. "Are you expecting me to choose between a muffin and a croissant? Because that seems like cruel and unusual punishment."

"Of course not!" Legs says with mock seriousness as he picks up the croissant and tears it in two. Then he picks up the muffin and tries to do the same, except it's a round mass of muffin, not a long, tearable pastry, so he mostly ends up smooshing part of it between his fingers, dropping huge crumbs and a few extremely valuable chocolate chips on the floor. "That went differently in my head," he says, and he probably means it as a joke, but it comes out sort of sad.

Right, I'm supposed to be trying to talk to him about why a black cloud of unhappiness has been following him everywhere. I could just out and ask him, but the moment doesn't feel right. "I'll get a knife," I say, hopping up.

By the time I return with a plastic knife, he's managed to pull the muffin into two mangled halves. They sit on our plates with the croissant halves—well, one croissant half. He's munching the other as he stares out the window, lost in thought. I set the knife down. "What are you thinking about?"

He finishes chewing his mouthful before answering. "Toronto's a strange city."

"I think I like it." I pop a bit of muffin into my mouth.

"I mean, I don't dislike it. It's just—there's a lake, right? Lake Ontario's—what, a few blocks away? But you'd never know it from here." He waves his hand toward the window, which hosts a view of wide concrete road and sidewalk and brown and gray buildings that stretch up high enough that they fill the entire window, hiding even the sky.

"I think you could see the water from the top of this building," I say.

"Right. It's like an arms race of water views. One building's built with a nice view of the water, which means the next has to be taller to get its own view of the water, so then the next has to be even taller, and so on up and up and up."

He sounds sad, like it's a war against him directly, or maybe like it's a metaphor for something I don't quite understand. Once again, it's the perfect opportunity to ask him why he's so down, but once again, I hesitate. I don't know why. Usually, I have no problem saying whatever's on my mind. But I suddenly feel too aware of all the people chattering away at the tables around us. I stand, zip up my coat, and wrap my own croissant-muffin duo in a napkin. "Come on," I say.

"Come on where?" he calls after me as I head to the door.

"To find the water they've taken from you," I say, then slip out the door, leaving him to gather up his own coffee and breakfast and hurry after me.

Legs is right; the lake isn't far away at all. Eating our breakfast as we go, we march down a few gray blocks, passing under a highway bridge and past some enormous yellow construction machines getting their weekend rest.

And then there's the lake—gray and still, but in a different way from the still, gray buildings we passed.

The sidewalk along the water leads us to a manufactured beach built on a slab of concrete a half dozen feet above the water, with real sand and a dozen tables complete with heavy fake-wood deck chairs and bright-pink beach umbrellas scattered across the sand. "Sugar Beach," says a sign. In the cold, sunless morning, the place feels more like a graveyard than a beach. Or perhaps like a beach made by someone who's seen pictures of beaches in books but never actually been to one.

"How warm does it get here in the summer?" I ask.

Legs shrugs and sets his coffee down on one of the skeleton tables. I finished my own on the way here. "Hot, I think," Legs says. "Just as hot as Ohio or Massachusetts, probably." Ohio, where I'm from; Massachusetts, where Legs is from. He's based in Boston, though he travels a lot.

"I hope I get into Boston College," I say.

"Me too," he says, and I feel as warm as the coffee in my stomach. We've talked plenty of times about the fact that I applied to Boston College—Legs knows I applied only to states with senators I like, so when I get into politics, I'll be supporting the right kind of change—but the discussion's never before been so weighted around the edges.

"Hey, let's check out the water," I say, changing the topic before I can get my hopes up about any of it. I head toward the edge of the beach, and Legs picks his coffee back up and follows me. Along the edge of the dock, a short little fence acts like it's keeping us away from the water and the risk of falling in. The park designer must think people are idiots—which, admittedly, is mostly true.

Across the water, clumps of trees highlight an island, and industrial boats crawl past us. "Here you go, sir." I gesture toward the lake. "Your water, as ordered."

He smiles a half smile only.

I've procrastinated enough. "So, are you going to tell me what's bringing you down?" The question comes out more abruptly than I intend, but Legs straightens with purpose, not anger.

"I suppose it *would* help to talk about it, if that's okay with you."

I want to tell him that he can talk to me about absolutely

anything anytime, but instead I just say, "Of course. Talk away."

A cold wind off the lake makes us both shiver. "Well, let's just tear off the Band-Aid, I guess," Legs says once the breeze dies off. "My best friend, Brian—well, ex-best friend, I guess—told me our friendship is over."

I spit out a sympathetic swear, and Legs laughs unexpectedly. "Yeah, that's what I'd say if I wasn't trying to keep myself and my channel PG because of all the kids who watch it," he says.

"So what happened?" I ask.

His face clouds over again. "I screwed up. Big-time."

"Oh, come on, I'm sure it wasn't that—"

"It was. We made this friend at college this year, Steve. He's a really nice guy, the sort who'll email you his notes from a class you missed without you even having to ask or bring you by Nyquil when you're sick.

"But," he adds, "he's from down south, from Texas."

The way he says it makes me think he means the worst parts of Texas. "Uh-oh."

"Yeah. So he'd make these homophobic comments sometimes, not realizing that Brian's gay. Not that he should have made them if Brian wasn't gay. You know what I mean."

"That's terrible!" Anger roars up inside me. "I hope you dumped his ass."

Legs's jaw clenches, like he's shutting his mouth on words he wants to say, or maybe words he's afraid to admit. Right, he did say he screwed up. We all screw up sometimes.

"So you failed to call him out on it, huh?" I ask, taking a guess.

Legs's jaw unclenches. He nods in confirmation, slowly and sadly. "I'm not great at confrontation."

I have no problem with confrontation myself—obviously—but I get that it's difficult for some people. "And Brian ended your friendship over it? I'm sorry. That sucks!"

Legs sighs with relief, like he's glad to be past talking about his screwup and on to mourning his loss, and for a moment, I wonder if there's part of the story he's not telling me. Before I can ask, though, he says, "Yeah, we've been friends since we were seven years old. He came with me to my very first convention. Drove with me all the way across the country—even paid for half the gas, though I told him he shouldn't. It was actually Brian who came up with my username, LumberLegs. You know the type of friend."

I don't, actually. I've never had that close of a friend. Our school is small, and most of my classmates are still living in the 1800s. Standing here with Legs, I can imagine it, though. "I'm sorry. That's so hard." I put my hand on his arm.

"Everything at these conventions reminds me of him. We went to a lot of cons together. I've been trying not to talk about it around the guys, though, because I can picture exactly what they'd say if they knew I was crying about some guy."

"Ugh, yeah." I can picture it, too. "Cody's the worst some-times. I don't know what to do about it. But I hope you know that it's okay to cry about anything—guy or otherwise." I hate that little boys are told to suck it up and be a man whenever they cry.

Legs must think I mean it's okay to be *interested* in anyone, guy or otherwise, because he looks me in the eye and says, "To be clear, I'm not gay. Not that there'd be anything wrong with that if I was. But I'm not. You know, just in case you were wondering or anything." He drops his gaze back down to his feet. I want to believe the hint of red in his cheeks is from what he just said, but it could just as easily be from the chill of the wind off the lake. "I don't know, I'm just rambling now. Are you looking forward to the rest of the convention today?"

I want to press further on why he felt it was so important that I understood that he's not gay. Was it the same reason I wanted to make sure on the plane yesterday that he wasn't actually thinking of me as his sister? But maybe I'm more afraid of some types of confrontation than I realize, because instead I simply say, "Yeah, I'm really looking forward to spending the rest of the day dealing with Cody's little fanboys."

"Fans aren't so bad."

"Of course they aren't bad to you. They worship you, which probably feels fantastic." He opens his mouth to interject, and I hold up my hand. "No, shush, don't say anything. It's fine. It's okay that it feels fantastic. It's not like you've built a temple in your name and are encouraging them to idolize you. And besides, *you're* actually worship-able. Cody's the one with all these fifteen-year-old 'Codesters' running around with his face plastered across their chests, not realizing that the person they're worshipping is actually the devil incarnate. What kind of toxic stuff are they picking up on without realizing it? I wish I could show them all who he really is and watch them run away, screaming in fear." I don't actually wish that on him, of course, except that maybe then he'd actually listen.

Legs laughs, and it's nice to hear him happy. But then he keeps grinning at me.

"Stop looking at me like that. What is it?"

"You think I'm worship-able."

I grab the coffee from his hand. "Did I say that? I don't think I said that. You're imagining things. Oh, look at the time. I've got to be heading back to, you know, make sure the cameras are ready to go for the Meister panel and other very important stuff." I pivot on my heels and start walking toward downtown.

"I'll get you a shirt printed with my face on it," Legs calls after me, then runs to catch up with me, falling into stride beside me. "Or maybe yoga pants with my face plastered across the thigh?"

"You can have your face on my thigh anytime" is what I would say if I was in some alternate universe where I'm a braver, flirtier version of myself instead of this universe's supremely awkward self. "Ha!" is what I actually say.

We walk the rest of the way to the convention center together, brainstorming all the things Legs should start selling on his site with his face plastered across them.

"Oh, hand towels!" I say as we enter the hotel connected to

the convention center. We've already considered pretty much every type of clothing that exists, pot holders, comforters, pillows, mouse pads, and iPhone cases. "People can wipe off their damp hands on your rugged skin."

"That sounds very wet."

We wind our way through the hotel lobby to the convention center door. "I don't think you'd actually feel the water on your face," I say. "They're not magic towels."

"If they're not magic, what even is the point?" Legs pushes the door open for both of us, and we step into the convention center. It feels more chaotic than last night, somehow, even though there probably aren't as many people here yet as there were then. Legs and I both step to the side to take it in.

We're in a wide hallway, wide enough that there are short faux-leather chairs clustered into seating areas along the right wall behind a row of enormous cream pillars, and there's still plenty of room for the growing crowd of Legends of the Stone enthusiasts to walk through or mill about or stare up at the huge posters on the wall—including one big one of my brother. I don't know how I missed seeing that last night. Ick. No one needs to see Cody's face blown up as big as the sun.

The thing I didn't realize about geek conventions before is that some of the stereotypes about geeks are actually true. I mean, not across the board, but amid the brilliant cosplay and geek chic, there are the clusters of guys in sweatpants and oversize shirts, with questionable hygiene. Part of me wants to yell at them for giving nerds a bad name, but another part of me wishes I could wear sweatpants and an oversize shirt and not care if people thought I looked sloppy.

Except, don't actually be sloppy about the hygiene part, folks. Can we all agree right here right now that good hygiene is a vital cornerstone of the society we live in?

The day's just getting going, but there's already a group of these guys hanging out at one of the coffee tables playing cards. In the circle of chairs next to them is what looks like a whole extended family, with two young kids, parents, grandparents, and probably an aunt—all of them holding LotSCON tote bags emblazoned with the Legends of the Stone logo of a red shield, yellow lettering, and a bright-cyan diamond.

There are a lot more guys than girls here, as usual, though as I think that, a girl glides past in an intricate black and red shadow-lady dress that drapes over her shoulders, then somehow skips her exposed stomach before flowing down to the floor. Her curly red hair spills out all over the place in perfect chaos.

By the left wall, a couple of white guys in jeans and T-shirts whip out their phones and snap pictures of her as she passes without even attempting to ask her permission, which is so against convention etiquette—against general human etiquette, really—that it makes my blood boil.

I whirl around to complain to Legs, but it turns out Legs has been spotted.

A teen guy with spiky black hair and warm beige skin is

asking him for an autograph. We just walked a dozen blocks in downtown Toronto and no one we passed even gave Legs a second glance, but here at LotSCON, he's basically royalty.

Legs finishes signing the guy's foam sword. "Be awesome!" he tells the guy as he walks away. He turns back to me. "What's got you looking like you smell a rotting corpse?"

"What?"

He scrunches up his face in what I realize is an imitation of my own.

I force my own facial muscles to relax. "Oh, just some guys taking pictures of a girl in cosplay without her permission." When I glance back at them, one is taking a picture of the other standing under the huge photo of my brother. Of course they're Codemeister fans. Cody did the exact same thing at PAX; he took a picture of this girl in a skintight Gamora costume without asking her, and when I told him that's against the rules, he said, and I quote, "That's garbage. A girl who wears a costume like that wants to be looked at." The elastic band that exists inside me stretches tight and angry just thinking about it.

"Those guys over there?" Legs juts his perfect chin in the direction of the guys. "Let's go tell them to cut it out."

"Really?" That doesn't feel very Legsian. Legs is the best human I know, but like he said by the water, confrontation is not his strong suit. He once worried for a week about sending a fan an email telling her not to release her turtle into the wild.

"Yeah, I mean, Brian was right. I've got to be less afraid of doing stuff like that. What's the worst that could happen? Come on." And with that, we're marching over to the two guys, who look to be about my age. They've put away their phones and are flipping through their programs.

"Hey," Legs says once we reach them, and they both look up. The one guy's face lights up with recognition immediately, and Legs smiles at him. "We happened to see you guys take a picture of someone in cosplay without asking her permission, and we wanted to make sure you knew that's against the rules, so you don't get in trouble."

"You should never take a picture of someone without their permission," I add, feeling suddenly like a television PSA.

I expect them to bristle like Cody always does when I try to call him out on stuff. But instead, the Legs fan grins. "Oh, I didn't know that," he says. "Thanks, man. Hey, could I have your autograph?"

Is it the fact that Legs is clearly his hero that made the guy listen? Or is it something about Legs himself, and the way he spoke so calmly and kindly? I get too angry to talk like that.

Legs signs one's tote bag and the other's program, then tells them to "Be awesome!" before we walk away.

"They were surprisingly happy to be told they screwed up by a superstar YouTuber," I say to Legs after we're out of earshot. The realization makes me unexpectedly sad. If Cody didn't spend so much time being a dick, I could be encouraging him to make positive change like this. With his millions of subscribers, he could do so much good. "Thanks for doing that."

"With great power comes great responsibility, I guess." Legs laughs with relief, and I have to push away the desire that bubbles up to lean right in and kiss him on his beautiful, laughing mouth. "That was a lot easier than I expected," he continues.

Which gives me an idea. "Hey, you should talk to Cody! You're so good at it! Just tell him the stuff I said yesterday. Maybe he'd actually listen to you."

Instead of lighting up with excitement, Legs's eyes darken. "Talk to your brother? I don't know, Lainey. I'm not sure that's a good idea. You're better off asking Z or something."

Why would he be willing to talk to these strangers, but not be willing to talk to my own brother about something that matters to me? I want to argue with him. I want to tell him that I bet he didn't think these fans would listen to him either. I want to say that he'll never know unless he tries. But I'm too disappointed in him. And I hate feeling disappointed in someone I usually think of as one of the world's best humans.

So I drop it.

"Want to go check out a panel or something?" I ask, changing the subject, even though I can't imagine there's anything I'd be interested in seeing other than that girl gamer panel Legs mentioned that I apparently just missed.

He shakes his head. "Think I'll hide away somewhere. I'm not in the mood for telling people they're awesome right now." Right, he's still sad. Maybe if he wasn't so down, he'd be up for talking to Cody. I want to believe that.

I can't help but wonder, though, if it's not the sadness but just who Legs is. Is it easier for Legs to talk to strangers like those fans than to his friends like that homophobic Steve guy? Is this the part of the story Legs isn't telling me? That even after Brian asked him, Legs still wouldn't call his dickhead friend out?

"You don't always have to tell people they're awesome." The words come out harsher than I intended.

"It's my catchphrase. I kind of do."

"I thought your catchphrase was 'To the rift!'"

A group of guys passing us must catch my last few words, because they pump their fists and echo, "To the rift!" They grin at Legs, who's forced to grin back.

The grin falls off his face as soon as they pass. "I think I'll go chill in the VIP lounge like last night."

I shrug. "Okay. I'll join you."

"Oh, no, I'd feel bad keeping you from the convention."

"Yeah, because I'm such a LotS fangirl and would be devastated to miss even a minute," I say, and Legs laughs, the tension falling away between us. I enjoy playing LotS, but I play maybe once a month, if that, and I haven't even bothered looking through the schedule in the program. My gaming expertise is . . . low. At PAX, I referred to LotS as a MMORPG, then had to endure a rant from Noog about how girls know nothing about video games and how MMORPGs are games played with thousands of people online in the same world at the same time, not smaller multiplayer games with private servers like LotS, or something like that. I was too busy trying to keep myself from punching him in the face to pay proper attention.

Cody, of course, agreed with him.

So after spending several days at PAX East with those idiots, I'm a little conventioned out. "Honestly, it'd be nice to have a bit of quiet before I have to deal with Cody and the gang."

"All right, then. Let's go be hermits together," he says.

As we head off, I glance over my shoulder at those two guys, wondering if they'll actually start asking permission now. "Legs, do you think people can change?" I repeat the question I asked Willow last night.

He considers as we round a corner. "I have to believe they can."

I frown. If that's true, why wouldn't he at least try to make a change in Cody by talking to him? Well, regardless, I have to believe it, too. I have to believe that Cody can change.

I'm not giving up on Cody like Brian gave up on Legs. And if Legs won't help, I'll just find someone else who will. I'll just keep trying.

@LumberLegs: If I finally started selling merch, what should I start with: shirts, phone cases, or hand towels?
[1.4K likes]

@LumberLegs: Why do so many of you want to dry your hands on my face?
[2.2K likes]

EIGHT

SamTheBrave

WHEN THE GIRL GAMER PANEL FINISHES, BEFORE THE CLAPPING HAS COM-
pletely died down, the Asian guy sitting next to me leans over. His
arms and face are a little pudgy, like he never lost his baby fat, and
his beige Team Meister shirt has been worn so many times that
it's starting to fray along the collar. "Do you know when the Team
Meister panel is?" he asks. "I lost my program."

I'm 99 percent sure it's at one o'clock, but if they're his all-time
favorite gamers, 99 percent doesn't feel like enough, so I simply
hand over my own program.

"Thanks." He starts flipping through the pages at a leisurely pace. "Do you think they'd give me a new program if I asked?"

I want to try to get ShadowWillow's autograph as she's leaving, but she hasn't even gotten up from her seat onstage yet, so there's still time. "I don't know. They've got all the info online, though."

He taps his pocket. "I'm out of data. And he's grounded, so no phone." He points to the scrawny white guy beside him wearing gray sweatpants and a baggy black shirt with a shadowdragon on it. His brown hair is combed to the side, except for one rebellious strand in the middle that sticks straight up.

"The schedule's at the very back of the program," I say to the first guy. Then to the second, "Should you be here if you're grounded?"

"I'm not grounded," the white guy says—or at least, I think that's what he says. His voice is quiet and the room is loud. The seats have mostly emptied, but there are still lots of people milling about. Shadow is still onstage, chatting with the other panelists. I lean in closer so I can hear the guy's response. "Mom just took my phone away and replaced it with some antique that doesn't even connect to the internet. For emergencies or something."

"Why'd she take it away?" It might be rude to ask, but I'm curious. The only rebellious things about this guy are that stubborn cowlick and the fact that he's wearing sweatpants in public. (Not that I'm one to talk, since I almost did the same.)

He shrugs. "I stayed up all night doing rift raids the night before my great-grandma's birthday party."

"One o'clock," the Asian guy reports before I can react. "The panel's at one."

"Okay." His friend pulls a pen out of his sweatpants pocket and scrawls the time on the inner part of his right arm.

"Thanks." The first guy hands the program back to me. "I'm Mark, by the way. This is Leroy."

"No jokes about the name," Leroy spits out.

I throw my hands up in surrender. "Wouldn't dream of it."

"Good. Can I borrow your phone?"

He's looking at me. "Oh, uh . . ." I'd never ask a stranger to use their phone, unless I was calling 911 or something.

"I want to look up some stats for our tourney."

Then again, spending only a couple of hours at Opa and Oma's house without my phone is torture, so I can't imagine spending a whole weekend without it. I pull my phone out of my pocket and unlock it. "Yeah, I guess that's—"

Leroy takes the phone out of my hand.

"Who's SamTheBrave?" Mark asks, looking over Leroy's shoulder at the Twitch page I had open to show Code.

"Oh, that's me. I'm Sam, by the way," I add, realizing that I haven't actually introduced myself.

"That's so cool. Are you famous? Should I be asking for your autograph?" Mark stands and Leroy follows suit and I do too; I guess I'm going wherever they are, since Leroy's still got his face buried in my phone. As long as they don't go too far, because I still want Shadow's autograph.

"Nah, my channel's really small," I say as we start winding out of the row. "I'm actually hoping to convince Codemeister to check it out this weekend. If he even just tweeted about it once—"

"That'd be epic!" Mark says, jumping in excitedly. "What's your pitch?"

"My pitch?"

"Yeah, like say you only have ten seconds to convince him. Hang on. . . ." We stop in the aisle as he pulls his own phone out of his pocket, then presses a few buttons. "Okay . . . go!"

"Oh, um . . ." I pause for a moment to think, then remember his timer's running. "Well, I'm SamTheBrave . . . and I have a Twitch chan—"

"Time! You need some practice."

Shoot, that went fast. We start moving down the aisle again. "I'm sure I'll get more than ten seconds."

"Maybe. But I've heard those autographs go by really fast."

Why didn't I think to practice a quick pitch? I want to reach for a fidget ball in my pocket, but I don't want to have to explain what it's for, and I have a feeling these guys would ask.

"Okay, 27 speed and 43 attack," Leroy says, handing me back my phone. "27 speed, 43 attack," he repeats to himself, then pulls his pen out of his pocket and writes it on his arm beside the *1 p.m.*, though in smaller letters this time.

I glance back at the stage before we exit the room. Shadow is still up there. I can see her purple hair shining out from where she's talking to GrayscaleRainbow and Aureylian.

"So, *can* I get your autograph?" Mark says as we step into the hall, and it takes me a moment for me to realize he's talking to me again. "Maybe Code'll make you super famous, and I'll be able to prove that I knew you when." He pats his pockets. "I don't have anything for you to sign, though."

"You could sign my arm," Leroy says, holding it out.

"Maybe we'll run into each other after you guys get new programs," I say, and Leroy thankfully drops his arm. "By then, maybe I'll have convinced Code to check out my channel and I'll basically be famous."

"Maybe you will!" Mark says, and the fact that he's serious instead of laughing somehow makes me more nervous. "Practice that pitch, though. Ten seconds!" Leroy is already wandering down the hall. Mark starts walking backward after him. "Nice to meet you, Sam. Catch you around."

"Yeah, see you. Bye, Leroy!" I call after his slowly retreating back.

Leroy raises his ink-scrawled arm in the air and gives a not-unfriendly wave but doesn't look back, which for some reason makes me laugh.

With the two of them gone, I head to the doorway closest to the stage. I finally pull a fidget ball out of my pocket and roll it between my fingers so they don't wander to my face or arms without me noticing. It's not only when I'm nervous that I need them. My fingers are just as likely to slip out of my control when I'm bored or distracted or concentrating on something. Though admittedly I am the tiniest bit nervous. I mean, she's ShadowWillow!

When none of the panelists appear right away, I pull out my phone and check my YouTube comments to distract myself. There are three new ones.

> Lolololololololol

> Stumbled across this video, and it's hilarious. Checked out some of your other videos, and your recent ones are all top-notch. I've subbed and followed your Twitch channel, too! Looking forward to more.

> this is so dumb your an idiot. I bet your face is as ugly as this video and that's why you never facecam

I blink at that last message. It's just a troll, one of the internet's joyful spreaders of hatred and bile. I get the odd comment like this, and like Jones would say, you haven't made it as a YouTuber unless you get grammarless hate spewers commenting on all your videos.

It's just garbage that doesn't matter, and I should ignore it. I force my hand away from the pimple it's found on my face and read through the two nice comments again, trying to fill my brain with them instead. When that doesn't work, I shove it all out of my head and message Dereck and Jones instead: I'm going to try to get ShadowWillow's autograph right now.

Dereck's probably sleeping, since it's the middle of the night in Australia, but Jones's little face bubble pops up right away.

Ooh, are you going to ask her to show Code your videos?

My stomach twists. The thought didn't even occur to me. All that occurred to me is that I want her autograph, and why wait until her scheduled signing, if she's even doing one, when I could get it now? It didn't occur to me to wonder whether she might be connected to Code. I hadn't even realized all that shipping was still going on until people asked questions about it at the panel.

Before I can reply, I catch a blur of purple out of the corner of my eye. Shadow! She's coming out of the hall with a few people.

"Shadow! Could I have your autograph?"

She turns toward me, and for a moment, I wish I could be in my LotS skin instead of in this big, bumbling body that doesn't feel like mine, with the face that troll could sense through the internet is ugly. What if she thinks I'm too fat or too ugly or too gross to be worth her time? What if she thinks I'm rude for interrupting?

But when her eyes settle on me, she only smiles. "Of course." She reaches into her purse and pulls out a Sharpie in one smooth motion. "What would you like me to sign?"

I should have thought of this before! Why didn't I buy that magnet in the vendors hall? In my bag, I do have that cyan clay diamond that I found in the vendor's tent. It's big enough for multiple signatures, but if I had someone else sign it first, I wouldn't be able to tell Code that I got it specifically for him to sign.

The only other thing I have on me is my program, so I take my own advice to Mark and Leroy and hand it to her. The LotS logo, with its shiny diamond over a red and orange shield, takes up most of the cover, but there's plenty of room around it for signatures.

She takes it, smiling. Her purple hair is sort of shiny and mesmerizing. Her friends have fallen back, and instead of checking over her shoulder every few seconds to make sure they aren't leaving her, she's looking right at me. "What's your name?" she asks.

If I ever see Mark again, I'm telling him he's wrong about the ten seconds. It's been longer than that already.

"Uh, Sam." It's silly to stammer about my own name, but at least I didn't accidentally call myself Sammy boy.

The program is thin and flimsy, so she makes me turn around and uses my back as a hard surface. I shove away the thought of how hot that is, because that's not what this is about.

"There you go," she says once she's finished. She hands the program back to me. "Are you having a good convention so far?" She's even kinder than I expected her to be, and I try to slot this feeling away in my brain. If I ever make it big with my channel, who she is right now is who I want to be: someone who makes nerds feel even more comfortable in this nerdy world of ours.

I nod. "It's fantastic." I wish she was more of a streamer

instead of mostly a YouTuber only, so I could ask her to check out my Twitch channel for herself; then I wouldn't need Code at all. "I love this place."

She grins. "Me too. It's bananas how magical it is."

Maybe I really could ask her to show my videos to Code, like Jones said.

Maybe she'd do it.

Except something about that feels gross; it might seem like I wasn't interested in her autograph at all, just using her to get to Code. Which is definitely not the case. I adore her videos.

As if she can read my mind, she leans in and says quietly, "Thanks so much for your question today. It was fun to answer one that wasn't about Code."

Welp, that cinches it. "I love your channel," I tell her truthfully, and she grins big.

"It was really nice to meet you!" she says, which feels like the thing I should be saying to her, but before I can say that, she's gone, hurrying down the hall after her friends.

I watch her walk away, then realize I'm staring at her hips where her long, fitted shirt perfectly hugs the curve of her body, and I make myself stop watching her walk away.

I pull out my phone and stare at Jones's last message:

Ooh, are you going to ask her to show Code your videos?

I'm not sure how best to explain why I didn't. If I told Jones that I was worried about Shadow's feelings, Jones would probably laugh in my face and tell me that when I have a few hundred thousand subscribers like Shadow does, that's when I can worry about her feelings. Or maybe she'd tell me that I'm being sexist in some way. Am I?

Instead of trying to explain at all, I simply say, Nah. Timing wasn't right.

Jones writes back immediately; a chicken emoji pops up on the screen.

I roll my eyes, but she can't see that, so I write, Ha ha.

I am not a chicken. I'm doing the right thing. That's different.

I glance down at the program and realize that Shadow actually wrote something instead of just signing her name.

> Sam,
> Thanks for coming to our panel and for your super-kind question!
> Dream big!
> ♥ Shadow/Willow

I read through the words again. My big dream right now is to have Code check out and promote my channel.

But I did the right thing, and that's what's most important. Isn't it?

NINE

ShadowWillow

I CATCH UP TO Z, STILL GRINNING FROM THE RUSH OF SIGNING *ANOTHER* autograph—and this one for an actual fan of me, not just Code. Not that I don't love signing autographs for the CodeShadow shippers, too. I'll happily sign autographs for anyone who wants one. Though maybe one day it'll be mostly fans like that kid. I can dream.

Z looks up from his phone as I fall into step beside him and the others. "The guys are here," Z says. "And Lainey says Legs is in the VIP room, so I think I'll tell the guys to head there. You want to join us?"

Would I like to hang out with a bunch of famous YouTubers in a room where only VIPs are allowed to go?! "Of course!" I practically shout, and he quirks an eyebrow. "Did that come out too loud? I'm having a good day."

Gray and Marley announce they're heading for the food court, and I beg Marley for a photo with her in her impressive cosplay before they go—though it doesn't take much begging. Her face goes all shiny with happiness when I rant about how much I adore the elven crest stamped into her vest. "I love careful craftmanship," I say, and she tells me about the hours of work that went into it as Gray holds up my camera and we pose.

Z jumps into the picture at the last minute, and I joke-yell at him for blocking the crest with his very tall head, and then we take another picture with Z properly posing just behind us. When I check the picture after and discover that Z's giving us both bunny ears, I don't even care. It really is a good day.

We say goodbye to Gray and Marley and head toward the VIP room—a place that I have access to not just because I'm with VIPs, but because I *am* a VIP! Bananas! (Claire says I use that word too much, but sometimes things are just really really bananas, okay?!)

And that's when I realize: "So, is Code going to be there?"

"Should be," Z says. "I think they all came over here together."

"Right." I force my smile to stay on my face, but I feel like my heart is pounding through my teeth. This is it, then. I'm finally going to meet him in person, face-to-face.

This could be the big turning point in my career—well, the second one. That tournament was the first. And I want this one to add to that one—triple or quadruple it, even, and this time actually keep up the momentum.

I want more of this. More signing autographs, more questions from people in awe of my skills, more conventions surrounded by awesome people and brilliant cosplayers and fellow baby skunks just like me. I'm willing to work my butt off and do what I need to do to achieve it.

I want a reason to tell my dad that when I start university in the fall, it makes sense to go to school part-time, because getting a degree is important, but so is ensuring that my hopefully millions of subscribers stay entertained and interested. I want the advertising money to pay not only for school but for me to move out of my parents' basement altogether. I don't think Dad could complain about that. I think he'd be proud of that.

I want success.

But if Code and I don't hit it off, there's a good chance none of that will happen. Because I'm not playing up my relationship with Code if there isn't even the possibility of one. I'm not making something out of nothing; I need there to be at least a spark.

We weave through the crowds, passing a girl in a sexy mutant rabbit costume—not a monster that I'd normally think of as sexy, but she makes it work—and a guy with some shoulder pads and a foam sword who I think is trying to pass as a dwarf. "Do you ever cosplay?" I ask Z.

He shakes his head. "I'm basically all thumbs." He holds up his hands as if he's showing me proof. "I'd try to make a badass elf costume and end up as a wereboar."

"I mean, frothing wereboars are actually sort of cool."

"Not the frothing kind. Just a regular old smelly wereboar. Smelly because I'd forget to shower because I'd be too busy trying to figure out how I superglued fuzzy brown fabric to my nose."

I laugh. "No cosplaying for you, then. We can't have you damaging your particularly exceptional nose. I mean, it's probably your best feature." It's a joke, obviously, but now that I'm looking at it, he does have a genuinely nice nose—it's long and thin, like him, and it's dotted with tiny freckles that are so adorably delicious I want to sprinkle them on my ice cream sundae.

"Right?!" He taps the freckled bridge. "They should put this thing in a museum—except preferably not cutting it off my face, which I guess means I'd have to sit there in the museum, so I really hope they'd feed me, and I don't know where I'm going with this, so do you cosplay?"

It takes me a moment to register the question at the end of his ramble. I shift my purse on my shoulder. "I dabbled in high school. I love trying to turn fiction into reality. It's like waving a magic wand at a page or a screen and giving a character life—and the more accurate and detailed the result, the stronger your magic must be, you know?

"I haven't done anything this past year, though. I didn't really realize that until right now. I've been so busy with YouTube stuff that I haven't had time for much else."

He nods. We've stopped in the hallway beside a LotSCON-volunteer-monitored door that must be a back door to the VIP room. I must be even more nervous to meet Code than I thought, because I don't feel quite ready to go in. Z doesn't move to go in either. "So are you not in school then? Or working?"

"Just YouTube," I say. "I know I need to go to university. I mean, even if my channel takes off, that won't last forever, so I need something to fall back on." Apparently Dad has gotten into my head, because I'm reciting one of his lectures practically verbatim—and believing it. "But I have no idea what I want to do. I'm eighteen; how am I supposed to know what I want to do with the rest of my life? That's a very long time to be stuck as an accountant or a surgeon or something."

"You know you want to do YouTube, though."

"That's about the only thing I know. I'd do YouTube for the rest of my life if I could. Which is why my parents let me take one year—but one year only—to work on building up my channel. In the fall, I'm off to university no matter what—if I want the education fund they've saved up for me and if I want to keep living in their basement, that is."

"Lucky," Z says. "Your parents sound great."

"Yeah. They are," I say, and I mean it. "What are you going to school for?"

His mouth quirks into a grin. "Accounting," he says, and then he marches up to the LotSCON volunteer—not Lorne this time—shows him his badge, and holds the door for me with a flourish of his arm.

I laugh for about the millionth time this morning, then show my own badge and head inside.

We're entering the room from a different direction than last night, and it takes me a moment to orient myself. The chairs by the other door, where Legs sat last night, are now pulled into a circle and filled with people I don't recognize. Z steps past me and heads in the opposite direction, toward a couch and armchairs around a coffee table. A couch and armchairs filled with Team Meister!

They're all there—all except Oz, of course, who's in Australia. Code, Noog, Ben, and some older non-Meister guy I don't recognize, plus a non-Meister guy I recognize but don't remember the name of. Off to the side, Legs, Lainey, and Wolf are standing in a little half circle, chatting. Z basically runs over to them and wraps Legs in an enormous hug before Legs has time to realize what's happening. When Legs reemerges from being smothered, though, he's grinning. Z puts his arms around both Legs and Lainey. He starts to wave me over with the hand resting on Lainey's shoulder before she reaches up and swats his floppy hand off her shoulder.

I force my gaze away and look back toward Code, who looks up at me at the same time. He smiles, which makes me smile, which means we're both just staring at each other smiling, which is super dorky but also really really good news. "Willow!" he says at last, his voice a little too loud and deep for this tiny room. "Join us!" He gives Noog beside him a shove. "Dude, stop being a jerk. Give the lady your seat."

Noog hops up, apparently not at all offended. "My lady," he says in his slightly nasally voice, gesturing toward his abandoned seat.

I'm suddenly unsure what to do with my hands. I wrap one around my purse strap and let the other hang loose at my side, hoping it looks natural and not like a zombie appendage, as I stride over, step over the other guys' legs, and slip into the seat beside Code.

The couch is worn and very spacious, and I catch my critical error immediately; I've plopped down in the middle of the cushion instead of on the left side close to Code, which means there are miles of space between Code and me. We could fit a whole family of skunks between us.

Still, I'm close enough to see the tiny scar just above his right eyebrow and the way his cheeks ball up like cherries when he grins. Which he's still doing. "Hi," he says.

"Hi," I say back. And a million words pass between those two simple hellos—or at least, I think they do, until Code turns away and starts telling the guy across from him a story about someone on the plane who thought he knew Code from the movies, leaving me alone in my seat on this couch, with a million miles between us. Crap.

It probably means nothing. Maybe he promised to tell the guy that story and doesn't want to be rude and ignore him. Maybe he has a good reason for ignoring me now. Maybe.

Code stretches his arm out across the back of the couch as he rambles on. If I was closer to him, his arm'd basically be around me. But it's not. Not even a little bit.

I have got to do something. I look around. The coffee table is strewn with mostly empty takeout containers, phones, and that bag of dried bugs from this morning that Noog was going to use to challenge another YouTuber to a contest. It looks like they've all just eaten—the takeout, not the bugs—which means that if I want to keep hanging out with them until their panel, I'm probably skipping lunch. It's a good thing I stuffed my purse with granola bars.

Noog's gone off to dig through a bag in the corner, but Wolf, Legs, Z, and Lainey are standing nearby, and it occurs to me suddenly that they couldn't sit even if they wanted to. There aren't enough chairs. I mean, they're chatting away and don't look like they want to, but still, I could use this. "Hey, Lainey," I say, and she turns to me. "There's lots of room on the couch if you want to sit. I could scooch over."

She crinkles her nose like she can smell the invisible family of skunks. "I'm good, thanks."

Before I can consider whether her aversion's to me or to sitting generally or to something else, Z's hopping over Ben's feet, stepping over the coffee table, and smooshing himself between me and the guy on my other side who I really should have introduced myself to. I squish over to make room for him, and even though I was technically the evil mastermind behind the whole thing, suddenly being hip to hip with Code makes my heart pound so loudly, I'm sure that everyone can hear it. Especially Z, who I'm now hip to hip with on my other side.

Code doesn't stop his story, though, and for a moment I think it's all over and I've lost, but then Code's arm, spread along the back of the couch, touches lightly against my shoulder and stays there—not in a "his arm's around me" kind of way but close enough that I can't help but think that maybe, just maybe, it's intentional.

A grin spreads across my face. I let myself breathe in the magic of this moment only briefly before opening my purse and pulling out my phone so I can snap a picture of myself squashed between two Team Meister members, on a couch, at a LotSCON convention, where I was just a featured panelist.

Well, I try to snap a picture, but it's mostly my face, extra big, and the sides of theirs.

"Here, can I help?" Code asks, interrupting his own story to take my phone from me, his fingers brushing against mine. His arms are a bit longer than mine, so in theory he should capture a wider picture, but with his other arm still on the back of the couch behind me, he can't actually reach that far, and his attempt at a picture isn't much better than mine.

I laugh and good-naturedly snatch the phone back from him. "Here, Z, maybe you can manage better," I say, passing it over.

And sure enough, with his extra-long arms, Z captures all three of us perfectly in the picture.

"It's vlog time," Noog announces as I thank both Code and Z and put my phone away. Noog has resurfaced from the bag in the corner, holding a camera.

"Dude, you're so much better at remembering to vlog than I am," Code says. His arm is still behind me on the couch, touching ever so slightly against my left shoulder blade. "Codesters are always complaining I don't vlog enough." He pauses for a moment, then shouts at his sister, "Hey, Lainey, new job for you: you're in charge of filming my vlogs now. Can you head back to the house and get the Canon PowerShot camera? It's in the living room, near the computers where we were streaming last night." He glances at his phone. "If you go now, you'll easily make it back in time for our panel."

He wants her to walk all the way back to the Meister Manor to get his camera for him? If one of my brothers tried to boss me around like that, I'd smack him. In fact, I'd probably smack both of them, to make sure the other one didn't get any ideas.

Lainey doesn't smack Code, just frowns. "That's a long walk. Can't you use your phone or Noog's or something? There's like a dozen cameras lying around here."

"Mine's better, though."

She glances at the camera in Noog's hand, then back at her brother. "Isn't it the same as Noog's?"

"Yeah, but it's *mine*. Come on. I'll buy you something in the vendors hall. There's like some nerdy purses in there or something, right?"

At the mention of nerdy purses, her eyes narrow into a death stare. "A thousand dollars. Pay me a thousand dollars, and I'll do it." Guess she's not a fan of nerdy purses. I love a good nerdy purse—though like Lainey, I don't love being asked to do something the asker is perfectly capable of doing. But Code is probably nervous about making it back in time for his panel.

He laughs, but there's anger bubbling beneath it. "Do you have any idea how much I'm already paying for you for this trip?"

"Yes, I know exactly how much, because you've told me a hundred times. No deal." There's a reason I'd never work with or for my brothers; it'd probably look exactly like this.

"And heeeeeeeeeeere we have the VIP room at LotSCON!" Noog's high-pitched vlog intro saves us all from sibling-related nuclear warfare as Code throws on a cocky smirk for the camera. Lainey turns her back on Code, dismissing him. I slide farther back into my seat—bumping into Code's arm with my neck. He doesn't move his arm, and I don't move my neck, and this is it, we're about to be in a vlog smooshed together on a couch. If this doesn't stoke the rumor fires, I don't know what would.

Except Noog's camera slides right past us, maybe catching us in the frame, maybe not. "And that's where the doughnuts should be," Noog tells his future viewers, pointing the camera at an empty side table. "Except none of you have brought me doughnuts. I'm very disappointed in you all."

I need a way to bring his camera back on me—or rather, on me sitting here with Code's arm practically around me. I glance around the room, then at the coffee table, then finally at the bag of dried bugs. Perfect.

"Hey, Noog!" I shout, and his head swivels toward me but his camera doesn't. "If you're hungry . . ." I snatch up the package of dried bugs on the coffee table and hold it up. "I challenge you to a bug-eating competition later."

This time, his camera follows his head. "Say that again."

I settle back into the couch—back into the space outlined by Code's arm—and hold the bag at chest height. "I, Shadow-Willow, challenge you, Noogmeister, to a bug-eating competition later today."

Z grabs the bag out of my hand and scrunches his beautiful nose as he peers at the big black beetles on the opaque white packaging.

"Gross!" says Noog. "No one's going to kiss you if your breath smells like bug."

I'm sure he wouldn't have said that if it was Z or Wolf who challenged him; being a girl means my mouth exists only to be more or less kissable. I'm not about to say that, though. "What, you guys are so scared of bugs that you won't kiss a girl who's so *not* scared of them that she's eaten one?" I say it to all of them, but I turn to Code.

"I'm not scared of bugs," he says, and I grin. I can already picture the CodeWillow (CodeSHADOW) shippers parsing the heck out of that statement.

"Code's in, too," I say.

"Wait, what? I'm not eating no bugs!"

Z snort-laughs and holds his hand up for a high five, which I give him, because why not?

"Not eating no bugs means you're eating some bugs," Wolf points out.

"It's done," Ben says. "Code, Willow, and Noog are eating bugs tonight back at the Meister Manor." And because Ben is the boss man, his word makes it so.

Noog turns the camera on himself. "What have I gotten myself into?" he asks, hamming it up for the camera, even though he's the one who brought the bugs and was planning to issue a bug-eating challenge himself.

"You owe me big-time," Code says to me once the camera is off.

I simply shrug and try to give him my most flirtatious smile. "I think you owe me, for including you in this brilliant idea."

He shakes his head, but he's smiling, too, with his dimpled cherry cheeks. "We'll see," he says, and raises his eyebrows up and down a couple of times like that means something—and maybe it does. This is all going so much better than I could have hoped.

"So which one are you going to eat?" Z breaks in, and I lean over and look at the package.

"Which do you think would go down easiest?" I ask, and we debate the pros and cons of the smaller beetle with the giant pincers versus the bigger beetle with the ridged back. All of them are going to taste absolutely terrible, I'm sure, but who cares. The biggest content creator at this whole convention is flirting with me, and not only that, but Noog's vlog is going to show the whole thing happening. If that doesn't hook the shippers on my channel, I don't know what will.

And all I have to do in return is eat a bug. Not a bad trade. Not a bad trade at all.

@LumberLegs: So stoked to be hanging with the Meisters at LotSCON! It's always a good time when these guys are around! Woot!

[2.5K likes]

TEN

Lainey

I DON'T UNDERSTAND THE APPEAL OF GAMING CONVENTIONS. I MEAN, I GET that attendees get to preview new games and expansions or whatever. And the vendors hall usually has a few cool things in it, and the cosplay is always impressive.

But there are so many people. You have to line up to do pretty much anything, including use the bathroom or buy food, your ears are always full of a hundred voices talking all at once, and you can't even breathe without inhaling someone's perfume or garlic breath or stale sweat.

Even here in the VIP room, there are more people than chairs and the chairs themselves feel packed in. Beside me, Legs lets his shoulders sag as Noog finishes vlogging and turns his camera off, permission for Legs to turn his phony happy self off as well.

We didn't get very much hermit time, because the guys showed up earlier than expected, filling the small room with their raucousness.

I'd suggest to Legs that we get out of here, since there's some time before I'm supposed to help with the guys' panel, but if Legs won't talk to Cody, then I do want to ask Z to do it. Someone's got to.

I should have asked Z before, when he came over to say hi to me and Legs. Now, he's squashed on the couch between Shadow-Willow and a YouTuber named Squigglez. If I wait too long, the weekend will be over, and I won't see him again for months.

I touch Legs lightly on the arm and let him know I'll be back shortly; then I stride over to the back of the couch, rolling my eyes at Cody's arm, which is already around Willow's shoulders. Good thing I warned Janessa to stay off Cody's social media. I tap Z on his shoulder. "Hey, Z, can I talk to you?"

"Of course." He hops immediately to his feet, understanding right away that I don't mean here, in the middle of this big group of people.

Willow watches as he hops over Squigglez's feet and comes around the couch to follow me out of the room.

In the hallway, I lead Z over to the opposite wall, trying to get away from people, which is an impossible task. Even this back hallway is packed.

But when you're trying not to be overheard, I suppose the next best thing to a room with no people is a room with a lot of people. I lean against the wall, and Z mirrors me. "What did you want to talk about? The mess we left in the living room at the house? Did Noog plug up the toilet again? Oh, I know, you want to talk about koalas."

I blink at him. "Koalas?"

"Yeah, you know, do I understand that although they're cute and look cuddly, they'd probably swipe my face off if I tried to pick one up? I understand the need to give me the PSA; it's important information that everyone should know."

If I was worrying less about whether I'll ever get back the Cody who sang dorky songs with me in a canoe and wasn't on the verge of becoming the next #metoo headline, I'd laugh.

Z catches on to the seriousness in my face and shapes his own face to match. "Not koalas, I take it."

I shake my head. "Yesterday, Code joked about sleeping with a fourteen-year-old."

Z crinkles his nose. "Ew."

"Right?!" His immediate grossed-out reaction makes my heart leap with hope. Maybe I should have talked to Z in the first place. "He's made a lot of jokes like that this week," I continue. "And, I mean, hopefully he knows that those are lines he shouldn't cross in real life." I think of Janessa and her confirmation that he hadn't physically crossed her line, at least. "But even just joking about that stuff is . . ." I trail off, trying to find the right words.

". . . a promotion of rape culture and misogyny?" Z chimes in.

"Exactly!" Z is definitely the right person to talk to about this. "Anyways, I've tried to talk to Cody about it, but he won't listen to me. Do you think you could? Talk to him, I mean?"

Z sighs. "I wish I could."

I cross my arms. What the heck is with these guys refusing to step up? Being an ally is not that damn hard. "You can. You just have to—"

"No, I mean, I do. I've called him out lots of times."

I bite my lip. "You have?" It comes out more skeptical than I mean.

"Sure. I mean, I didn't at first. Code's the one who suggested adding me as a Meister in the first place, and I was in such awe of him. And he's a nice guy, generally, you know?"

"A nice guy?!" My still-lingering anger spikes my left eyebrow upward.

"Sorry, you're right, that's a terrible excuse. Being a 'nice guy' doesn't excuse jokes like that. Nothing does.

"But I swear I speak up now, though," Z continues. "Sometimes he says things, and I'm like, 'Whoa, buddy, you did not just say that.' I mean, I try to do it nicely, but I do tell him."

My anger is fizzling away. It's hard to be angry at Z, who's obviously making an effort. *Unlike Legs*, the voice in the deepest part of my brain whispers before I push it away. "Has it ever worked? Calling him out?" My heart sinks as the words slip out; I already know the answer.

Z frowns. "Does he listen to you? Because he doesn't listen to me. Know what he said last time I tried to call him on his crap?"

Nearby, a guy walks around the corner wearing one of those blow up T-rex costumes, which has nothing to do with LotS; even though it's a LotS convention, it seems like anything dorky or nerdy goes. I shake my head.

"He said that I was just jealous that he has way more subscribers that he does."

Of course he did. Hamster dickhead. "Yikes," I say.

"Yeah. Not a great look. Honestly, I don't think he's going to listen to anyone but his subscriber count. That's what matters to him most."

The T-rex guy's friends laugh as he tries to pick something off the floor with his stubby arms. I clench my fists in frustration. "Why don't you guys kick him out of the group?"

The edges of Z's eyes crinkle in confusion. "For a few inappropriate jokes? If an inappropriate joke disqualified someone from being a Meister, we'd be a team of no one."

I stare at him. I thought he got it; he seems like he's trying so hard to get it, to be an ally. But I suppose the fact is that the guys' jokes are things he sees, not feels. He doesn't have an elastic inside him—or maybe he does, but he doesn't have to feel it pulled tight with every obnoxious joke. He knows the theory, can spout the right words, but he doesn't understand it, not yet, not fully. "You're not making me feel much better about the state of the world, Z."

He laughs, and I want to believe that, like me, it's because if he doesn't laugh at these things, he'll cry. "Uh, if you want to feel good about the state of the world, you probably need to move to a different planet. On this one, even the koalas will kill you." Z arches onto his tiptoes and cranes his neck. "Though I'm pretty sure that person who just walked past was eating a LotS cookie. The world can't be that bad if there are LotS cookies in it, Lainey."

I laugh so I don't cry. "An excellent point."

Z stops tiptoeing to try to see over the person's shoulder and turns back to me. "Sorry. I'm easily distracted." He glances over his shoulder again, then back. "We were talking about Code."

I shake my head. "No we weren't. We were talking about how you were going to go run after that person to find out where the cookies are so you can bring back a whole tray."

"Heck yeah, we were!"

"Go go go!" I wave him off, and he goes running.

I lean against the wall again, not ready to return to the VIP room, where I might overhear my big brother spout off offensive joke after offensive joke. I sigh. Cody won't listen to me, he won't listen to Z, and Legs won't even try to talk to him. What else am I supposed to do? I have to do something. I'm not giving up.

Z has fully disappeared, but his words play back in my head. *I don't think he's going to listen to anyone but his subscriber count.* Or his subscribers generally? Maybe that's the answer.

Maybe if I could find some comments his followers have made on his videos, then show those to Cody, he'd finally listen. I whip out my phone to look at some video comments, then remember that I'm outside the US and only have a tiny bit of data on the international plan I got—which I'm not wasting on my brother.

I pull out my map, find the playtesting room, then head in that direction.

The room is almost full, but I snag an empty computer near the back. As long as I'm online, I decide to check my email and various social media. There are numerous messages from Janessa, following my helpful warning to her to stay off Cody's social media.

> Why?
>
> Is Cody talking about me?
>
> I looked on his social media. I can't find anything.
>
> What am I watching for?

I roll my eyes.

> I told you not to go on his social media.

I'm about to log back off when the little dots appear indicating that Janessa is typing a response. I tap my fingers on the table while I wait. I'm sure I don't have a lot of time before Cody starts pinging me wondering where the heck I am, since I'm supposed to be on duty.

I'm about to give up waiting and log off when her message appears.

> Right, but you wouldn't tell me why. What else am I
> supposed to do?

I shake my head. It's sad when women don't trust other women. And annoying. What's the point in trying to help her if she's not even going to listen?

I could explain to her about Willow, but I've already wasted enough time waiting for her idiotic response. And besides, she's really better off not knowing.

It's nothing, I write. Forget I said anything.

And then I log out and close the window before she can distract me any further. I have things to do.

I switch over to YouTube and find Cody's channel. I pull up his latest video, press Pause, then scroll through the comments, looking for a callout.

> Teddybeer: LOL
>
> SueNanPat: I don't get this game at all
>
> Goldberg Gutenberg: I almost pooped my pants when those lights went out!!!
>
> RevolutionaryWomen: this video is a metaphor for life
>
> ISweatRootbeer: "AAAAAAAAAAAAAAAAAAAAAAAAA"— Codemeister
>
> Buffy1982: y didn't you play this with shadowwillow?!?
>
> XXMUSCLESXX: your such a wimp
>
> LlewyDAD: CODESTER FOR LIFE!!!!!!!
>
> Betty Felon: If you like this, check out my channel! I play horror games and post every Tuesday, Thursday, and Sunday.
>
> IKerryAboutYou: I <3 <3 <3 <3 <3 <3 you
>
> Good Will Hacking: hahahaha
>
> The Empress: My toddler walked in while I was watching this and now he knows the F word. Oops.
>
> theoutlawinlaws: CODESTERS UNITE

Nothing. He must not say anything grotesque in this one, or surely at least someone with a username like Revolutionary-Women would have something to say.

I click to another, press Pause, scroll through the comments. More of the same drivel.

My eyes glaze over halfway down the page. Does he not say anything terrible in this video either? How is no one outraged at him? How is it possible that Cody-the-big-mouth-meister doesn't have a million people ranting in his comments about how terrible he is?

At that convention I helped Cody with six months ago, Z and I got in a big debate about the book *Ender's Game*. I told him I couldn't like any of Orson Scott Card's books, because I thought the guy was a terrible person, while Z argued that you have to look at a book's merit (or lack thereof) separate from the person who wrote it. We had some pretty great arguments zipping back and forth until Cody yelled at us to stop killing his buzz by talking about such boring things.

And though I disagreed with Z, I could understand his point. With YouTubers and streamers, though, it's different. Cody doesn't just create entertainment; he *is* the entertainment. If Cody's videos were really separate from him, people wouldn't wear his face. Or write fanfiction about him and the rest of Team Meister. Or ship him with Little Miss Leggings ShadowWillow.

Which means the things he stands for should matter. The things he believes should matter. Don't these people care?

I click on the first video again, pick up the headphones on the table, and put them on.

Honestly, I've watched almost none of Cody's videos. This one's a solo video of Cody playing through some horror game with a facecam in the top corner. His intro is an incomprehensible mash-up of clips of him spewing out random nonsense noises, put to music. I skip ahead in the video and catch Cody midscream as a jump scare catches him off guard. Skip ahead more, and he's squealing and joke-shouting at his viewers that he'll never forgive them for making him play this game. Skip ahead even more, and there's another high-pitched scream, caught somewhere between hamming it up and legit scared.

I switch to another video, this time a collab with all of Team Meister. They're playing some war game, and when I skip around this time, it's mostly them shouting at each other to "Go go go!" and "Hide! It's a plane!"

But then Ben dies, and Cody starts tea-bagging his dead body, and I sit up straight, thinking I've finally found something. But the next moment, the rest of them have joined in—even Z—and they're all laughing and making dick jokes.

Oh, right, boys become complete idiots when they play video games.

Though I don't watch Cody's videos, this one brings me immediately back to Cody and his high school friends in Mom's basement, shouting at each other just like this while they waved around controllers.

Guys hug the line so closely while playing that it could be easy to miss if one stepped over it briefly here or there. And so many of his fans are guys. Maybe Cody censors himself enough that no one's noticed a pattern. It's either that or everyone's noticed and no one cares enough to say something.

The idea that no one cares makes me want to vomit. I log off the computer and hurry away before I see something that tells me it's true. I refuse to believe that it's true.

Back in the VIP room, the coffee table now boasts napkins piled with cookies iced red and yellow and cyan, like the LotS logo, and the entire group seems to be debating whether cookies, cake, or ice cream is better.

Everyone except Legs, who's managed to grab a basic plastic chair from somewhere and is sitting in the circle like he's part of it, but who's staring into his lap, mind far away. Any frustration I feel toward him withers away. He's grieving the end of a friendship. He can barely hold a conversation; why would I have thought he'd be up for something neither Z nor I have managed to accomplish? I'd suggest that we ditch this whole thing and actually go somewhere far away, except I'm still supposed to be on duty in my role as roadie or whatever.

Which gives me an idea; I can get out of here by doing what Cody wants. I stride up beside the couch and smack Cody on the arm. "Hey, loser, I'll get that camera for you. Where is it again?"

Both Legs and Willow look at me in surprise. Cody narrows

his eyes at being called loser, but only says, "Great. It's the Canon PowerShot. I got it out of my bag last night to show Ben and didn't put it back. I think it's in the living room on the coffee table." Right. Beside all his beer cans, probably. He glances at his watch. "Rush and get it now, and you can make it back in time to man the camera for our panel."

Instead of snapping at him for bossing me around, I simply say, "Will do," give him a smile, and give Legs a pointed look as I move toward the door.

He hops to his feet. "I'll join you. I could use a walk."

No one else pays any attention as we grab our coats and head out into a back hallway, then hurry outside, away from any fans who might stop Legs.

Once we're out in the bright sunlight, Legs raises an eyebrow at me. "So, you really want to do a favor for your brother, huh? What's the plan? You going to grab the wrong camera to tick him off or something?"

"No . . . I just—I offered because it looked like you needed to get out of there, okay?" Something about admitting that I did it for Legs make my cheeks flush hot.

"Oh!" Legs says, and gratitude pours out of him in a way that makes all his muscles relax. "Well, thank you then. And I'm sorry I'm so obsessed with thinking about Brian right now."

"You're not—"

"I am. It's not just thinking about Brian, though, that's got me down. When someone tells you something like that—that they don't want to be friends with you anymore—it makes you question everything about yourself."

I want to say something encouraging, but if he didn't even talk to their dickhead friend after Brian asked him to—if that's the part of the story he's not telling me—then maybe that's something he *should* be questioning. I don't say that, though. Not now, when he's grieving. "Hey, so I was talking to Z," I say, trying to distract Legs from the heaviness of his thoughts. "Know what Cody told him when Z warned him a joke was offensive?"

"What?"

"He said Z was just jealous of his subscribers."

Legs frowns. "He must have been joking, right?"

It's my turn to frown. "You have got to stop believing the best in people," I snap, and Legs's dark eyebrows shoot up in surprise. "Sorry, it's just—I know it's hard to believe, but sometimes when people say bad things, they mean them."

"And sometimes they don't," Legs points out quietly.

And sometimes people don't say anything at all when they should, I think. If no one is willing to speak up, if no one is able to get Cody to listen, my own brother could end up in jail. Or at the very least, go on making his crude jokes forever. That thought alone is enough to make my stomach twist with nausea. I wish I never had to hear him make another sexist joke. I find it hard to believe that not one of his subscribers feels the same way.

"Hey, does Cody make crude jokes when you guys do videos together?" I ask Legs.

Legs considers my question. "No more than the average guy, I guess."

"Really?" I ask, my voice full of skepticism. "But he makes them all the time with you guys in person."

"Yeah." Legs groans with apparent annoyance at Cody before continuing. "Remember, though, that we're performers. We turn on and off parts of ourselves every time we record or stream. While somehow still being real, approachable human beings." He sighs.

"Right." Apparently Cody shuts off his dickness the same way Legs shuts off his sadness.

Legs and I walk in silence as we pass a wrap place that's channeling the scent of bacon directly onto the sidewalk. Legs stops for a minute to study the place. "Z said he and ShadowWillow haven't eaten," he says, changing the topic. "I think I'll stop here on the way back and grab them some wraps."

I want to ask more about Cody, but I don't want to dwell on how Legs hides his sadness from viewers. It must be exhausting. "Good idea," I say, breathing in the crispy goodness for a moment before we get going again.

"Hey, so funny story," I say, helping with the topic change. "I messaged this girl from my school that Cody dated, and like an idiot, she did exactly what I warned her *not* to do. I thought Cody was the one at fault there, but maybe you're right and Cody's not always the bad guy."

"You messaged Cody's ex-girlfriend?" Legs asks, sounding like I just told him I messaged the president's private number. "Are you guys friends or something?"

"No. She's new and quiet and hangs around with the cheer-leader girls, though I don't think she is one. I just wanted to help her out. Women helping women, you know?

"Oh, and I guess I messaged her to make sure Cody hadn't, I don't know, date-raped her or something." I'd almost forgotten about why I messaged her in the first place. "He didn't, by the way."

As we stop at a red light, Legs shifts from foot to foot, not looking at me.

"What? What is it?" I demand. "Tell me."

Legs shrugs. "I don't know. Was that—was it wise? Messaging her like that?"

I cross my arms. "Why wouldn't it be? I'm not afraid of talk-ing about the hard things with people." Like you are, I almost add, but don't.

"No, I just mean . . . what if he *had* done something terrible? What if it was the worst night of her life and all of a sudden the perp's sister is messaging her demanding to know what hap-pened?"

"I didn't say it like that," I snap, though admittedly at the moment I can't remember exactly what I did say. I'm sure it was fine, though. Wasn't it?

The light changes, and we both move forward, Legs a split second after me. "Sorry, I shouldn't assume," he says. "You prob-ably worded it carefully and thoughtfully."

"Right!" I say. "Exactly." Though even as I say it, I think of the panicked rush I wrote that first message in, on the plane. I slip my hands into my pockets to hide them from the wind that still feels like winter. Then something occurs to me: "Hey, look at you," I say, taking a hand out and smacking his arm. "You just called me out on something!"

"Yeah, and I feel terrible about it," Legs says, and he's so serious about it that it makes me laugh.

"But now I'm going to look at those messages I sent Janessa and see if I could have worded them better," I say as I decide to do just that. "You're making a difference. That's what I want. For the world to be better. For Cody to be better. For us all to be better."

"Me too." Legs bumps his shoulder lightly against mine as we walk. "Though can't we avoid making people feel worse about themselves in order to get there? Can't we build people up instead?"

I swallow back a lump in my throat as I nod noncommittally. I really want to agree with Legs on something. And yeah, I do want to build people up.

But sometimes you have to burn them down first. Sometimes you have to burn whole villages to the ground before you can build something better in their place.

And I'm sure Legs doesn't agree with me on that.

So I just nod as a sadness settles into my stomach. Because if Legs and I are pointed in completely opposite directions, how could we ever come together in the middle? How could there be any hope for an "us" at all?

ELEVEN

SamTheBrave

A TEXT COMES IN FROM MOM WHEN I'M GRABBING A SLICE OF PIZZA IN THE
food court.

> How's it going, Sammy love?

By "it," she means my quest to get Code to check out my
channel. If I told her about not asking ShadowWillow, would
she be proud of me, or would she be disappointed that I didn't
even try?

> No sightings yet. Just finished wereboar vs mutant
> rabbit panel. Having fun. Meister panel's in under an
> hour.

The Band-Aids on my fingers are starting to annoy me—I can usually only handle wearing them for a few hours at a time—so I toss them in the garbage and then look around the food court. The tables are all full of groups of people eating together. A few tables away, a group of kids around my age gets to their feet, and I hurry over to grab the table before someone else does. There are three of them—two girls and a guy—and they're laughing at some joke as I slip into one of the three empty seats they leave behind.

Maybe someday that'll be me and Dereck and Jones. For now, I eat alone, the same way I do at school. I suppose there are some things that even the magic of LotSCON can't fix.

I text with Mom a bit more—she's spent the morning checking out the CN tower—then Mom signs off to head to the bookstore, and I need to head to line up for the Team Meister panel.

Except there's a new bump on the underside of my left arm, halfway between my hand and my elbow. It's tiny. Not quite a pimple, just an imperfection. I know that tearing it from my skin won't fix it, won't make the wrong right. I know this in my brain, but my brain has about as much control over my fingers' actions as over my dick's reactions.

I outline it with my stubby fingernails, trying to get a grasp on it, mapping out the perimeter. I'm a surgeon preparing to extract a tumor, a gardener planning to dig up a weed. Slowly, carefully, I dig my sharpest edges in. Remove the wrong, bit by bit. Remove the part of my skin that doesn't belong.

I do not want to bleed. I never want to bleed. I take my time, move carefully, try to get it right.

I bleed anyway. Surprise, surprise.

I sigh and fish a Band-Aid from my pocket, rip it open, and pat it on, pressing down to stop the blood.

When Mom first noticed the bloody Kleenexes that found their way into our bathroom trash can more and more often, she thought I was cutting myself, which I guess scared her because apparently depressed people who don't seem outwardly depressed are the most at risk or something.

I'm not depressed, though. I told Mom that, and some test Dr. Murphy made me take confirmed it.

It's not sadness that makes me peel off my skin, that makes bits of skin and blood find their way under my nails like I've been in a brawl. I don't do it to hurt myself. (In fact, when it hurts, that's sometimes enough of a trigger to get me to stop.) I don't *want* to do it at all. My fingers do it anyway.

I grab my phone and check the time.

12:40.

Crap. Crap crap crap. I wanted to be in line for the panel twenty-five minutes ago!

Stupid picking trances ruining my life.

I shove the last remains of my pizza crust and paper plate onto the tray and dump them in the trash, then rush out of the basement food court, consulting my program, trying to read the map and weave around people at the same time. I wish I could be my LotS character instead of bumbling down the hall as my own oversize self. I feel too big and too slow.

I pound past a group of archers, down a hallway, past that sexy mutant rabbit girl from this morning, up the escalator, past the shadowdragon, and down a wide hallway. And there it is: the very very very long line.

It starts at the auditorium entrance and stretches down both sides of the hall to somewhere completely out of sight—in both directions. I don't even know which way I should walk to find the end of it.

Crap.

If I end up near the very back of the room, that's fine, but with this line, I might not even get in at all. If I don't, I could hang around and hope I see Code when he leaves, but what am I going to say then or later at the autograph signing if he asks what I thought of the panel? What kind of fan am I going to look like if I admit that I didn't line up early enough?

I choose a direction and start to walk in it, though before I get more than a couple of steps, I hear, "Sam! Hey, Sam!"

I don't know who'd call my name like that, so it's almost certainly not directed at me, but I turn anyway, because it's instinct or something.

And there, maybe fifteen people from the entrance, are Mark and Leroy, waving frantically at me. Well, Mark is waving frantically. Leroy meets my eye and salutes me, then goes back to looking at the program he's got in his hand.

I stride over. Maybe they know which direction the end of the line is in. "You guys got new programs," I say.

"Yeah, turns out they're practically throwing these things at people over in the registration area," Mark says. "I told Leroy he should get his own this time in case I lose mine again, but he refused because apparently he doesn't need one."

We both look over at Leroy, whose face is buried in it, and share a grin.

"Needing one is not the same thing as wanting to look at yours because I'm bored," Leroy says into the book.

"He's got a point," I say. "Hey, do you guys know where the end of the line is?"

"Who cares! Join us!" Mark steps out of the multi-people-thick line to make room for me in it.

"Oh, no, that's okay. I don't want to butt in line." I glance at the people behind them, who are sitting on the ground, huddled over their phones, paying no attention to us at all.

"I've seen a lot of people join other people in line," Leroy says without looking up. "It seems to be socially acceptable."

I look down the long, thick line. I hate butting in line, because it completely disrespects all the people who weren't lost in eating pizza and tearing their skin apart and who actually managed to make it here on time, but nerd people are good people, and maybe Leroy's right and they wouldn't care.

"Okay," I say, stepping into the space Mark made for me. "Thanks." I finger the edges of my newly placed wrist Band-Aid, waiting for the angry mob to tar and feather me—but when I glance around, no one's even looking at me. At school, if you saw me with a couple of people, you'd assume that they were threatening to dickpunch me—a threat that rarely comes true, but never fails to make my balls shrivel up in fear. But here, I realize, people probably assume that Mark and Leroy were simply saving a place for a friend, and for some reason the thought makes my heart go sort of squishy. Not that I'd admit that to anyone.

"Man, this line is so long," I say to Mark, since Leroy's now busy copying something from the program onto his arm.

"They should be letting us in soon," Mark says. "Hey, pull up one of your videos for me to watch."

"Oh, um, yeah, okay," I say, because if I'm going to have the guts to show one to Code, I should be up to showing one to Mark. Besides, maybe he'll want to subscribe.

I get out my phone and flip to the highlights video I pulled together last night. It's only seven minutes long, and it includes a sped-up montage of the hours and hours I spent expanding my castle over the rift and herding the shadowwolves (and dying a lot). After the montage is the footage of me and Jones—my trap, then my realization that I've trapped myself, too.

I'm pretty pleased with how the video turned out, and the positive comments on it keep coming in—even more than usual, I think—but as I hand over my phone, my stomach twists. I've never watched someone watch my videos before.

Mark has conjured headphones out of somewhere, and he

plugs them in and pops the earbuds into his ears, then presses Play.

It's less intimidating to watch than I expect, because by about one minute in, Mark is laughing so uncontrollably that the people around us keep glancing over. I don't even care that they're staring; that's *my* video that's making him laugh like he's a voice actor for a studio laugh track. When people comment things like "LOLOLOL" on my videos, I assume the video maybe made them smile a bit, and they're saying LOL because that's internet speak for "This was okay and I sort of half smiled once or twice, and I'm going to write this to be polite," but maybe when they're watching, they really are laughing out loud. My heart grows a half dozen sizes larger at the thought.

When the doors open and the line starts moving forward, Mark's only partway through the video, but instead of putting it away, he shuffles along behind me and Leroy, headphones still in his ears, eyes on the phone, chuckling regularly. Leroy and I nab three seats in the second row, and as Mark slips into his seat beside us, he lets out one big guffaw that fades into giggles as he pulls his headphones out.

"That was hilarious, man," he says. "That setup . . . it must have taken you forever! And those deaths . . . and the realization at the end! Top-notch. We definitely have to connect you with Code."

"My turn," Leroy says, holding out his hand.

I've somehow ended up sitting between them. Leroy reaches

across me to Mark and trades his program for the phone, like holding both would be too much to juggle—though he keeps his pen—then slips the earbuds in and slides the video back to the start.

"You're most definitely going to end up famous," Mark says. "You have got to sign my program. Maybe date it, too? This thing's going to be worth a million bucks someday."

"Uh, yeah, sure, if you want me to," I say, and he hands his program to me, then reaches over and takes the pen from Leroy's left hand. He gives it up easily, never looking away from the screen.

Turns out it's hard to focus on signing your name when you're busy watching a guy watch a video you made out of the corner of your eye. Leroy doesn't laugh the way Mark does—loudly and freely—but his mouth keeps twitching up at the edges, and when I die for the third time while herding shadowwolves, his bony shoulders shake with silent laughter.

When a LotSCON volunteer gets onstage and announces Team Meister, the place erupts in applause and hooting and cheering. I clap, too, but instead of looking at the stage, I find myself watching Leroy, who presses Pause and takes the earbuds out of his ears. He's partway into the bit where Jones is taunting me.

I expect him to hand my phone back, but instead, he holds it on his knee and wraps the headphones cord around his neck as he claps with his left hand against his other knee.

Maybe I should want my phone back. Maybe I should be reaching for it, because it's mine, not his. Instead, I feel strangely honored. With Leroy holding my phone like that, paused but not put away, it feels like my video is the real show and the panel is an interruption Leroy's forced to tolerate.

I grin to myself as I lean back into my chair and let out a cheering hoot as Team Meister—minus Oz—take the stage less than fifteen feet away from us. Code saunters across the stage, right in the middle.

Mark leans toward me and whispers, "See that door over there?" He points across the room at a door barely visible around the corner of the stage setup. "That's where they came out of. So that's where we have to go afterward."

"Afterward?"

"To show Code your video. They'll be in there."

A LotSCON volunteer stands outside the room like a bouncer. It's some kind of private space, like a green room or backstage area. "I don't know." What if it's against the rules? "I don't think they'll let us in."

"Maybe they won't. But we have to try."

I'm about to say no again when the door opens and Shadow steps out, striding across the room to a front-row seat on the other side of the aisle, and I remember how kind she was this morning. This isn't school, I remind myself. This is LotSCON, where we're all nerds together. This is LotSCON, where I belong.

"Okay," I whisper back to Mark. "Let's do it."

TWELVE

ShadowWillow

I DON'T KNOW HOW LEGS FIGURED OUT THAT I HADN'T HAD LUNCH, BUT WHEN he returns, he hands me a wrap that smells so delicious I could kiss that boy. But won't, obviously, since Code is the one I'm trying to connect with. He and the guys have migrated to the chairs by the auditorium entrance, ready to take the stage when needed, so I sit on the couch alone, scarfing down the chicken-and-bacon wrap.

The older guy who had been on the couch on the other side of Z for a while is leaning against the wall, and when Lainey enters the room after Legs, he pushes himself off the wall and hands her the video camera and tripod he's been holding. "I believe this is your job."

She takes it from him without a word. "Hey, Willow, I'll save you a seat."

My mouth is full of bacon and lettuce and wrap and I can't respond, but I give her a little wave of thanks and chew more slowly now that I don't have to rush as much.

"Me too, kiddo," wall guy says. "Get me a seat."

Lainey heads toward the door without acknowledging him.

"Hey, Lainey! Did you hear me?"

She swirls around and gives the guy a sickly-sweet smile. "Why yes, Jimbo, I would be happy to save you a seat even though you're doing nothing but leaning on your ass. Especially since you asked so nicely."

I snort into my wrap, then take another huge bite to hide my grin. Lainey marches out of the place while Jimbo glares at her and mutters something under his breath. I hope I get more opportunities to chat with Lainey. She seems like someone I'd get along with.

As I eat, I check my notifications and mentions on my phone and check the reactions to the picture of me and Code and Z that I posted. There are a number of responses already, including one "OMGOMGOMGOMGOMGOMG #CODEWILLOW." I laugh. I hadn't realized we were a hashtag already. As I stuff another bite of wrap in my mouth, I click on the hashtag and scroll through some of the comments. Most are similar to the first, but then one jumps out at me: "I think Willow's just using him. She's such a—"

I swipe the app closed before I finish reading the comment, my cheeks flushing hot. It's not the name-calling that bothers me—well, of course it bothers me, but it's not exactly new. I've been doing YouTube for a few years; I'm used to being called names. It's the other part of it that has my face and neck burning, the allegation that all I'm doing is using him. Because I'm not. Am I?

I look up at the guys by the door. Code and Wolf are on their phones. Noog is vlogging again. Ben is talking to Jimbo. Z happens to look my way, and his face splits into a grin, which makes me grin. I can't help it; the guy's happy energy is infectious.

I look back at Code, who's poking at his phone, face lit up by its white light. He's not smiling, so his cherry-round cheeks have flattened out, but his perfectly smooth skin looks kissable enough. And I'm not making something out of nothing. We had our spark. The wink last night, his arm practically around my shoulder on this couch. I wouldn't have drawn Noog's camera our way if there was nothing to see.

A LotSCON volunteer pops his head in the room then and tells the guys it's almost time for their entrance. I shove my last bit of wrap in my mouth, then fish for a piece of gum in my purse. By the time I make it to the door, the guys are already entering to thunderous applause. Legs, though, is still in the back corner of the place, looking at a print on the wall. "You coming?" I call across the room to him.

He shakes his head. "I've seen them on lots of panels. Going to take advantage of the empty room." He adds quickly, as if I might have thought he meant something suggestive, "Not anything weird, just a bit of quiet. You'd better head in."

He's right about that; the applause is dying down. "Enjoy your bit of quiet," I say, then enter the auditorium.

I have to walk across a small open space, past the stage, to the seat in the center front that Lainey's saved for me between her and Jimbo, and for a moment, I feel fully exposed as my skunk self in front of the jam-packed room of people. But then some other girl in the front row leans over to her friend and whispers something, and her friend looks right at me, and they both grin. They don't look like they think I'm just using him. And it's not my fault if simply walking out of a door makes the rumors fly.

ShadowWillow came out of the same room Code did.

ShadowWillow was at Code's panel.

ShadowWillow and Code, sitting in a tree . . .

Of course, the rumors probably call me Willow, not Shadow-Willow or Shadow. My eyebrows scrunch together as I slip into my seat.

Onstage, the guy I thought I recognized is introducing himself as Squigglez, a YouTuber I've heard of but have never watched, and explaining that he'll be moderating the panel, and that they'll be taking some questions from online and some questions from the crowd. They've got the stage set up like my panel from this morning. There's a long table with five chairs—Noog, Ben, Code, Wolf, and Z, in that order—and three mics to share between them, with Squigglez standing to the side at the podium.

On the floor in the aisle is a mic that people are already rushing to line up at even though Squigglez hasn't started taking audience questions yet. On the other side of the aisle, there's a camera operated by a LotSCON volunteer, which is probably streaming this live. Lainey must be taking video for the Meisters to use later.

As the guys all introduce themselves to more thunderous applause, I look around. We're in the same room as Legs's Q&A last night, but it feels bigger now, especially compared to the one from my panel this morning. This one's four times the size of that one, and every single seat is filled, unlike our only mostly full one from this morning—which is not a surprise considering that theirs is scheduled in a prime slot and we got the filler early-morning slot.

Suddenly, the panel I was so excited to be on this morning feels like a joke.

"The first question is a very important one," says Squigglez with mock seriousness. "Over or und—"

"Under!" Code shouts before Squigglez can even finish the question, and the whole auditorium bursts into laughter at some joke I'm not in on. An inside joke between Code and his millions of fans. Life goals.

Maybe someday I'll be up on that stage, and I'll shout out, "Avocado sundae!" and the whole place will explode with laughter. Or maybe I'll keep getting relegated to the girl gamer panels that no one comes to because they're scheduled at the unimportant nothing times.

"You have a lot of newer fans," Squigglez continues. "Can you explain to them how Team Meister originally came to be?"

Ben takes the mic from Noog. "Code and Wolf and I met on a PvP LotS server a chunk of years ago—"

"*My* PvP server," Wolf cuts in.

"Right. Wolf's server. I'm not sure multiplayer even officially existed then, but Wolf had done some hotwiring of the code or something—"

"Uh, maybe don't mention that at a Legends of the Stone convention," Wolf says, and laughter ripples through the place as he gives a guy in the background in a LotSCON shirt a cheesy grin and a wave.

"Don't worry, man, if you get carted off to LotS prison, we'll send you lots of shadowcake," Noog says.

"And conjugal visits from an elf!" Code adds, then turns to the same LotSCON volunteer. "You should add that to the game." More laughter.

"I'm pretty sure you can find that on the internet if you know where to look," Noog says.

"Annnnnnyway," Ben says, which makes the room fill with the most laughter yet. Once it finally dies down, Ben tells the rest of the story of how he and Code and Wolf discovered they were all fledgling YouTubers and decided to form a group, which they called Team Meister for reasons none of them can remember, but which Code and Ben both claim was their idea, and which Wolf says he had nothing to do with, as he would've come up with something better. They added Oz shortly after forming, then Noog a while later, and then Z.

"You're one of the few gamer groups that require members to change their names to a team name," Squigglez says once Ben's done his story. "Gavin M from Twitter wants to know: was it hard to give up your individual identities and become a Meister?"

"No! I love my Meister bros," Noog says, and Code reaches down the table and gives him a fist bump.

Z takes the mic from Wolf. "It wasn't an easy decision for me, actually."

"Dude, this"—Code points at himself—"is always an easy decision."

Z chuckles along with the crowd before continuing. "I mean, I love these guys. They've done a lot for me, and they're like family. But you do give up a bit of yourself by joining a group like the Meisters. I mean, this isn't like Hermitcraft or Stoneworld, with a shared server and occasional collab. The Meisters are tighter than that—they give more than that, but they also require more than that, which is mostly epic and awesome but does require some compromise."

"You regretting joining us, Z?" Noog jokes.

"I only regret joining you, Noog," Z says, which makes Noog snort with nasally laughter. "I don't regret joining the group," Z continues, refusing to get derailed from his serious answer, which is reason #7,391 today why I need to start watching his channel religiously. "I did need to give it some serious thought before I agreed, though. I had loyal viewers, and I was worried how it would impact them if I was suddenly no longer answering to myself and to them. But ultimately I decided that I could grow more as a person and a content creator if I had this group of talented guys pushing me and holding me responsible for Meister-worthy content."

"And the chance to grow your subscriber count," I mutter under my breath, feeling a stab of envy.

"Plus, who's going to refuse the opportunity to see Wolf's brilliant tactics up close and personal," Z adds, punching Wolf in the arm.

"Get a room, you two," Code groans, scrunching his nose in disgust, and the room fills with laughter again.

Squigglez opens the floor to questions then, turning to the long line at the mic that they'll never get through. Their first few answers devolve into more and more silliness, and I'd be rolling my eyes if I wasn't busy taking in the way the whole crowd ripples with laughter at every inside joke that flies over my head. I want this. I want this so badly it hurts.

The next question comes from a short white guy in impressive dwarf cosplay, with huge silver shoulder pads and a shield that looks just like the LotS logo shield. "My question is for Code," he says, his high-pitched voice shaking with nervousness. "My name is Morgan. I don't know if you remember me, but a couple of years ago I gave you a watercolor of you searching in a dozen different caves for the diamond."

"Dude! Morgan!" Code jumps in. "Of course I remember you. That watercolor was amazing! I've got it up on my wall in my office!"

I stare at Code in awe. He has millions of subscribers. He's probably been given hundreds of pieces of fanart. Does he really remember this one guy, this one piece of artwork? But there's no trace of lying in his face. His dimpled, round, suddenly-looking-very-cute face.

"Morgan, my man, what's your question?" he asks.

"Right, um, I was just wondering," he stammers, though he's beaming. "Is there anyone you're hoping to do more collabs with?"

"Good question. Collabs are my favorite! There are probably a dozen people I want to do more videos with, but right now, probably . . . Willow!" Code says, and it takes his arm thrown in my direction and all the people around me suddenly staring at me before it sinks in that he's talking about me. Someone in the crowd wolf whistles, and my face flushes hot as titters pass through the crowd.

"Are you dating?" someone in the crowd shouts, and I assume Code'll just ignore it, but he leans in to the mic and says very seriously, "No comment." Then winks at me. On camera.

It's so obviously theatrical, but still, I find myself grinning. Because superstar content creator Codemeister winked at me. Because his fans—who will hopefully become my fans—will be talking about this for days. And because can you really be using someone if they're using you right back?

@LumberLegs: Heading to a bookstore to grab a book or something for my mom's birthday. Any suggestions? [1.1K likes]

@LumberLegs: NO, I'M NOT BUYING MY MOM FIFTY SHADES OF GRAY! SHE'S MY MOM!!!!! [2.7K likes]

@LumberLegs: Okay, that's it, you're all cut off from the internet. You're awesome and I love you, but internet privileges officially revoked. :P [2.6K likes]

THIRTEEN

Lainey

WILLOW BLUSHES WHEN CODY WINKS AT HER. AND SMILES. GROSS.

I could make a whole big thing of it on camera, turning to catch her reaction beside me before zooming back in on the stage, but there's no way I'm playing into their little drama. I keep the camera pointed at the stage and that's that.

Honestly, I'm not even sure I caught the wink on camera. If not, Cody'll probably yell at me later when he finds out, but if I remind him that I walked all the way back to the Meister Manor just to get him his vlogging camera, maybe he'll get over it.

I have to give Cody credit for one thing, though: he really

does have that guy's painting on his wall. I've stood staring at it before, because it's so atmospheric, with a huge lava-filled rift and Cody's LotS character in a dozen different places, searching for the diamond.

And that's not the only picture Cody's got on his wall. He's got one wall in his apartment that's completely covered in fanart—from impressive paintings to crappy sketches that look like they were done by toddlers. He values every single one.

He doesn't just care about his subscriber count; he cares about his subscribers, period. If his subscribers would speak up, would he listen to them too?

And just as important of a question: if his subscribers knew what he was really like, would they even speak up in the first place?

The panel finishes not long after Cody's disgusting wink, and when the applause finally dies down and the guys are off the stage, Willow turns to me. "Do you need help?" She gestures to the camera and tripod. Her teeth are so perfectly straight that she could be in a toothpaste commercial, but her smile still feels genuine. She's as nice as Canadians are stereotypically supposed to be, so why isn't she as progressive, too? Why is she blushing at someone as misogynistic as my brother?

Though maybe she hasn't seen that side of him yet. Apparently he's able to hide that side of himself from his viewers, so maybe he hides it from the girls he likes, too. Maybe he's been throwing on the charm for her. Maybe they simply haven't spent enough time together yet for her to see.

I ignore her question and replace it with one of my own. "How well do you know my brother?"

She looks over her shoulder to the VIP room door the guys have disappeared into, then back at me. "Not very. Why?"

If I told her right here, right now, what a jerkwad Cody can be, would she believe me? Probably not. She barely knows me. Better to let her see for herself; Cody can't hide that part of himself for long.

"No reason. Never mind. I'm good. You head back and join the guys." Which, after offering to help one more time, she does.

It doesn't take long to bundle up the camera and tripod and head toward the VIP room, but by the time I get there, Willow and the Meisters are all back inside, and three dorky Codesters are talking to the LotSCON guy, trying to convince him to let them in.

"We don't have to go in. Just ask him to come out," the Asian guy says.

When we were at PAX, a Codester with Cody's face printed big across his chest spotted us getting into our hotel elevator and went sprinting across the lobby to hop in just as the doors closed. He rode up eleven floors with us, oversize shirt reeking of BO (come on, man, I don't care whether your clothes fit, but can't you at least remember to put on deodorant?), and recited to Cody every scene in the last video Cody had posted and his corresponding feelings.

Cody tried to be patient with the guy, saying, "That's cool, man," from time to time, which surprised me, even though I know how much he loves his fans. When the guy got off the elevator on our floor and started to follow Cody to his room, though, Cody finally snapped, like he'd just learned for the first time what it's like to have an elastic band inside. He yelled at the guy to F off, and when we finally got free of the guy and back to our room, Cody was shaking with some combination of rage and possibly fear.

Later, I tried to tell Cody that women have to deal with those kinds of personal space violations all the time, and he said, "Would you stop making everything about women?" His elastic was clearly still pulled tight about it, and for a moment, I almost felt sorry for him, so I didn't push it.

These guys outside the VIP room, who're probably a couple of years younger than me, look a little less clueless, but not a lot. The Asian guy in the middle has this worn-out beige Team Meister shirt on that should have been thrown out a dozen wears ago. On his left is a chubby white guy in a Codester shirt who at least has the decency to look sort of embarrassed at what they're trying to do. On the other side is a scrawny white guy in sweatpants—sweatpants!—who's staring in the opposite direction, watching the crowd file out of the hall.

"We just want to show him something," continues the middle guy.

An idea comes to me. Maybe I can use Cody's elastic to my

advantage. I hold up my badge to the LotSCON guy and squeeze past them, then turn back to look at them. "I'll ask if he'll come out," I tell them. "But don't get your hopes up," I add as the middle guy's eyebrows shoot up in excitement. "He probably won't." I feel bad for using them in my plan, but it's for the greater good. Or at least for ShadowWillow's good.

Inside the VIP room, I lean the tripod against the wall, then survey the room. Legs has disappeared off somewhere, but Cody is on the couch beside Noog, with Willow standing close by, looking on. Perfect. If I can't get Cody to change, maybe I can at least force him to reveal his terrible side to Willow. She might not be my favorite person, but girls need to look out for each other, and every girl should know the truth about Cody.

Plus, once she knows, maybe she'd talk to him about it. He didn't listen to Z, but maybe if it's a girl whose leggings he's trying to get into, it'd be different.

I stride over to the little circle. "Hey, Cody," I say, "there are three elevator fanboys outside, desperate to talk to you, refusing to leave."

Cody vaults to his feet. Yep, he's still sensitive about it, just as I expected.

"Not this again," he mutters, quieter than I hoped. I glance over at Willow, who's watching. Good. If I can just push his fear into anger, maybe he'll spout off at the mouth a bunch and Willow will know to steer clear.

"You scared of a few fans, Cody?" I laugh.

He scowls at me. "Don't be stupid. I'm not afraid of elevator fanboy creeps."

Noog glances up at Cody, then returns to his conversation with Wolf and Ben. Grumpy Cody is nothing new to any of them. "Aw, Code just wears his heart on his sleeve," Ben said when I complained to him once about Cody.

"What's an elevator fanboy?" Willow asks.

Cody's eyebrows furrow together under his beanie, like he's about to start ranting, but then he turns to her and slips on his I'm-a-famous-streamer mask, hiding his anger faster than I knew he was capable of doing. "Nothing," he says. "We had this kind of creepy experience with a fan in an elevator. Thought the guy was going to knife me or something, but he didn't. It's actually a funny story looking back." He smiles at her, all charming, and she smiles right back.

I stare at Cody. He has never looked at me and thought, "Maybe I shouldn't be my worst self around this person. Maybe I shouldn't yell or use slurs or make offensive jokes in front of them." Never ever.

And I mean, I know that being around your little sister is different from being around a girl you're trying to impress, but still, would it be too much to ask for a little respect?

Apparently it would.

Which is exactly why I need someone other than me to get the message across to him. Someone he'll listen to. And maybe he'd listen to Willow, but if he doesn't show her his bad side, she's never going to believe me that he needs a talking to in the first place.

"So are you going to speak with them or not?" I snap. Not that it matters now.

"Oh, um . . ." He glances at me, then at Willow. He doesn't want to talk to them, but also doesn't want to make a bad impression. "Why don't you take them to our network's table in the vendors hall and give them each a Codester sticker. Tell them if they come to the autograph session later, I'll sign them." He flashes another grin at Willow, like he's some sort of superhero.

"Who designed your stickers?" Willow asks as she strides over to him, and Cody starts to tell her about "this great designer" he knows, and that's it, I'm dismissed, unimportant. While Willow still fawns over him like he's the greatest.

That did not go as planned.

I head back toward the door but pause before going through. I don't want to go out there and deal with three fanboy Codesters. Though as I glance over my shoulder at Willow and Cody lusting over each other, I realize that I don't want to stay here either. So I push out the door.

The Codesters are standing to the side against the wall, the two chubbier ones leaning together over a program while the skinny one watches me exit the door. He taps the other two on their shoulders simultaneously, and they straighten at the same time. Tweedledee and Tweedledumb. Great.

"Is he coming out?" the Asian guy in the Team Meister shirt asks. I want to believe he's a general Team Meister fan instead of a Codemeister fan specifically, but then he wouldn't be asking for Cody specifically and looking at me with such hope. Why couldn't they all be wearing Z shirts or Wolf shirts? Aside from the fact that they're friends with Cody, those guys are actually decent human beings.

I shake my head. "He had to rush off to another event," I lie.

The Team Meister guy's face falls.

"Darn," the guy in the Codester shirt says, then mumbles something to himself about one chance left. Screw the stickers; I'm not going to do that much work just to perpetuate their unhealthy obsession.

I step back from them and pull out my phone, dismissing them, and check for messages from Legs. There's one from him fifteen minutes ago, telling me he went nearby to grab a book for his mom's upcoming birthday, and asking if I want to go for a walk once he gets back. *Sure*, I message back, then slide my phone back in my pocket. And since the whole thing has taken me about twenty seconds, when I look back up, the three guys are still there.

I happen to meet eyes with the guy in the Codester shirt, and he says to me in this really genuine way, "Thank you for trying. It meant a lot."

I sigh. Stupid heartstrings.

"If you all come with me to the vendors hall," I say, because I'm apparently a huge pushover, "I can give you each a sticker, and

Cody said he'll sign them later at his autograph session." Maybe I can give them Team Meister stickers instead of Codester ones.

"Dude!" says Team Meister guy, elbowing Codester guy in the side. "Perfect conversational in!"

"I actually bought something for him to— Never mind." He turns back to me. "Thank you. That's super nice, though I don't want you to have to go out of your way."

"Hey, I want a sticker!" the skinny guy pipes up.

"Come on, then," I say as I start walking across the auditorium. Out of the corner of my eye I catch Tweedledee and Tweedledumb trying to talk to each other with their eyes, except communication goes poorly and they both try to fall in beside me and end up bouncing off each other. The Codester one goes around to my other side, while the skinny guy follows behind.

"We're Mark and Leroy," Team Meister guy says, pointing to the skinny guy instead of at his Tweedle brother. "And that's SamTheBrave. He's a streamer. Have you heard of him? No? Well, you're going to. He's absolutely hilarious. I just started watching his videos and he's already one of my favorites if not my very favorite. You should check him out. You work for Codemeister, right? Or are you a streamer, too?"

SamTheWhatever clears his throat.

"Never mind. I'll let you two talk," Mark-or-Leroy says as we step out of the auditorium into the big hallway with the giant poster of Cody's face. Then he falls back with the skinny guy, becoming Mark-and-Leroy. I'm left walking down the hall and into the big open registration area with SamTheWhatever, whose face has become adorably red, like he's nine years old and someone mentioned girls' underwear.

"You have very enthusiastic friends," I say.

"Oh, I just—" He breaks off and glances behind him, then smiles. "Yeah, I do."

We pass the big dragon thing, and I step onto the escalator. Instead of stepping on beside me, they all fall in line behind me, one after another, leaving room on the left for people to walk past. And for a moment, I have this vision of the four of us as the Beatles on Abbey Road or as the Fellowship of the Ring crossing one of those big mountains in a line, and I can't help but laugh to myself. We'd be a funny fellowship.

At the top of the escalators, I show my badge and they show their wristbands to the LotSCON volunteer in the red shirt, and then we're in the big, chaotic vendors hall that takes up the entire top floor of the convention center—though it's still much smaller than at PAX.

The Meisters' YouTube network's table is in the back corner, so I wind past the nearby exhibitor booths, weaving my way through the crowds of people, at least a quarter of them in varying levels of cosplay. We pass a guy and a girl dressed all in black, thick layers of it in various textures of fabric cascading off them, matching veils over their faces, even their hands painted black. I have no idea what they're supposed to be, unless it's something to do with the shadows that fill the farthest reaches of the Legends of the Stone rifts. I've only been in those parts of the game once or twice. I'm happy to just build my house on the surface and let other people clear out the rifts—or turn them off on our server altogether.

The alleys between the booths are busy and full, so it's not until we reach the back of the hall that SamTheWhatever is able to fall in step beside me again.

"So, *do* you work for Codemeister like Mark said?" he asks. He's eying my badge, which has turned around backward and is showing nothing except its white back with tiny print. I keep it that way.

"I'd rather not talk about it."

"Okay," he says, dropping it immediately. He fiddles with a Band-Aid on the outer part of his wrist as we weave our way between some artisan booths to the big-name brands along the side wall. Then he drops both hands and straightens his shoulders. "Well, if you ever want to check out my channel, it's easy to find. SamTheBrave. Here, I'll write it down for you." He pulls his program out of his tote bag and Mark-or-Leroy hands him a pen, and I'm about to tell him that it's okay, I'll just remember it, when I realize his hand is trembling. It's subtle, but enough that writing his name while we walk looks super difficult.

I stop walking so he can stop walking, and he sets the program down on a nearby table and finishes writing, then rips off that corner and hands it to me. "You can call me Sam," he says.

Perhaps he's trying to talk up his channel to as many people at this convention as he can. I can't really fault him for that. I know enough streamers and YouTubers to know what a tough business it can be. It's not like posting a cat video that goes viral; Legs and Cody and everyone else all work their butts off every day.

I slip the scrap into my pocket, even though I know I won't use it. Aside from the odd Legs video, watching people play video games just isn't really my thing. I smile at him as I do so, though—but then looking at him makes me see his Codester shirt, which I had forgotten about when we were walking side by side. Ugh.

"Why do you watch Cody's videos, anyways?" I spit out.

Sam tilts his head in thought before answering. "I watch his streams, mostly. The energy of them is incredible—everyone laughing and cheering him on." There's longing in his voice.

"And he's funny!" pipes up the skinny guy.

"Right, yes, he's funny," Sam parrots.

"Well, come on, then," I say, and once again the three of them trot after me like they're puppies and I've got a dog biscuit. At the network's table, I wave to the guy who helped me find a spot for Cody's sticker boxes yesterday, then slip around the back of the table. I grab three palm-sized stickers of Cody's logo—at least they're not the ones of his face—and then return to Sam and his buddies.

I study the three of them—Mark-and-Leroy all wide-eyed and expectant, Sam's face still tinged red from his fumbling attempt to gain a new viewer. They're not so bad, really. Almost sweet, honestly. Maybe Cody really is good at censoring himself, and they don't realize the truth.

What would they do if they knew? Or do they already know and they just don't care?

I need to know.

"Hey, if you found out that Cody was a misogynist jerk, would that bother you?" The question pours out of me.

Sam pauses for only a moment before saying, "Of course it would."

The tightness inside me loosens the tiniest bit. And as it loosens, the dark, wavering tendrils of an idea start to creep through the cracks. "How much would it bother you?"

Sam's eyebrows furrow with what I think—I *hope*—is worry. "Is he?"

"I didn't say that. Would you stop watching?"

The bigger half of Mark-and-Leroy pipes up. "Of course we would."

Sam is slower to respond, cocking his head as he gives it honest thought. "I hope so," he says at last. Which is enough. The dark tendrils solidify into a black mass in the middle of my brain. I know what to do. I know how to do it.

"Cool." I thrust the stickers into their hands. "Have a great day." I start to march away.

"Is he, though?" Sam calls after me.

"Again, I didn't say that," I call back over my shoulder.

I won't have to say it.

When I post a video to the Codemeister channel with clips of Cody mouthing off behind the scenes, it'll do the talking for me. And when Cody's subscribers—at least the ones like these good boys—tell him with the clicks of their unsubscribe buttons, maybe Cody will finally have to listen. Maybe he'll finally realize he has to change.

I'm sorry, Cody.

I'm sorry, but I have to do it. For Janessa's sake. For Willow's sake. For Cody's subscribers' sake. And, especially, for his own sake. I have to save my big brother by burning him to the ground.

FOURTEEN

SamTheBrave

"WHAT WAS THAT ABOUT?" I ASK AS THE GIRL STALKS OFF.

"Apparently Codemeister's a misogynist jerk?" Mark says uncertainly.

"She didn't say that," Leroy says. "In fact, she specifically said she didn't say that."

"Thanks for the recap," Mark says with a nervous laugh.

"I got your back." Leroy gives him a little salute.

"So . . . what do we do with this . . . noninformation?" I ask.

Mark shrugs. "Nothing? Like you said, it's noninformation. You can't judge someone based on something someone else didn't actually say about them."

"Yeah, that's true," I say, though the words sit uneasily in my stomach. My hand reaches for the Band-Aid on my wrist, though I catch myself and draw it back. "I'm guessing she's not going to show my videos to Code," I say.

"Hmm, no, probably not," Mark says. Then he slaps me on the back. "But at least you got some practice. And we've got free stickers."

I nod. It was nerve-racking talking to that girl (why didn't I ask her for her name?) about my videos, but Mark's right; it was good practice. And she was nice about it. Of course. Everyone here is nice.

Beside me, Leroy is waving over the guy behind the table. "When does the lineup start?" he asks, tapping a sign on the table that says:

Team Meister

Autographs

4 p.m. Saturday

Right. This is where they're having them.

"The line's started already." The guy points toward a nearby wall, where those retractable rope-fence things shape out the place where a long line will go. At the front, there's a little clump of seven or eight people, some sitting and some leaning against the wall, standing.

"Ooh," Mark says. "Should we go get in line?"

"Already?" I glance at the time on my phone. "The autographs don't start for over an hour." I didn't come here to spend my whole time waiting in line for things. Waiting feels like lost time. I could be wandering around this magical place, maybe running into Code at a vendor's booth or in line for ice cream. Code's not going to be in the lineup of people waiting to see himself.

"People are already lining up, though. What if they run out of time and don't get through the whole line?" Mark asks. "Isn't your whole reason for being here to talk to Code?" He starts moving in the direction of the line, Leroy trailing after him. "Why risk it?"

He has a point. A very good point that should have been the point I was already making to myself, especially since last time I almost missed being in line entirely. I'm starting to think I'm not cut out for this real-life self-promotional stuff, though Mom'd probably smack me upside the head—in a loving way—if she ever caught me thinking this way.

"Sammy, you're cut out to do anything you're willing to work hard for," she'd say.

Which is why I follow Mark and Leroy over to the wall to sit in line over an hour early—well, that and also because I've just realized that hanging out with them in line sounds more fun than wandering around the convention all by myself.

Once we've filed through the rope fence to find our place in line, I pull out my phone and find myself on Code's Twitch channel, staring at it. It's not live now, of course, but simply staring at the page takes me back to that first stream I watched of Code's. He was playing LotS with a couple guys, and his viewers were all yelling in chat that he had forgotten to equip his armor as he went running into a rift screaming, "Victory is mine!" And then he died to an unbuffed wereboar and his thousands of viewers about lost it with laughter, and so did I.

And I don't think he said anything misogynistic or terrible in any way, but really, I was so enamored with watching his nonstop busy chat that maybe I wouldn't have noticed if he did.

"I need to hit the washroom," I say. "Can you guys—"

"Hold your spot? On it." Mark spreads out his arms like he's reserving extra space.

"Thanks, man," I say, and then weave my way back out of the fenced-in line.

In the bathroom, I ignore the stalls and head over to a corner, where I switch to Code's YouTube channel and pull up one of Code's recent videos on my phone. I don't have headphones with me like Mark did, so I turn the volume down quiet and hold it up to my ear. A guy at a urinal glances over at me, but I turn my back to him and press Play.

It's a pretty typical Code video. He's creeping through the dark hallways of a horror game, shrieking at an incredibly high octave any time something jumps out at him. Aside from the shrieks and grunts, he doesn't say anything particularly coherent except to rant and swear at us, his audience, about how he's probably going to die and it's all our fault for making him play this game and—scream!

I switch to a multiplayer video, which is mostly just chaos, as he and his buddies run around on a tiny LotS map trying to slaughter each other.

I've watched a lot of Code's streams in preparation for this weekend, and I don't remember him saying anything bigoted in any of them. Surely if he did, I would have noticed, right? I want to believe I would have noticed.

I message Jones. Do you have any reason to believe that Codemeister is a terrible human being?

Jones's face bubble appears in chat. I don't watch a ton of his videos, but no. Why? Has he asked you for your soul and you have to decide whether it's worth giving it to him?

My shoulders relax a little. Jones is the kind of person who would definitely say so if she'd heard Code say some bad stuff. She calls me on my crap all the time.

I tap out a response. Exactly. What do you think? Could we still be friends if I had no soul?

Dereck's face appears. He must have just gotten up. Ask if he'll take your brain instead. I've always wanted a zombie friend.

Jones: Zombies still have brains, idiot. They're just infected brains.

Dereck: Do they? Are you sure? Well, ask him if he'll settle for infecting your brain instead.

My laugh echoes through the concrete box of a bathroom. I'll see what I can do.

I slip my phone away, wash my hands, and head back out to Mark and Leroy. I've been gone for so long that they probably think I just took a big, long, constipated dump.

The line for Team Meister autographs has grown substantially while I've been in the washroom, so I guess I should be thanking Mark for making us get in line. It's already curved back and forth through the fenced-in grid a few times.

I study the lined-up people as I pass. There's a short black girl with a tall white girl, a group of Asian kids, a couple of black guys, and two girls in dwarf costumes holding hands. The growing line is way more diverse than my whole school, which makes sense since this is Toronto, not Stratford—a place I'm pretty sure no immigrant has moved to ever (aside from Opa's German parents, I suppose), and lots of them are girls.

More evidence; I've been worrying for nothing. That girl must have genuinely been talking in hypotheticals. Maybe she was wondering about someone else's career, but using Codemeister as a comparison.

"You're bleeding," Leroy says when I make it back to them. He points to his jawline.

I tap my own jawline, and my fingers come away red. Crap.

I spend the next half hour with a Kleenex pressed to my face, though it's not so bad, really. Me watching a ton of Code's streams and never realizing he was a sexist jerk would have been a whole lot worse than me having a bit of blood on my face.

Mark chatters away to me for a while about the LotS-based card game he and Leroy play, and then the two of them get into an intense debate about whether it's better to stack the deck with swords or shields that goes completely over my head. I check my phone again to see a rambling string of messages from Dereck about how he's watching the replay of my stream last night and it's hilarious, though not as good as the stream where I played Battlegrounds with random strangers and pretended to be all sorts of eccentric people—doing things like talking nonstop to one guy about how much I love Cheez Whiz, or singing Disney parodies to another girl every time we got a kill.

Which bolsters me up enough to admit something to him. I'm nervous. About meeting Code. I force myself to type the words instead of writing them into my skin.

Nervous? Are you kidding me? It's no different than when you were playing with those strangers, talking to them about all sorts of crap.

Jones pokes her head in too. Dereck's right. You can talk to anyone. Remember in that stream when you asked that guy if he still sleeps with a stuffed animal and he said yes?

I chuckle. I think he was joking.

Jones: Regardless, it's no different than this.

Dereck: What she said.

It feels different. Online, I'm SamTheBrave—prankster, streamer, shadowlord.

Here, I'm—well, me.

Though as Mark and Leroy continue to argue about their LotS card game and I overhear the people behind us discussing whether it would be more fun to cosplay as an elf or a dwarf, I remember: being me here is not the same as being me at school.

Here, I'm the same as everyone else.

I can do this.

I'd better be able to do this. After this, the Meisters don't have any other events scheduled. And yeah, I might see them around the convention, but I also might not. This is my best shot.

I thank Dereck and Jones, then open a new window on my phone and type out an intro for myself, because Mark is right: winging it won't do. Once it's written, I repeat it to myself over and over inside my head. "Hi, I'm SamTheBrave, a streamer and YouTuber. You should check out my latest Twitch stream in which the prank I spent twelve hours preparing for goes terribly wrong. Spoiler alert: it involves Shadowwolves and a hot girl and me trapped in a closet." Hopefully Jones'll forgive me for referring to her that way (or rather, hopefully she'll never find out).

"That looks good, man," Mark says, looking over my shoulder. "You going to pitch it to any of them other than Code?"

I shake my head. "I don't want to be that guy who won't stop talking about my channel to every single person I meet."

He glances over to the signing table, where five chairs are

set up in a row. "Guess it would sound pretty ridiculous if you pitched it to all five guys one after another."

"Exactly. And Code streams the most, aside from maybe Ben, but Ben doesn't have that many followers." I've watched one or two of Ben's streams, and they're a lot quieter and less epic than Code's. "Hey, do you have any paper?" I ask Mark.

"Only this." He holds up his program.

"Yeah, me too," I say, pulling out my own. I flip through it, trying to find a clear spot somewhere that isn't marred by schedules or fine print. I settle on a page near the back that has an advertisement with a castle on a gray background.

I fold around the advertisement, then around the castle, marking off a small, plain rectangle of gray. I fold the page back and forth and back and forth along the lines, then carefully start to rip it.

"What are you doing?" Leroy asks. He's sitting cross-legged on the floor beside me. I don't think my legs bend that way.

I survey the autographs line that winds through the rope-fence zigzag, then along the far wall. "I don't think there's going to be much time," I say. "Definitely not enough time to show him a video. So I need an alternative. Pen, please."

He passes over the pen, and I set the small gray rectangle on the floor and lean over to write on it clearly: SamTheBrave. It's just like I did for that girl, but tidier and more legible. "If I ever do something like this again," I say, "I'm paying for proper business cards." I pass the pen back to Leroy.

"Yes!" Mark says. "You should do that! And you could wear a sharp black suit. Or maybe even a tux!"

"Uh, it's still a gaming convention, not prom," I point out.

"What if Codemeister was going to be at your prom?" Mark asks.

"Oh, in that case, full tux, gold-plated business cards, and I'd give Code a corsage to match his dress, obviously."

Mark laughs and Leroy looks at me like he doesn't really understand the joke, and then there's cheering, and we whip around, and there's all of Team Meister—well, except Oz, obviously—walking across the room to file into their chairs, looking like total badass superstars. We all cheer, too, and some people browsing a nearby stall turn to stare and to puzzle out who we're all lined up to see.

Code is in the very first seat and then the others are after him in some order that I can't keep straight in my head because Code is right there. And the line is moving already, as each person in line walks up to Code, gets his signature, then moves to the next Meister down the line.

And suddenly, I hate that we lined up so early and are so close to the front of the line, because I am not ready. I'm not. Not not not.

I reach for my phone to reread my spiel, but Mark's pushing me from behind, and there isn't time, because I'm there, I'm right there, and Code is in front of me saying, "Hey, man," and my mind goes blank.

For one long second that stretches to eternity, I stare at him. And then I grin. "I brought something very special for you to sign," I say, and then I pull out the cyan clay gem I bought and hold it out to him. I thought it would just be a silly joke from an old series of his, but it goes even better than I possibly imagined, because he snatches it up and holds it over his head and shouts, "The Stone!" and all the Meisters and everyone around us laughs.

I've said it before and I'll say it again: these are my people.

And my nerves are magically gone, so as he signs it with his Sharpie, I say, "By the way, I'm a streamer, too. My channel's SamTheBrave, and I do ridiculous pranks that I spend way too much time on. Like last week, when I spent an entire weekend moving my entire castle over a rift to prank one of my girl friends, only to end up locked in a closet, surrounded by shadowwolves."

He chuckles as he hands the Stone back to me. "That's cool, man."

"Like I said, my channel's SamTheBrave if you want to check it out." And then I reach out and hand him the rectangle of gray with my channel name on it.

And he takes it.

He takes my makeshift business card in his hand and says, "Thanks," and then I'm moving on to Noog signing the Stone and then Wolf and Z and Ben or maybe Ben then Wolf then Z or who knows because I'm filled with the lightest, brightest euphoria I've ever experienced.

"It worked!" I whisper excitedly at Mark and Leroy when they step off the metaphorical conveyor belt. "It actually worked!"

And I turn back to grin at Code, at the Meisters, at the world!

Which is when I catch Code give a flick of his hand. An intentional flick. A flick that sends something fluttering to the ground like it's garbage. A little gray rectangle.

It settles, discarded, on the convention floor.

FIFTEEN

ShadowWillow

THE BUG IS BIG. ABOUT THE LENGTH OF MY THUMB, IT SITS SHINY AND BLACK in my palm, ready for eating. At least it's all dried out and brittle and doesn't look at all alive. I slip it back into the bag just as Z enters the room. He cocks an eyebrow. "Checking out the eats?"

"I washed my hands first," I say.

"Oh, good. Because the thing I was most worried about eating in that bag was your germs." He laughs.

"Does that mean you're joining the challenge?" I seal up the bag. "Top-quality stuff in here."

He shrugs. "All the cool kids are doing it."

"I'll take that as a compliment." I toss the bag at him, and he catches it just in time. "Where are all the guys?"

"What am I? Chop suey?" He makes a face, though whether it's at my question or the bag of edible bugs he's holding, I can't tell.

"Chop suey?"

"Well, I'm obviously not chopped liver. I mean, look at how handsome I am!" He gives an impish grin as he gestures at himself. His hair seems to have grown two inches since this morning and added at least ten new angles to the directions it sticks up.

"You're right," I say. "You're at least a Polish composer."

"A . . . composer? What?"

"Yeah. Chopin. You know, it's spelled C-h-o-p, like chopped—never mind, it was funnier in my head."

He stares blankly for a moment, then lets out a burst of laughter. "Shadow, you've got the same sense of humor as me."

"You mean finding things that make absolutely no sense hilarious?"

"Exactly!" He steps toward me and sets the bug bag back on the counter, and as he does, his arm grazes mine, and heat flushes right up my arm, across my neck, and into my face. I turn away before he can see, pulling on the kitchen tap to rinse the invisible bug guck off my hands.

You're here to see Code, I remind myself. "So, Code and the guys?" I ask again. The wink at the panel was great, but still, the buzz could die off just as quickly as last time if I don't secure something more with Code. And, you know, maybe we'd actually be good together and all that.

"Should be here soon," Z says. "They stopped for more beer. Where are Legs and Lainey?"

"Around." I try to gesture toward the backyard and upstairs in a single sweep but probably look instead like I'm about to take a sweeping bow.

Back at the convention center, I could have gone with the guys to their autograph signing, but I don't want to scare Code off by following him around like a lost puppy, so I decided to go with Legs and Lainey back to the rental place. It felt weird to have such an epic LotSCON pass, then be leaving so early, but then again, I was walking down the streets of Toronto and then on a long detour down by the water with one of my idols, talking about all the words that are different in Canada versus the US—toque versus beanie, keener versus brown-noser—and that's an experience more valuable than all the money in my bank account. (Plus a lot more than that, because even with the new income that's been coming in from all the subs I've gained, I'm still pretty darn broke.)

But then I wanted to stop at a corner store and pick up a few things, so they went back without me, and when I got in, Legs was in the backyard on the phone and Lainey was upstairs showering, so I chilled by myself in the kitchen, putting things away and considering what I've gotten myself into with these bugs.

If I want to be memorable, I'm going to need to eat one of the big ones. And if I'm going to eat one of the big ones, I'm going to need to psych myself up.

Lainey wanders into the room then, holding the small camera she was using earlier in the VIP room. She's got on a new T-shirt—one with the cast of *Hamilton* cartooned fabulously across the front—and her brown hair has that light, fluffy-bodied look of having recently been blow-dried without a straightener. "Is Cody back yet?" She bites the black elastic off her wrist, then pulls her hair into a ponytail without looking into a mirror, which is possibly the most badass thing I've ever seen. If I tried to do that, I'd end up with huge loops of hair sticking out in random places.

"What's Z? Chop suey?" I say.

"Hey! Joke stealer!" Z says, but he's grinning. "Better be careful or I'm going to engineer a way to make you eat this entire bag of bugs!"

"Oh, good. I could use some more protein in my diet." I grin back at him, and the warmth of the grin travels all the way to my toes, as it strikes me for approximately the ten millionth time today that I am here, at this convention, with Team Meister, making my YouTube career dreams come true. Hopefully.

"So . . . Cody?" Lainey says, and we both swivel our heads to look at her.

"He died," Z says. "Sorry."

"Oh, gosh," I say. "Shipping his body back over the border's going to be rough. I bet you have to sign a lot of forms and stuff."

"It's fine. There's no body. He was consumed by shadowdragon fire."

I scrunch my eyebrows, then shrug. "All in all, not the worst way to go."

"I hate you both," Lainey says. She turns to leave, but Legs strides in the door she's about to exit through. LumberLegs! Again! Every time I see him, my giddiness intensifies.

"Wolf just texted me that the guys are on their way."

"*Mais sans Code, qui est mort*, obviously," I add.

"May what?" Z asks.

"It's French. I said, 'But without Code, who's dead.'"

"Ah. Your country's weird. Like look at this." He swings open the fridge and pulls out a jar of ketchup. "There's French on it! And on this!" He holds up a package of sliced ham.

"That's how we do things."

"Hey Z, you beat the rest of the guys back?" Legs cuts in.

He shoves the food back in the fridge. "Yeah, they stopped for beer."

"More?" Legs eyes the arrangement of beer cans on the counter.

"Yeah, Noog's very excited that he's legal drinking age here. Not that it stops him back home. They'll probably try to get you to drink a ton too, since even you're legal here, apparently. Drinking age is nineteen, right?"

Legs only shrugs, so I jump in. "Yeah, it is." Which I know even though I don't drink a lot, either. I've got more important things to do with my time.

"Joy," Legs says, voice thick with sarcasm.

"Not a big drinker?" I ask.

"More like not a big fan of Cody, Noog, and Ben drinking," Lainey answers for him, though Legs doesn't disagree.

"People without a lot of inhibitions to start with shouldn't guzzle down things that loosen their inhibitions," Legs adds, and Z laughs.

Legs turns to Lainey. "Want to get out of here before the drinking starts? Maybe go down to the water? Or out for dinner?"

She's staring at the camera in her hand—the one she got for Cody earlier—like it's some precious jewel. She pulls her eyes away from it and looks at Legs. "I wish I could, Legs, but I ended up telling Cody that I'd handle his vlog camerawork for him."

"You did?" His eyebrows furrow in confusion and surprise. Honestly, I'm surprised, too. Volunteering to do extra stuff for her brother doesn't seem like her thing.

"You could stick around here, though," Lainey suggests.

Legs stares at her for a long moment, as if he's trying to figure out how to get out of the alternate universe he's somehow slipped into. Then, as though he's realized he's trapped and there's no way out, his shoulders sink. "Nah, I don't think I could handle it right now. I'll catch you later, okay?" He touches her arm, gently, then disappears out of the room, leaving Lainey staring after him like she wishes this were the climax of some rom-com and she could go running after him.

"I didn't think you were going to do the vlog camera stuff," I say.

"I have every right to change my mind, okay?" she snaps.

I throw my hands up in surrender. "Sorry. Of course you do."

"So, what toppings do you guys want on the pizzas?" Z asks,

jumping in to save me from any further Lainey wrath.

We're still in the kitchen, debating pizza toppings, when Code and the rest of the guys get back. As soon as Code steps into the room, hefting a case of beer onto the counter, Lainey opens the fridge, pulls out a cold one, and hands it to him. Whatever she said earlier about how obnoxious he is when he drinks, she must have been joking.

With Code and Noog and Ben and Wolf all back, the noise level increases exponentially, and as we all move out of the kitchen and into the living room, Z has to shout to be heard: "Pizza toppings! What do you want for pizza toppings?"

"Pineapple," Wolf says, at the same time that Ben says, "Anything but pineapple!"

And then pizza toppings suggestions are flying around the room.

"Pepperoni only!"

"Every kind of meat they have!"

"Mushroom."

"Bacon."

"No mushroom."

"Bacon!"

"Green pepper."

"I don't believe in veggies."

"Bacon!"

Z hops up on the arm of a chair, almost hitting his head on the not-very-high ceiling. "Enough!" He holds his arms out, a king waiting for his subjects to quiet to a silent reverence, which the guys actually do. "You have all lost your right to choose. I am going to order whatever I want to order, and y'all will live with it." He taps on his phone, apparently putting in the order.

Code laughs. "The king has spoken!" he says. Apparently we're both thinking of Z standing up there as a king. Another reason we might be good together, right? Great minds and all that.

Before I can approach Code to try to strike up some flirtatious banter or something, Lainey grabs his arm and takes him to a corner, where they talk quietly for a couple of minutes. It's too loud in here to hear the whole conversation, but Lainey holds up the vlogging camera and Code grins widely in response. And I do catch Lainey's suggestion that she film some candid shots for the vlog, in addition to the normal vlogging camerawork she's already doing. Code gives her a thumbs-up, and then she slips quietly into a chair in the corner and pulls out the camera, apparently ready to vlog it up.

Code, on the other hand, marches across the room and plops onto the couch.

Noog plops down on the couch beside Code before I can snag the seat.

I'm tempted to go over and chat with Lainey for a bit, but then Noog says, "What's this stuff?" and waves at the grocery bags I left on the coffee table.

"Oh, I picked some snacks up. Canadian stuff." I move to the coffee table and start sorting through the bags, pulling all-dressed chips, Aero and Caramilk chocolate bars, and ranch Crispers out of the first bag. "Since you're in Canada, I thought we could do a video of you guys trying Canadian junk food."

Code's brow crinkles with displeasure, and my brain jumps with a panicked thought that maybe I've crossed a line by daring to suggest a video idea. Code frowns. "I don't know about—"

"That sounds awesome." Wolf snatches up the bag of all-dressed chips. "What do these taste like?"

"Like all-dressed chips," I say.

"That's helpful," Ben says with a laugh.

"I don't know. They taste like themselves. How would you describe the taste of . . . I don't know, cheese, to someone who's never had cheese?"

"I'd say it tasted like a cow was milked in heaven. I'm trying it." Wolf starts to open the bag, but I grab it before he can pull the seams apart.

"Not until the video!" I kneel beside the coffee table and shove the chip bag back into the plastic grocery bag.

"Then you have to tell me what it tastes like," Wolf says.

"Fine, let me think." I settle cross-legged onto the floor. "They taste like . . . like a barbecue chip and a salt-and-vinegar chip had a baby, sprinkled it with maple syrup, and hung it over a fire to be smoked."

"Gross," says Wolf.

"Awesome," says Noog at the same time. "Clearly we need to do this video." He leans forward and starts looking through the bags.

"Oh, I have an idea!" Z pipes up. He's still standing on the arm of the chair. He slides his phone into his pocket, apparently done ordering our pizza, and hops to the floor with a thud. "We should combine it with the bug-eating challenge. We could play Mario Kart or something, and if you win, you try a Canadian snack, if you lose, you eat a bug."

"Ooh, I like it," says Wolf. "It adds something unique to a challenge that's been done before. Though Mario Kart might be too long of a game for this type of a challenge. Viewers will want us to hurry up and eat the gosh-darn bug already. Is there something else we could play?" He grabs a beer off the side table, then flips around one of the chairs by the computer system in the corner and settles into it.

"We could just have a spinner that lands on something good or bad," Ben says. "That'd be quick and easy. I mean, aside from the fact that we don't have a spinner. I guess we could draw slips from a box or something instead?"

"What about Pictionary?" Z suggests.

And as the ideas start to fly around, I start to understand what Z was talking about earlier on the panel, about the benefits of working with other YouTubers. If I was doing this myself, I'd have sat in my basement and done a basic Canadian snacks video and a different bug-eating video, and they'd have been fine. But this is better than fine. They're taking my idea and making it better, building on it, making something exceptional.

I tune back in to Wolf saying, "We could do video game trivia. Get it right, try whatever Canadian thing you want. Get it wrong, eat a bug."

"No way," Noog says. "You'd destroy us."

"It's not Wolf's fault he's got an encyclopedic knowledge of all things video game," Z says.

"What if we answered trivia questions about each other?" Ben suggests. "We could each write a handful of questions about ourselves, then toss them in a hat."

"Good one," Z says, settling onto the floor beside me.

"Viewers are going to want to see Willow and me answer questions about each other," Code says, and my neck flushes with its inescapable heat. "Could we make that happen?" He waggles his eyebrows at me in mock seductiveness, and I wonder if he has any interest in me beyond wanting to please his viewers. Should that thought make me sad?

Lainey's been sitting quietly in the corner, intermittently lifting the camera to take what I assume is potential vlog video and lowering it back into her lap. I wonder if she caught Code's eyebrow waggle on camera, and if it'll make it into his channel's vlog. Is it wrong that that thought makes me happy?

"I've got it," Wolf says, and he explains to us his idea. We'll each write five trivia questions about ourselves with increasing difficulty. On our turn, we'll pick someone to answer a question about, and that person will read the next question on their list. Get it right, choose any Canadian snack to eat. Get it wrong, and that person will choose a bug for us to eat.

"I love it," I say, and I mean it. This is what happens when you throw a bunch of creatives together. This is what happens when I get to work with people so much further ahead in the business than me. Gold. Pure gold.

We spend the next while getting set up. When the pizza arrives, Code yells at Lainey to hurry up and go answer the door, and instead of yelling back at him to stop being an asshole, she presses stop on her recording and trots off to get them.

I can't help myself. I lean over to Code and say quietly, "Maybe you should treat your sister better."

"She's working for me," he says, and apparently he thinks that's a good enough reason, because he hops up to go scarf down a dozen slices of pizza and doesn't say anything more about it. For a split second, I want to smack him, but I push the feeling away. Nobody's perfect, right?

We continue setting up while we eat. Wolf passes around paper and pens so we can jot down our questions; Noog loses his questions for a while and then finds them in a pizza box on top of the Hawaiian pizza. By the time we're finished eating, we're ready to go.

A table is set up on one side of the room, with the snacks and bugs spread across it, and we squash in behind it, settling into chairs that are so close together they've become a bench. Code slides in after me from one direction and Noog from another. Z follows behind Noog, and the thought that I'd rather have Z's leg pressed against mine than Code's skips through my brain before I shove it away.

This is about Code, not Z, and I can't judge Code based on the way he and his sister fight. Conventions are stressful, and if someone walked in on me and my brothers fighting, they'd think we were all terrible human beings. And besides, Code's thigh and shoulder feel warm and soft against mine, and it's kind of nice.

The camera is set up across from us, on a tripod, and Wolf's fidgeting with it to make sure the lighting's right and we're all in view. Lainey's back in her chair in the corner, still intermittently filming things for possible vlog footage, looking more and more disgruntled over the course of the evening—perhaps because Code has been treating her like a servant robot instead of a human.

Ben slips in on Code's other side. "Is this whole bug-eating challenge overdone? There are so many videos about it."

"Uh, maybe a little too late to be pointing that out, dummy," says Noog.

"We've got a ton of unique stuff in ours," Wolf points out. "The Canadian snacks and stuff." He nods at me, an acknowledgment of *my* awesome idea, and my heart fills with rainbows.

"Confurzzle did one recently, and I think it's already at a million views," Z points out.

"Yeah, but he's black," Code says.

"What's that supposed to mean?" Z asks, taking the words right out of my mouth.

"It means that everyone's so excited about this 'black gamer' that he gets a free ride because he's black, while the rest of us have to work our butts off to get a few views," Code says, making air quotes around "black gamer."

What in a bushel of overripe bananas is that supposed to mean?!

There are so many things wrong with Code's statement,

and judging by Z's raised eyebrow, he thinks so, too, but Wolf announces, "Aaaaannnd we're rolling," and presses Record on the video before either of us can say anything. He rushes into his seat, and then he and Ben start into an explanation of the game and introduce me as a special guest, while Code and Noog interject with random crap.

I study Code as he jokingly tells Wolf to get to the point already. Maybe he didn't mean his comment about Confurzzle like it came out. After all, it's true that there's a lot of excitement that there's finally a mainstream YouTube gamer who's black in a world full of white guys and the odd white girl. And it's true that it's made his channel very popular very fast. Everything else probably just came out wrong. I hope.

I glance over to where Lainey was sitting to see if she had a reaction to Code's comment, but she's gone.

There isn't more time to think about it, because Wolf's explanation is done and it's Z's turn, and he's twirling his finger around like his hand's a spinner, then halting it in my direction. So like I do a dozen times a day or more, I take my annoyance and I push it away and I put on a smile.

"Me?" I ask, perhaps a little too flirtily, because Code's forehead crinkles, then immediately smooths over. Even though I know my questions by heart, I make a show out of cupping my hands around my paper, trying to hide it from Code and Noog as I unfold it and ask my first question: "What do my viewers call me for short?"

"That's too easy," complains Code.

"It is," Z agrees. "They call you Shadow."

Code frowns. "No, they—"

"That's right!" I cut Code off with a cheery grin before he can say something awkward again. I'm not trying to embarrass him; I'm just trying to set the record straight. "From time to time, I get called Willow, but most people call me Shadow. It's what I prefer."

"Nailed it!" Z says, then reaches across the table and snatches up the Caramilk bar, breaks off three whole pieces, and pops them into his mouth. "Mmmm, caramel-y. I'm buying a dozen of these to take back home with me."

Noog is up next, and he chooses Ben.

"How old am I?" Ben asks.

"A million and—"

"If you get it wrong, you have to eat a bug," Wolf reminds him.

"I mean, not a million. You're twenty-nine. Which is basically the equivalent of a million."

"Correct," Ben says.

"I want this," Noog says, grabbing up a Kinder Egg.

"What is it?" Wolf asks.

"It's a Kinder Egg," I say. "I can't believe you guys don't have them down south."

"We do now, but they're different," Ben says.

"Do we?" Wolf asks. "I've never seen them."

"Well, they were a staple of my childhood," I explain. "They're a chocolate eggshell with a toy inside."

"Hey!" Noog says through a mouthful. He's somehow ripped the foil wrapper off and shoved the entire egg-sized candy into his mouth. "There'sh shomething in here."

"Yeah, a toy, you doofus," Code says. "She just said that."

I laugh. "I guess I understand why they're outlawed in the US now."

Wolf smacks Noog's arm. "This is why we can't have nice things. Our entire country, I mean. Because you'll eat them."

Noog spits out the smaller orange egg from inside the chocolate shell. It lands on the table, coated in chocolate Noog-spit.

"Dude! Gross!" Code says.

"Let me just . . ." Noog snatches up the egg and struggles with the saliva-slippery thing, finally popping it open and pouring out a few green and white plastic pieces onto his hand. "What the heck is this?"

"You have to put it together," I say.

"Well, screw that." Noog drops the pieces on the table, and we all laugh.

It's my turn next. "Hmm, let's go with . . . Cody," I say, purposely using his first name instead of his username.

He twists his body to look at me, squishing Ben out of the way. "Okay. What's my favorite movie?"

"Your favorite movie? Have we talked about this? How am I supposed to pick your favorite out of the billions of movies that exist?"

He tries to give me a clue by lifting his arms in an upside-down biceps flex and making an angry face, which could mean about a thousand things.

"No cheating!" Wolf says. He's holding a tiny roaring dinosaur, put together from Noog's Kinder Egg pieces.

"Uh, *The Hulk*?" I guess.

"No!" Code says, sounding genuinely put out. "*Nacho Libre*!" He flexes his arms again. "I'm Jack Black! I'm a wrestler."

"Dude, you totally looked like the Hulk," Noog says.

"I've never seen *Nacho Libre*," I admit.

Code's eyes bug out at me. "What?! World's funniest movie. Jack Black's a monk turned wrestler and he runs around in this leotard and cape, and look, you're just going to have to watch it with me."

Honestly, it doesn't really sound like my type of movie, but a million people are going to watch this and that's probably not what they want to hear, so instead I say, "You name the time and place."

I mean it as a *Hamilton* reference, but Noog goes, "Ooooh," which I guess means it's working as some kind of sexual innuendo, too, so good job, self.

"You got it wrong," Wolf points out. "That means you eat a bug."

"Pick a big one!" Z shouts.

"Shush, you!" I point my finger at him, and he scrunches his nose at me, and I scrunch mine back before turning back to Code, who's got the bowl of bugs in his hand.

Code reaches across and holds it up to the side camera for a closeup before drawing it back and turning to me. "I'll go easy on you," he says, and his implied "because you're a girl and I'm a gentleman" makes me want to roll my eyes.

He picks out a salted and seasoned ant that's no bigger than my thumbnail and tastes like a potato chip, but I make a big deal out of eating it anyway.

We continue on like that, tossing trivia questions around. Code gets my favorite color right—in retrospect, that one was probably too easy, since I wear my favorite color every day on my head—and tries out dill pickle potato chips, and then Ben gets one wrong and has to eat a centipede and looks about ready to faint, but somehow he forces it down and then guzzles an entire bottle of water.

Wolf and Code get in a big argument about what Code wears to sleep. "You don't sleep in the nude," Wolf insists. "We've roomed together multiple times and you've got those Pac-Man PJ pants."

"I meant when I'm at home, and that question wasn't meant for you," Code says, which maybe should make my heart go pitter-patter but instead makes my stomach flip-flop. Code makes Wolf eat this big old beetle that Wolf scarfs down without batting an eye, insisting it tastes like peanuts.

I intend to choose Code again when it comes back around to me, but for some reason I find myself picking Z instead.

"What's my favorite movie?" he asks, and the way he widens

his eyes in response to my eye narrowing makes me think that wasn't his next question at all.

"Guys! Asking what your favorite movie is doesn't count as an easy question!" I protest. "There are seven bajillion movies out there. How the heck am I supposed to know which one?"

"So what's your answer?" Z bats his wide eyes at me.

"I don't know." I swivel to Code. "What was yours?"

"*Nacho Libre.*"

"Right, that stupid *Nacho Libre* one, then." I thought Z would have a better question than Code. I don't know what he's going for here.

Z shakes his head. "Nope. It's *Your Name.*"

My heart skips a beat. "As in the anime?" As in the anime I've watched approximately one dozen times?

"That's the one." He grabs the bowl of bugs, fishes out the biggest one, and holds it out to me. "Here you go."

"Dude!" shouts Ben. "That's nasty."

"Let it be noted that I went easy on you," Code points out, as if that's a good thing.

I take the bug, letting it sit in the palm of my hand, then hold it out to the camera. Something about Z's grin and raised eyebrows makes me think he knows that it's exactly the one I was holding in the kitchen earlier. The one I was psyching myself up to eat, because the bigger the bug, the more interesting I seem, and the more viewers I get. In theory.

Maybe Z chose a question I would fail on purpose. Maybe his question wasn't so bad after all.

The bug's shiny black armor looks impenetrable, like it's about to break my teeth. And it is thick, promising meaty insides. Unlike the ant I ate earlier, which simply tasted like salt, this one's going to have a flavor beyond just its seasoning.

I hold the beetle close to my face. Its pointy head looks ready to stab me.

"Do it! Do it! Do it!" Noog chants, pounding the table along with his words.

"I'm going to barf," Ben moans.

Why, exactly, am I doing this again?

Oh, right, for the viewers. That's reason enough. So I plug my nose, open up, pop it in whole, and chew and chew and chew.

@LumberLegs: It's a super-awesome night for a stroll by the water alone. So quiet. So spoooooooooooky.
[1.1K likes]

@LumberLegs: MUTANT TREES BY THE WATER ARE EATING ME! HAAAALLLLLPPPPPPP!!!!!
[1.5K likes]

@LumberLegs: Survived the mutant trees. Need ice cream to celebrate my victory. Best ice cream places in downtown Toronto?
[1.2K likes]

@LumberLegs: Some LotSCONers found me! Check out this super-awesome dragonlord cosplay!
[1.4K likes]

SIXTEEN

Lainey

IT'S EASIER THAN I EXPECTED, CATCHING CODY'S BIGOTRY ON CAMERA.

I mean, at the same time it's exactly what I expected, because that's who Cody is, and it's only gotten worse the last while as saying racist and other terrible things has become the new normal. I sprawl backward onto my bed with a sigh.

I gave up spending time with Legs to try to catch Cody on camera; I had to see whether my idea could work.

I have to admit that I hoped I'd discover I was all wrong about Cody, that if I was watching for them, the problematic things he says would turn out to be so rare and unusual that it'd be impossible to catch any on camera.

But it only took two hours. Another sigh pours out of me, like a boiling kettle releasing steam.

Cody doesn't normally talk much about race, probably because our whole family is white and all his friends are white, and out of sight, out of mind, apparently. But he says things like that once in a blue moon. Last time, it was at Friday dinner at Mom's house, and Cody and I got into a shouting match about it, until Mom kicked me out of the room for "turning a nice dinner into a political debate." If I had my way, every dinner would be a political debate until those two finally got with the program.

I reach for the camera I dropped beside me on the bed and sit up. I scan through the videos, find the last one, then fast-forward through it, pausing until I find the spot, and play it back. Cody's words are disappointingly clear. He really said that.

I shake my head. Cody, you're giving me no choice.

I lie back down on the bed, thinking through my plans, until the door creaks and I sit up to see Willow striding into the room. I slip the camera into my sweater pocket, like it's evidence I need to hide.

"Toothbrush. Need my toothbrush," she says, hurrying into the bathroom. When she pokes her head out a minute later, her toothbrush is sticking out of her mouth and she's foaming around the edges like a rabid dog. "Whadja doon uppear?" she asks through the foam.

I shrug. "Just checking my messages."

Which reminds me: I log on to see my chat with Janessa. There are a few more messages from her, demanding to know why I told her to stay off social media, before she must have realized that I disappeared again. I scroll back to look at my very first message:

Hey Janessa, I'm probably the second-last person you want to talk to, but I need to know: Did my brother cross any lines with you or pressure you to do anything you didn't want to? I . . . just needed to check.

That's not so bad as a message, is it? I was nice about it.

And she said she was fine, and I'm sure she meant it. She's one of those people who are always smiling, who might as well be one of those cheerleaders she's always hanging out with. So no harm, no foul, right?

Except Legs said I shouldn't have messaged her in the first place, just in case it did hurt her. Like it's more about the principle of the thing. Is it wrong even if no one got hurt? Did I screw up? And if so, what the heck am I supposed to do about it?

I shove my phone away so I don't have to think about it just as Willow emerges from the bathroom, teeth shiny-white and clean. Instead of leaving, she sits on the edge of her bed.

"How were the bugs?" I ask.

"I tried to imagine I was eating nuts on the top of a delicious banana split."

"Did that work?"

She laughs and wipes her sleeve across her mouth. "Not in the slightest."

I shake my head. "Why the heck did you do it, then?"

She shrugs. "It's a tough world, YouTube. You can't just post a half-decent gaming video once a week and expect to rake in the views. Besides, it was pretty neat working with the guys to plan the video. I haven't done anything like that before. This whole trip's been pretty incredible."

For some reason, her comment about how hard it is makes me think of that guy today who sales-pitched his channel to me like he was desperate for every viewer. I get up and slip my fingers into my jeans pocket, and sure enough, the scrap of paper he wrote on is still there. I should drop it in the trash now, but something makes me keep it in my pocket, even though it's destined to be forgotten about and put through the wash a few times before eventually turning to lint and getting caught in the dryer filter. Watching video gamers just isn't my thing. Poor kid. I hope he finds his niche. At least he's got some friends.

Willow pulls a ChapStick out of her purse and starts shining up her lips. And actually, her cheeks look pinker, too, like she freshened up her makeup in the bathroom. Like she's got someone to impress.

Surely she's not still all googly-eyed over Cody. She's seen his bad side now; it was right in front of her eyes.

"Hey, Willow, you heard what he said, right?"

"What who said?"

"Cody. About Confurzzle."

"Oh, yeah." Her brow furrows with concern. "He didn't mean

it like that, did he? Did it just come out wrong?"

What the heck is with everyone assuming that people don't mean what they say? If it walks like bigotry and talks like bigotry, maybe it really is bigotry! But I'm tired of trying to explain that to people. "Why don't you figure that out for yourself?" I snap.

She frowns. "Oh, okay." And then she returns to staring at herself in the bedroom mirror, trying to straighten one strand of her hair that's developed a small wave when the rest of it is straight. As though she's definitely still trying to impress. As though she's already dismissed his comment as unimportant.

Maybe she's as bad as he is. Maybe they deserve each other.

I glance at her to make sure she's not watching, then Google her on my phone. ShadowWillow. Maybe she's actually some alt-right leader. Do they have the alt-right in Canada?

The first thing that pops up is her YouTube channel, where her most-watched video is some tournament she did with Cody. Gross. And the comments are full of CodeWillow shippers. Double gross.

The video's from only a few months ago, and yet it's her most-watched video already, which is kind of weird, since she's apparently had her channel for a few years.

Willow turns to me. "Do you think I should wear my *The Adventure Zone* shirt tomorrow or my Legends of the Stone shirt?"

The mention of my favorite podcast makes it hard to stay grumpy. I close the search window on my phone. "*The Adventure Zone*. Definitely." I don't *actually* think she's an alt-right leader.

Maybe she's just in that infatuation stage with Cody where she won't be able to see logic until she snaps out of it.

Her face lights up, her eyes twinkling with her own obvious love of the podcast. "Did you start listening to *TAZ* after Legs mentioned it in his videos?" she asks.

My heart twinges at the mention of Legs. I should go find him once we're done talking. I shake my head. "No. I did start listening because Legs recommended it, but not in one of his videos. I mean, I'm sure he did mention it, but I don't really watch them."

Her eyes go wide at that, as if she's an anime character. "You don't watch Legs?! Who do you watch, then?"

I shrug. "No one." I'll watch the odd video Legs sends me, when it's one he's proud of, and it's cool to see him in action, but watching other people play video games is not the sort of thing I do for fun on my own.

She stares at me for a long moment in silence, this difference in our interests stretching into an unbridgeable chasm between us.

But then she says, "You like *TAZ*, though?" and I say, "I don't *like TAZ*, I *adore TAZ*," and then we're talking for five minutes about our favorite story arcs and characters and about how I didn't think I'd like it because three brothers and their dad playing D&D and other games doesn't sound like my kind of thing, but how Legs made me promise to listen to at least seven episodes before giving up on it, and by then I was hooked.

"Are you guys dating?" she asks suddenly. "You and Legs?"

And she's so easy to talk to that I almost tell her the truth. I almost tell her that no, we're not, but I want us to be, except how are we supposed to date if we can't see eye to eye on the important stuff?

But the fact is that though she might be easy to talk to, I still barely know her, so instead I simply say, "No."

"Do you want to be?" she asks, all hush-hush and giddy like we're BFFs gossiping. When I narrow my eyes at her, her cheeks— no, her whole neck—flushes pink. "Sorry, I shouldn't have asked. I go all baby skunk and say things I shouldn't sometimes."

"Baby skunks can talk?"

She laughs at that, and the awkwardness between us falls away—for now. I've never figured out how to have conversations with people that run smoothly, like a car on a highway on cruise control. It's more like being in a jam-packed rush hour, with stops and stalls and sudden lane changes and people honking at each other in frustration.

Willow leans over and pulls a shirt out of her bag. "I should probably go with Legends of the Stone tomorrow, though. Since it is LotSCON and all. I don't want to confuse people."

"Who cares! You do you. It's just a signing."

"Yeah, but it's my first ever signing. So I care."

Now it's my turn to wordlessly blink at her. "How is it possibly your first signing?" I ask at last. "You have hundreds of thousands of YouTube followers."

She scrunches her lips up, then says, "Most of those are recent. Like in the past few months."

The past few months. Things start clicking into place in my brain. "Like since your video with Cody?"

A little crease appears between her eyebrows. "I mean, it's not like I didn't have subscribers before that. I worked hard to build up my channel. But yeah, that helped. A lot."

"You must have been pretty stoked when he invited you this weekend then."

"Of course. Wouldn't you be?"

I tap my phone against my palm. So she doesn't care about Cody, she only wants his subscribers. Which I couldn't care less about, except that it means she's not all blind from lovesickness after all. She should be able to see right through him.

And ignoring Cody's bigotry because she's clueless and lovesick is one thing, but ignoring it because she wants his subscribers is a million times worse. It's a choice.

I hop to my feet as the chasm spreads between us again. "I'm going to find Legs," I say, and I'm surprised to hear the words come out normal instead of echoing across the great divide between us.

Though the chasm must be doing something, because her response doesn't make it across the space between us before I'm gone.

At the bottom of the stairs, I run into Cody. He's got another beer in his hand. Earlier, I hoped he'd get drunk so there'd be a greater chance of him saying something I might catch on camera.

Now, I wish he'd switch to root beer.

"Willow upstairs?" he asks. He leans against the banister like he's super chill, but his hopeful gaze slides upward.

My heart twists for him. I think he might actually like her. And while maybe the only way I can help him become a better person is by outing him as a bigot to his viewers, here I can help him simply by telling him the truth. Or at least what I suspect is the truth.

"Cody, I think she's using you."

His gaze darts back down to me. "Of course she is." There's no alarm in his face; he's still leaning against the banister, relaxed.

"You knew that?"

He sets his beer down on the railing post. "She wants sub-scribers, and how else is she supposed to get them? Girls don't make it to the top."

I stare at him. I want to believe that his words are a profound commentary on the misogynistic state of the gaming world, and a pledge to help talented, hilarious female gamers break through that glass ceiling. That's not what he means, though. It's never what he means.

I'd call him out on it, but I'd rather not be filled with a desire to punch my own brother in the face. Again. "So it doesn't bother you?" I ask instead.

"It's what the viewers want." He takes a sip of his beer before adding, "And besides, she's hot."

Which is quite enough Cody for me, thank you very much.

"I'm going out," I say, and then I slip past him, grab my coat, and walk out the front door.

Out on the porch, the cold night air prickles against my skin. I wrap my coat tightly around me, sit on the porch step, and pull out my phone. I text Legs: Done with vlogging. Want to hang out?

It suddenly occurs to me that he could be back at his hotel room in a depressive early sleep, or out somewhere where he won't think to look at his phone.

Before I can properly start to wonder what I'll do in that case, his reply text comes in: Sure. You still at the Manor? I'm not far. I'll be there in ten.

Great, I reply. I could ask him where he is and meet him halfway, but it'd probably take half that time just to coordinate, and besides, walking around Toronto by myself on a sunny Saturday morning is one thing; walking around Toronto by myself in the dark is another.

While I wait, I pull up Legs's social media. Apparently he's been having a grand adventure chilling with mutant trees and eating ice cream. There's a picture of him in the middle of a group of fans, and he's grinning ear to ear, and for a moment I'm filled with the most intense FOMO of my life.

But then I remember what he's going through, and I zoom in on the picture, and sure enough, he's wearing his fake grin, the one that doesn't reach his eyes. He probably wanted a quiet walk alone, and instead he got fans and smiling for photos and telling people they're awesome.

My FOMO slips away, replaced by guilt. Maybe I should have gone with him, but I had to see whether my idea had any chance of working. And now that I know it does, I really should be in the house, trying to get more video, but there'll be plenty of time for that tomorrow. For now, I'm going to do what *I* want, and what I want is to spend time with Legs.

I always want to spend time with Legs. Though I'm not looking forward to explaining to him my plan.

I look up then, and there he is only half a block away. I hesitate for only a moment before hopping up, slipping my phone into my pocket, and striding to meet him.

"Hey," he says when I'm a few feet away. His cheeks and nose are windy pink in the edge of the light of the streetlamp.

"Hey. Looks like you were having quite the adventure."

"Adventure?" He steps into the streetlamp's full light, and it illuminates his whole face—the real one, not the one he wears for fans. As he studies me, his eyebrows are relaxed, his jawline soft, his mouth curving naturally down at the edges. He's not trying to look happy or excited or anything at all. He's just himself.

"Yeah, the difficult kind where you have to act all happy for fans when you feel anything but. I'm sorry."

He shrugs. "Ah, yes. Thanks. Can you please use your time machine to go back in time a few years to tell me not to build a persona that's so darn happy all the time? It's exhausting."

"I'm on it. I will start working on building a time machine

tomorrow, and once it's finished, future me will go back in time and do exactly that."

We both freeze simultaneously, then after a moment, we both look around like we're expecting the whole world to have changed.

Legs pats his cheeks. "Still sore from smiling. Nothing's changed."

"Look, man, it's not my fault if you refused to take future me's very sage advice."

He gives a soft chuckle, then points in the direction he came from. "Want to go to the park?" he asks. "There are some benches where we can sit."

"Sure." There's a quiet tension between us. We've spent the evening apart, and whatever conclusion Legs has come to about it, it's not the right one. Maybe he thinks I'm tired of his grief. Maybe he thinks I'm tired of him.

He turns a corner, and I mirror him too late and bump into his shoulder, and it's like every atom in my body shouts, "Hallelujah" at the touch, and yeah, if he thinks I'm tired of him, it most definitely isn't true.

I'm not sure how to correct it, though, because how do I tell him that I spent the evening trying to get a clip of Cody being a bigoted jerk so I can compile a video and post it to his channel behind his back, hopefully causing Cody's fans to blow up in horror and anger at him? How do I explain to Legs that I'm thinking of causing major devastation to Cody's YouTube career?

And most importantly: how do I tell him all that without making him hate me?

Legs is the kind of person who tells all his fans to be awesome because he really does mean it, the kind of person who always listens when people speak, the kind of person who sees the good in everyone. He's not the kind of person who would understand that sometimes you need to burn something down in order to build it back up again. So how, exactly, do I tell him that's precisely what I'm planning to do to my own brother?

That every time I think about it, it solidifies more and more from idea to plan?

We make it to the park, which has paved pathways winding through trees and shrubbery and not much else, considering that there's still another month until spring is officially here, same as back home.

There's a park bench in a corner, and we head there together like our minds are in sync, except I know that they're not, because Legs doesn't know that I'm a little bit evil. I plop down on the bench. It's cold through my jeans.

"How was your evening?" Legs asks as he settles onto the bench a respectful foot away from me. He's definitely got it all wrong.

If we were in a TV show—one of those sitcom ones like *New Girl* or *The Mindy Project*—the writers would have a heyday with this moment. It would be the first off-again in a five-season-long on-again-off-again saga that revolves around stupid miscommunications, where all they need to do to sort things out is to frickin' talk to each other, but they never ever do.

Not that we're a couple, we're just friends, but still, I'm not living my life like that. And if we did become more than friends, I'd want our relationship to be based on honesty and open communication and all that corny but still super-important stuff.

Which means that even if Legs isn't going to like it, I have to tell him.

"So, you should know that I'm a tiny bit evil," I say, ignoring his question. "But it's for the greater good. And I really really really wanted to spend this evening with you—it sounded a million times better than hanging out with those idiots—but it was my only chance to put my good-slash-evil plan into action."

"Oh?" Legs says, eyebrows raised as if to say, "Tell me more."

And I want to tell him more, I do, but right at this moment, I can't find the words. So instead I unzip my coat and fish the vlogging camera out of my sweater pocket, find the right spot on the right video, and play it for Legs, turning the volume down low in case this cold park isn't as empty as it looks.

When the video finishes, Legs frowns. "Have you ever read through any of the comments on Furzzle's videos?" he asks. "Some of them are pretty atrocious."

"Ugh, I bet." For a moment, I wonder if any of those comments are from Cody, and my stomach twists with nausea at the thought.

Legs furrows his brow and opens his mouth, and for a moment

I think he might say something angry about Cody, but then he closes it again and simply looks at me, expectant, waiting for further explanation.

It's my turn to frown. "Your face is telling me that watching this video didn't magically unlock for you every thought in my brain. That's disappointing."

Legs laughs. "I . . . don't think so? Unless you're thinking about burritos."

"I mean, I'm always thinking about burritos."

"Aren't we all?"

I try to smile, but my mouth goes all pinchy instead.

Time to tear off the Band-Aid. "I'm planning to ruin Cody's YouTube channel."

The smile falls off Legs's face. "What?"

I shove the camera into my coat pocket and stand. "I don't know what else I can do. I've tried talking to him. So many times. He won't listen.

"You won't talk to him. Z has tried to talk to him, to no success. What am I supposed to do? Just keep letting my brother make racist comments and joke about sleeping with fourteen-year-olds? I'm not going to let that happen!" I'm pacing in front of the bench, unable to sit still while I explain. "The world is broken, and my own brother is part of the problem. I have to change that, have to change *him*."

Legs chews on his thumbnail as he considers my words. "My mom always says, 'You can't change other people; you can only change yourself.' Which I think is good adv—"

"No," I say, cutting him off. "I've heard that before, and I don't believe it. Are you just supposed to let an alcoholic be an alcoholic? Or a cheater be a cheater? Or a bigot a bigot? If it's someone you love, isn't it wrong to do nothing? Shouldn't you have talked to your homophobic friend like Brian wanted you to?" I regret the words as soon as they slip out of my mouth. I don't want to rub it in that Legs has lost his longtime best friend. That's not what this is supposed to be about.

Legs looks more confused than angry, though. "You think I didn't talk to Steve about it?"

I wish I could take the words back, but they're out there now, so might as well be honest about it. "Well, you wouldn't talk to Cody, so I assumed . . ." I trail off, unsure of myself now.

"I didn't want to talk to Cody because he's your brother."

"My . . . brother?" I repeat, not sure how that's relevant.

"Yeah. What if I got mad at him and punched him in the face and from then on your family only ever thought of me as the guy who beat up your brother?" It's dark here in this park, but still, I'm pretty sure Legs's cheeks flush red.

"You'd punch someone in the face?" I say to distract from the fact that my own cheeks are probably just as red.

"Well . . . a metaphorical punch."

I laugh, then break off. "So you did? You spoke to Steve?"

"Of course I did." He should be angry at me for assuming he didn't, but he's apparently too perfect a human, because there's no malice in his voice. "It was definitely awkward at first, but I think he's finally starting to get it." He frowns. "It's too bad that wasn't enough for Brian." There's a hardness in his voice that's new. When he's talked about it before, there's only ever been the softness of sorrow, like the mushiness of a rotten apple, fallen from a tree and forgotten.

I slip back onto the bench. "What do you mean?"

Legs's frown dips so low it almost falls off his face. "He cut off his relationship with Steve, and he wanted me to do the same."

I frown for probably the fiftieth time. "He wanted you to stop being friends with Steve?" In all my brainstorming about how to deal with Cody, cutting him out of my life has never even crossed my mind. Though he's my brother, which makes it different. If the Meisters or Willow were to finally kick Cody to the curb, I wouldn't fault them for it. In fact, I sort of wish they would.

Legs nods in answer to my question. "Steve's a good friend. We've gone camping together, and we went to his grandpa's funeral, and he showed up at my house with all the *Star Wars* movies to watch together when I was sad about . . . a thing."

I'm guessing the "thing" was a breakup, and even though we're in the middle of some fight or debate or I don't know what, the fact that he's avoiding mentioning anything about another girl to me makes my heart flip in place once or twice.

"He's a homophobe, though," I point out. I think I agree with Brian, I realize; shouldn't the fact that he's homophobic be the end of the story?

"That's changing, I think," Legs says. "And even if it wasn't, how would he ever change if he was only ever around people who agreed with him?"

"So you *do* think you can change him."

Legs chews his lip again for a moment, then says, "No, I don't. But if he decides he wants to change, I'll be there to help him."

"Why don't you tell him that, then? Tell him it's sayonara until he decides to be a decent human being!"

"Because two wrongs don't make a right, Lainey."

There's a heaviness to Legs's words that makes me think he's referring to more than just homophobe Steve. "Are you talking about my plan for Cody's channel?"

He sighs and slumps backward on the bench. "I don't know. Tell me again what you're planning to do and why."

So I tell him again the whole story—about Cody's crude joke in the airport, about Janessa, about talking to Z. About how Cody refuses to listen. About how the only other way I can think of to force Cody to listen is to make his subscribers do the talking.

I turn to Legs, suddenly hopeful. "Unless you have any other ideas!" If something less drastic would work, I would happily do it.

But Legs only shakes his head sadly. "I don't, sorry. I can't think of anything that would make him change unless he wants to." Then he adds, "So, what if it doesn't work? What if you do all that and cause all that pain and anger, and in the end nothing happens? What if you do all that and he doesn't change?"

I shake my head. "It'll work." It has to. I can't believe my brother is so far gone that even something this big wouldn't make a difference. "And if it doesn't," I add, "at least I'll have tried." We sit there in silence as the leafless tree branches rustle above us in the breeze. At last, I ask, "Do you think I'm a terrible person?"

"It's not the choice I would make, but no. I understand why you're doing it." He shifts his whole body toward me on the bench and stares at me with an unexpected intensity. "And Lainey, knowing who you are and what you stand for, I could never think you're a terrible person. Even if I don't always agree with you."

I look down at my lap so he hopefully can't see my cheeks flushing hot again, then decide that's silly and look him in the eye again. "I'm glad you don't always agree with me. How would I know when I'm wrong if you did?"

Which reminds me of what he said earlier about Janessa, of how I shouldn't have messaged her in the first place. And how am I supposed to expect Cody to listen when I call him out on his crap if I don't listen when people call me out on mine? I pull out my phone. "Hey, so I think you were right. I shouldn't have messaged Janessa. If Cody had hurt her, I could have made things so much worse for her."

He nods, but there's no judgment on his face. "Do you want help figuring out how to apologize to her?"

Apologize? It's not like I actually hurt her. "No, it's fine," I say, then stop myself. Cody has never once apologized when I wanted him to. If Legs thinks I need to apologize, I should listen.

"Actually, yes." I pull up my chat with Janessa and hand it over to him. I might be good at burning down worlds, but I could probably use some help building broken ones back up.

Legs scrolls through my conversation with Janessa, then tilts his head in thought. He starts to type, thinks, types some more, until finally he hands the phone back to me.

I look at the unsent message.

Hey, Janessa, I'm sorry I worried you. I saw that people were blaming you for your breakup with my brother, and that seemed unfair. I'm guessing it's not your fault at all, as Cody doesn't have the greatest track record with girls. I'm sorry for what you're going through. If there's anything I can do to help, don't hesitate to ask.

I look at Legs, then back at my screen. He's good at this. "That's perfect," I say as I hit Send. "Thank you." I'm proud of us. Legs is learning to call people out, I'm learning to apologize when my big mouth gets the best of me. People *can* change for the better. Cody just needs a little something to jump-start him in the right direction. Or a big something.

"We make a good team," Legs says, breaking into my thoughts. I grin because he's right. Maybe we don't agree on everything, but his disagreement makes me stronger and wiser.

Which makes me realize what I have to do. I have to tell him. I have to do it because I am not going to risk being stuck in one of those five-season-long miscommunicating story arcs forever. That is not going to be my life.

And so I take in one deep breath. And then I say: "Legs, I like you. Romantically, I mean. Just so you know."

For a long moment, my words hang in the air between us, colored with fear and bravery that writes them visibly across the night sky.

I want to look away, but I force myself to meet Legs's eyes. And when I do, my heart skips a beat, because in his eyes, the whole sky of stars is sparkling.

"I like you, too," he says. "Romantically, I mean." And he grins and slips his hand into mine, lacing his wind-chilled fingers with mine, pressing his soft gamer's palm against mine. And that is that.

SEVENTEEN

SamTheBrave

I CAN'T STOP SEEING MY MAKESHIFT BUSINESS CARD GET TOSSED TO THE ground like it's trash—like *I'm* trash. It replays over and over in my mind.

Mark and Leroy didn't see it. Mark chatters away to Leroy about how awesome that was, how well it went, how I'm going to be famous.

My phone buzzes, and I pull it out and unlock it, hoping for a message from Dereck or Jones that'll distract me.

It's not. It's a YouTube comment.

> This is garbage. I want these seven minutes of my life back.

My throat tightens as I stare at it. *This is garbage.* I try to blink it away and focus in on the couple dozen nice ones, but instead, I find myself scrolling to the other comment from this morning.

> this is so dumb your an idiot. I bet your face is as ugly as this video and that's why you never facecam

My business card is trash. I'm trash. My videos are garbage. My face is ugly. I've heard all these words before, and worse, spat at me in the hallways, shouted from a car in the parking lot, scrawled on a piece of paper slipped onto my desk in civics class, muttered into my ear with a hand on my throat or a fist in my gut.

And now here, in this place I thought I belonged.

"You want to join us for the card tournament downstairs?" Mark asks. His words are far away.

I shake my head and mumble something about not feeling great.

And then they're gone and I'm texting Mom to come pick me up.

I want to go home.

One of these days, I'm going to wake up and discover I have no skin left.

Mom waits twenty minutes into our drive before reaching over and handing me a Kleenex. She's learned that sometimes pointing out that I've lost control only makes me feel more out of control. It's like pointing out to a depressed person that they're still in bed, or like telling a drunkard that they're drunk. I'm fully aware I'm tearing off my skin, thank you. If I could stop, I would.

I press the tissue against my lower arm, where half a dozen tiny bumps no longer exist. The Kleenex comes away spotted with blood. I stare at the dots of red, a sign that I have lost—though I knew that already. This whole day has been a loss.

I push the Kleenex back against my arm and hold it in place.

"Want to talk about it?" Mom asks.

I shrug. "Plan didn't work."

"I'm sorry, Sammy." She reaches over and pats my knee. "Well, we knew it was a stretch, right? And at least you tried! Did you have a good day anyway?"

Did I? I'm sure there were moments I liked, but all I can think of right now are those YouTube comments. Sitting alone in the cafeteria. Those girls at the shadowdragon escaping before I could even try to talk to them. That gray piece of paper swirling to the floor.

"I don't know. Sometimes, maybe? I don't think I'll go back tomorrow. I've run out of chances with Code, so what's the point?"

"Aw, Sammy boy. I'm sorry. Maybe we were focusing too much on your goal. I want you to work hard to reach your dreams, but not work so hard that you forget to have fun. Go tomorrow and just enjoy yourself!"

Are there places people can go where the words don't follow them? Where they aren't written off as someone who doesn't belong and shoved discarded to the floor?

I thought I had found one, but maybe I was wrong.

"I'll think about it," I say, though I'm leaning toward not.

Mom's phone, which is sitting in the cupholder, chirrups. She points to it, which is my sign to check the message for her. I swipe her passcode and pull up her texts. It's from Opa. Great.

"Opa wants to know if he can stop by tonight and pick up that crokinole board," I tell her. Just what I need to cap off my failure of a day.

Mom glances at me out of the corner of her eye. Apparently I look too pathetic to have to deal with Opa, because she says, "Tell him he can come Monday evening."

"It's okay, Mom. He can come tonight." If I'm going to be in a crap mood anyway, might as well take advantage of it and get an Opa interaction out of the way. It's better than having him spoil a good day.

"Are you sure?" Mom asks.

"Message already sent," I say, which will be true in ten seconds.

We listen to a crime podcast for the rest of the drive. A couple more YouTube comments come in, but I turn off my notifications and don't read them.

When we get home, Mom tells me to grab the crokinole board and set it by the door, and I suspect she's hoping what I am: that he'll grab the board and go. Fat chance.

Mom and Opa have a weird relationship. They love each other, but they don't ever seem to actually like each other. So, same as my relationship with Opa, I guess. Even in my annoyance, I can still taste the Apfelkuchen Opa saved for me yesterday because he knows it's my favorite.

I could go work on a video while I wait for Opa to arrive, but if I'm on my computer when he gets here, that's a sure way to inspire a lecture. And maybe it's deserved, because apparently my videos are a waste of time anyway.

Instead, I sit at the kitchen table, finishing the last of my homework. I don't have much to do, since I did almost all of it at Opa and Oma's yesterday.

The doorbell rings as I start on the last row of math problems. I sigh as Mom plods to the door. Maybe this will be the one time when Opa will duck his head in and then leave, without needing me to basically line up for inspection or even say hello at all. Universe, after today, you owe me this much.

But after their quiet, murmuring exchange, I hear a booming, "Where's the boy?" followed by thumping footsteps coming my way. Universe, you're a jerk.

I shove myself to my feet as Opa enters the kitchen. He wears almost the same thing on the weekend that he'd wear on any workday—crisp gray pants, a white collared shirt, and a navy sweater vest. The only thing missing is his tie. You'd think our school was a private one with uniforms; it's not.

"Hi, Opa," I say.

"Hey, champ." He pulls out a chair and slips into it, then calls to Mom, "Eva, put on a pot of tea!"

I slip back into my own seat. I guess we'll be here awhile.

Mom walks into the kitchen and flicks on the electric kettle without a word, though she's probably seething.

"Sammy," she said to me once after Opa left, "if you ever shout at me to do things that you're perfectly capable of doing yourself, I'm going to box you upside the head."

When I asked her why she doesn't box Opa upside the head, she told me not to talk about my opa that way, though she laughed when she said it.

"Doing your homework, I see," Opa says, and he taps my math textbook with three firm thuds. "That's good. All your teachers say you're doing well in your classes. Eva, he's like you that way!"

"What's that?" Mom wanders over and clunks a mug and box of teabags in front of Opa, then tears open a box of maple leaf cookies as she slides into the seat across from me. She holds them out to me, and I take one. Not as good as apple cake, but Mom works long hours and I have my Twitch channel and afternoons at Oma and Opa's, so neither of us has time for baking. Maybe I should give up streaming video games and spend my time baking instead.

"You two are going to die at fifty if you keep eating that garbage," Opa says.

Mom twists a cookie apart and pops the entire icing-less cookie half into her mouth. "Dad, I think you were saying something nice about Sam," she says between chewing.

"Yes, well . . ." He trails off, then clears his throat. "Sam is doing well in school. No complaints from any of the other teachers."

I bite into my cookie whole. The maple of the icing is sweet and smooth.

Mom smiles at me. "Yes, he certainly works hard at it."

Opa turns to me. "Now just think what you could achieve if you stopped playing all those video games."

I stop chewing.

"Dad, we've been through—"

"And you're always alone. Success isn't only about good marks, you know. You've got to learn how to connect with people, how to make friends. That's how you really succeed in this world. You do things for people, people do things for you, mutually beneficial. We call that symbiosis."

Thanks, Opa. A reminder that I have absolutely no friends at school and that I ate lunch alone even at LotSCON is just what I need right now.

"Dad! It's not that simple," Mom says.

Opa turns to her. "He's got his head in that phone all the time. You can't make friends if you can't even look people in the face. I walk into the cafeteria at lunchtime, and there are these clusters of kids all staring into their little black boxes, not interacting, just filling their brains with garbage. If Sam put his phone away and started talking to people, he'd make friends in no time."

Oh, and the phone lecture again. There's always the phone lecture. Opa doesn't understand that my phone is the one place I do have friends. Or that his taking away people's phones is what loses me friends.

"I've tried making friends. I get punched in the stomach."

Opa's eyes widen. I'm not sure if it's because this is the first he's heard of me getting beat up at school or if it's because this is the first time I've ever talked back to him.

Mom's lips purse. I've never told her this before either. She wants to ask more, I can tell, but she's not going to ask with Opa here.

Opa's eyebrows settle into decisiveness. "Sam," he says, "there are bullies everywhere. You have to ignore them. And for goodness' sake, stop picking at those pimples. That can't help."

My hand falls from my face as my mottled skin flushes hot.

"Dad, we've been through this," Mom jumps in. "It's a disorder."

I tune them both out as she tries to explain dermatillomania to Opa for about the hundredth time. I pinch my fingers to keep them from returning to my face as Opa's words play over in my head. *There are bullies everywhere. You have to ignore them.*

I stare at him as the unexpected truth of those words settles into my stomach.

"Everything is diagnosed as some disorder nowadays," Opa says before I tune them both out again. I watch Mom's mouth open and close, watch Opa's eyebrows sit in their steady, unmoving place of confidence.

There are bullies everywhere. Even in families. Even in my own kitchen.

You have to ignore them.

I stand to my feet, cutting both Mom and Opa off with the movement. They turn to look at me. "I have to type up my essay for history," I say. "It's a requirement."

Mom raises an eyebrow at me. She knows it's a lie. But maybe she also knows the truth of Opa's words, knows that sometimes the only way to ignore someone's poison is to walk away. Even when they're family.

"You go, Sammy," she says. "Homework is important."

"I don't know why these teachers insist on essays being typed up," Opa says. "The last thing these teens need is more screen time."

I hurry out of the room before I hear anything more.

I should feel big, not small, for walking away from Opa's comments, but I don't feel like Thor or Worf or Chewbacca. I feel more like little hobbit Frodo, who's just gotten into his canoe to paddle off to the darkest part of Mordor alone, because he doesn't trust a soul not to steal the ring of power before it's destroyed.

Upstairs in my room, I pull out the diamond Code signed. It's supposed to be a glorious reminder of the one place I belong; instead, it's turned into a symbol of how I apparently don't belong anywhere. I throw it into the back of my closet, then thud down onto my bed, where I think about all the lunch hours I've sat alone. I add them up in my head. Ten months a year—or nine and a half, I guess, since classes end halfway through June—minus Christmas break and March break. So probably thirty-six weeks a year, five days a week. That's . . . 30 plus 150 . . . 180 days last year of me sitting alone, plus almost that many again this year. High school's really going well so far.

When I watch *Lord of the Rings*, Frodo always feels like a hero for heading off to Mordor alone, knowing he can't trust his fellowship anymore. But maybe it's not heroic, maybe it's stupid. He could have had the help of badass, long-lived hero king Aragorn, not to mention a sharp-shooting elf and a hilarious dwarf. But he didn't.

At least he had Sam, in the end. I don't even have that.

My fingers are smeared with blood. I don't even know from what or from where.

"You're bleeding," I hear Leroy's voice say in my head from earlier today, and it strikes me in retrospect that there was nothing judgmental in his words. He didn't say it was gross or that I was gross. It was a fact: I had blood on my chin.

Now I have blood on my fingers. I don't want it to be there, didn't choose for it to be there, but there it is.

I open my bedside table and pull out a box of Band-Aids. I plaster them on my wrist, on my arm, on my face. I put a big Band-Aid across my forehead where a new pimple's sprouted that I'm itching to empty but haven't touched yet.

I find the bloody spot—on the back of my neck—and spread a Band-Aid over it, then take off my blood-dotted shirt and rinse off the collar before throwing it in the laundry.

I switch to a worn black shirt I love that says "Pizza and Winglings" and has a cartoon of a couple of winglings from LotS sharing a pizza on the front. When we were leaving the convention, I saw some girl wearing the same one, and it made me wish I had worn it instead of the stupid Codester shirt.

I plop down at my computer. There are multiple YouTube notifications. I should ignore them, probably. If I get another one calling me garbage and dropping my hard work to the floor like trash, it might break me for good. But I can't help it. I click the little bell and read through the comments.

MortalWombat and asfdeLOL have declared war against each other, each proclaiming they'll defeat the other in the battle for highest "First!" count.

Two new people have left generic "nice vid" comments, and Canuckosaurus says he (or she) died laughing.

I can still see the comment from earlier, but Opa's ironic advice flits through my head again, and I click away from it.

I write thank-yous to the first two, then click on Canuckosaurus's comment and reply with, "I'm very sorry for your family's loss. Please have your ghost tell them to tell me where I should send the funeral flowers."

A small grin creeps onto my face. I know, I know, you're not supposed to laugh at your own jokes. Try and stop me.

I scroll back to look over the other nice comments from this morning. The "OMG THIS IS AMAZING I LOVE YOU SO MUCH!" pops out at me. It's just above the comment that calls me ugly.

Maybe Opa is right on so many more levels than he knows. Maybe it's not that I don't belong in this gaming world either. Maybe it's just that there really are bullies everywhere. The thought makes me hopeful and sad all at once.

I haven't heard Opa leave yet, which means I'm a hostage in my own room for a while.

I click over to Twitter. "Impromptu stream in ten," I tweet, adding a link to my channel. I post the same thing on all my other social media. It's not on my schedule to stream today, but it's only a problem if you say you're going to stream at a particular time and then don't, not the other way around. And besides, what else am I supposed to do?

I test my mic and my recording software, get my screen layout set up, open the chat, and move it to my second screen.

BlastaMasta742, one of my regulars, is already in chat.

BlastaMasta742: what are you gonna play?

Normally, I follow a schedule, but since this is impromptu, I could do anything. Though honestly, I'm not feeling up for much. I put up a generic blank screen, turn on my mic, and start the stream.

"I haven't decided yet what to play," I say. "Maybe some Hearthstone?" I could go for a mindless card game I've played a thousand times.

BlastaMasta742: you should try out your
warlock rush deck

"Good idea, man," I say aloud, then open Hearthstone and switch it to my main screen so my viewers—well, my one viewer—can see it.

I play a game, chatting with BlastaMasta742 between moves. It took some practice when I first started streaming—checking for comments periodically, then responding aloud. Well, I shouldn't say when I first started. When I *first* first started streaming, there wasn't anyone in chat at all.

At least I've got BlastaMasta742.

That's more than at school.

A new name pops up in chat that I haven't seen before.

> xxMeisterFanxx: Yes! You're streaming! Didn't
> miss it! BRB!

"Uh, hi, Meister Fan. Bye, Meister Fan," I say. What I want to say is "Don't be a Meister Fan; they're stupid!" But I don't.

I take another turn. BlastaMasta742 tells me what cards he thinks I should play, and he's usually right.

xxMeisterFanxx appears back in chat.

> xxMeisterFanxx: I destroyed Leroy at the
> tourney today
> NotLeeroyJenkins: That's only because you
> had the luckiest first 3 rounds ever. The odds
> of that are . . . hang on, I'll calculate . . .

I halt the cursor over the card I was planning to play next. "Mark?"

It takes a moment for my words to stream, then for chat to update, so I play the card, then check chat.

> xxMeisterFanxx: in the flesh!
> xxMeisterFanxx: or the digital!
> xxMeisterFanxx: electronic
> xxMeisterFanxx: whatever
> xxMeisterFanxx: why aren't you clearing out
> your LotS base, man? Clearing out those

wolves is going to be a fun time!

BlastaMasta742: ooh! yes! do that!

"Uh, I don't know," I say, still amazed that Mark and Leroy are actually in my chat. They live an hour away, so I figured I'd never see them again after today. They did seem to like my videos—Mark sure laughed a whole lot—but it didn't even occur to me that they might check out my stream, especially not on the very same day. "It'd be hard to clear them out alone."

NotLeeroyJenkins: The odds are 1 in 1024

xxMeisterFanxx: get your friend to help

BlastaMasta742: yeah, get jones

It's Saturday night. Jones is probably out with her boyfriend or doing something people with friends actually do. "Oh, I don't think she's—" I stop myself. That's Opa talking, or my scabs talking, or Code talking as he flicks my name to the floor. The fact is that Jones is more likely to spend an evening on our LotS server than anywhere else. She lives out in the boonies and can't drive yet, so what else is she supposed to do? "Okay, let me message her."

I pull up my chat with her and Dereck on my phone.

I'm streaming. Want to help me clear my base of those shadowwolves?

Her message comes back right away:

You mean the ones you killed me with?

Uh, yeah, those ones

Dereck's face appears. I'm in!

There's a pause, then Jones's response: Give me ten minutes.

Half an hour later, I'm in the closet in my LotS castle with nothing but a flowerpot in my hand, shadowwolves snarling outside my door, and two friends armored up and on their way to grant me aid.

My stream chat has only a few people in it, but they're people I like, and as I misjudge Jones and Dereck's ETA and go running out of my closet and get utterly destroyed by shadowwolves, and as the chat cheers me on and laughs hysterically, I realize something: I am not alone.

A while later, once all the shadowwolves have finally been killed, Leroy and Mark start telling BlastaMasta742 all about LotSCON in chat—though nothing, thankfully, about my (failed) attempts to gain Code's interest. Then Mark writes:

> xxMeisterFanxx: Sam you meeting us there tmrw?
>
> xxMeisterFanxx: how about at the shadow-dragon at 10? We can go vote on the LotS expansion options.

And I hesitate for only a moment before saying, "I'll be there." Because I might not have gained Code's promo today, but I think I gained something else.

EIGHTEEN

ShadowWillow

I RUN INTO CODE ON MY WAY DOWN THE STAIRS. HE'S SITTING NEAR THE bottom, drinking a beer, clearly waiting for me, since his bedroom's down in the basement, and he has no reason to go upstairs and no reason to be sitting in the hall by himself. Code doesn't strike me as the type of person to need alone time—though I suppose I shouldn't jump to conclusions.

He stands and grins at me, then accompanies me to the bottom of the stairs before saying, "Want to go hang out in my room for a bit?" He's got a toque on again now that we're done filming, and a hoodie, and he looks warm and sort of cuddly.

I chew my lip as I consider it. It might be nice to get to know him better, to figure out whether there could be a real spark between us, or whether we're painting glitter on Styrofoam and hoping viewers will see it as a star.

But then he leans close to me and says, "I've got condoms, if that's what you're worried about."

I blink at him as my neck and face flush warm. Is he so famous that all he has to say is "Want to go back to my room with me," and bam, a girl's hooking up with him?

Or does his comment say more about who he is as a person than about his fame?

Or maybe it's neither of those things, simply the fact that he's twenty-one and I'm only eighteen. Eighteen, and it's not like I'm a virgin, but I've only had one real boyfriend, and we broke up a year or so ago because he got accepted to University of Victoria in British Columbia, and if he was going to be across the country while I was going to be here, I didn't see the point.

By the time I'm twenty-one, will I feel as casual about sex as Code apparently does? More important, will I have millions of subscribers like Code does?

"Why don't we hang out in the living room for a while?" I suggest instead.

Code is taking a sip of beer, which hides most of his expression, but his eyebrows dip downward, and for a moment I worry that my unwillingness to hop into bed with a guy I barely know has screwed me over, that succeeding in this business will require a part of me that I'm not willing to give.

And then I'm thinking of the girl gamer panel from this morning, and the fact that it was scheduled at a crap hour in a tiny room, and I'm suddenly wondering whether GrayscaleRainbow and Aureylian and IsabelPlaysGames and Emmaleie were scheduled for any other panels, or only that one like me. And then I'm wondering whether any of them have ever felt pressured to sleep with a guy for the sake of her career, and I'm thinking of GrayscaleRainbow and the dick pics she gets even though she has a girlfriend and how guys always assume I'm going to be crap at every game even when I'm ranked Diamond or higher, and this little flicker of rage burns abruptly inside me.

But then Code finishes his sip, gestures in the direction of the living room, smiles at me, and says pleasantly, "All righty then. After you, m'lady." And I extinguish the rage flame inside me, because in this gaming world, there's nowhere for it to go but out.

Code burps then, loudly, and I laugh—because what else am I supposed to do—and follow him down the hall.

In the living room, I settle onto the couch, and Code hands me a beer like his own, which I pop open, then set on the coffee table with no intention of drinking, because once you've smelled a drink as someone's burp, it loses its appeal.

Across the room, Noog, Z, and Ben are piled in front of the monitors with controllers. "Die!" Noog shouts, and Z replies with a cry of, "Not on my watch!" while Ben stares at the screens with intense concentration.

I'm about to go see what they're playing when Code plops himself down on the couch beside me, close enough that the side of his knee bumps hard against mine before he settles into the couch, thigh pressed the length of mine. He reaches out and takes a strand of my hair, lets it slip through his fingers. "So, you dye your hair purple?"

And suddenly I'm thinking of Code's comment earlier about Confurzzle. I tried to ask Lainey about it when she brought it up, but she immediately got upset and I didn't want to push it. I wish I could ask Code now what he meant by it, but I don't want to upset the guy who holds the future success of my channel in his hands. So instead, I lower my voice in a fake whisper. "Actually, I only pretend to dye it, because if people knew the truth, they'd freak out. I was born this way."

Code gapes at me. "Really?" He grasps another strand of hair and stares at it like it's a unicorn.

I force myself to laugh. "No, not really. How drunk are you?"

"Got you!" Noog shouts, and I look up in time to catch Z tearing his eyes away from us and back to the screens. He swears.

"You win," Z concedes. He puts down his controller.

"Dude! What happened? We were ahead!" Ben moans.

Z shrugs and stands. "I was worried about Noog's confidence. He hasn't won one in a while." He pats Noog on the shoulder.

"You didn't let me win," Noog declares. Then, "Did you?"

"I'm going to get a drink of water," I say, standing so quickly that I forget Code is holding a piece of my hair, and it gets jerked from his fingers with a painful tug on my scalp. Still, I feel like a bird freed from a trap.

I take my time in the quiet kitchen, and by the time I make it back into the living room, Wolf's reappeared out of nowhere, and Code is complaining about the Canadian cold that Wolf apparently brought into the room with him, and Noog and Ben have settled onto the couch beside Code, which means the most logical place to sit is in the big armchair in the corner, so that's what I do. And any grin on my face is because I'm here with all the Meisters and it's utterly bananas, and not because Z is sitting on the arm of the chair that I settle into.

"So what are we going to do at LotSCON tomorrow?" Ben asks as Z smiles at me and I smile back.

"We have got to get our votes in for the next expansion," Wolf says. "People online say one of the options is skyrifts, like normal rifts but splitting open high in the sky, with all new sky-related mobs."

"Holy crap, that sounds amazing," I say. With all the excitement of hanging out with the Meisters, I forgot that LotS had announced they'd have a booth showing off concepts for three possible expansions that attendees could vote on.

"We'll definitely have to vlog that," Code says. "Where's Lainey?"

"Bro! You actually remembered that vlogging is a thing!" Noog gives Code a high five.

"Lainey's out with Legs," I say.

"Those two need to hook up already," Ben says.

"Dude. That's my sister." Code crinkles his nose in disgust.

"Yeah, and she and Legs are in luuurrvve," Noog says, which gets him a hard punch in the shoulder.

"What time should we go tomorrow?" Wolf cuts into their banter. "Lines were really long today, and with word getting out about the skyrifts, I think they'll be even longer tomorrow. So maybe late morning?"

"I have my signing at one tomorrow," I say, and my stomach twists. What if no one shows up? What if the few obscure people who wanted my signature got it already, and now tomorrow it'll be me, my Sharpie, and the whole convention staring back at me, wondering who I am and who the heck thought I should get my own autograph time?

Z shifts on the arm of the chair so he's looking at me. His knee taps my arm. "Do you need help setting up and stuff tomorrow?"

"Oh gosh, I don't know. Do I? I've never done one before."

Z's eyes light up. "Your first signing."

I nod. It's sort of embarrassing to admit, but none of the other guys are listening, just talking about all the different expansion options and what they hope will win, and I know Z won't judge me.

"I'm not going to miss helping out with your very first signing," he says. "Someone needs to be there to take a picture of it at the very least!" He must catch the panic in my eyes at the thought that he'd tweet to the whole world that it's my first signing, because he adds, "For your scrapbook or whatever."

"I don't think there will be time to get into the expansion voting before it. If the guys are going late morning, that probably actually means, what, noon? You shouldn't have to miss that to help me out."

"I think Gray and Marley are going in the afternoon. We can join them, then meet up with the guys after."

I think it's finally happening—I think I'm finally feeling like a real YouTuber—because the idea of spending a day with a bunch of famous content creators doesn't sound bananas at all. You know, aside from the signing autographs part, which is exactly one metric ton of bananas.

For the rest of the evening, I play some Smash Bros. with Z and Noog, then chat rift strategy with Wolf, then chat all sorts of randomness with Z and Ben, then put a blanket over Code, who's fallen asleep on the couch, drool pooling on the pillow.

And as I stare down at him, I realize this: I feel nothing for him. He's crude and sort of bossy and whines about the success of people we should be raising up. As I study his round face, there's no pitter-patter of my heart, no swirl of excitement going right down to my toes.

Perhaps it should worry me, but as Z walks with me to the stairs, I feel a bubbly sort of freedom. If nothing's going to happen with Code, anything could happen.

"Good night," Z says.

"Good night," I say. And although we say nothing more, as I float up the stairs, my heart feels all warm and fuzzy in my chest.

Do skunks purr? Because as I brush my teeth again and pull on my PJs, I'm pretty sure my baby-skunk heart is purring.

I dig my phone out of my purse, then collapse, exhausted, onto the bed with it. It's blinking with approximately one million notifications. Right. I put it on silent when we went to record the bug video.

I check my messages from Claire first. There are about a dozen of them, all along the lines of:

Did you lick Code's face?

Did you ask Wolf to marry me?

In that video, you look close enough to lick Code. Did you lick him? Marissa?!?!!?

Exchanging messages with her yesterday feels a million years ago. So much has happened since then.

I want to tell her that really, Z's the most interesting Meister of the bunch, but first, I need to know: What video?

She must be up late studying, because her response comes immediately: Noog's vlog. You're practically sitting on Code. Did you sit on him?

I had forgotten about Noog's vlog from earlier today, when I sat beside Code for the first time, the thrill of it making my arm hairs stand on end. That feels like a million years ago, too.

I tap in my reply.

Actually, Code's . . . Well, I'm not sure we have chemistry.

Oh, that's disappointing!

I know, right?!?

Except I don't actually feel disappointed at all. My heart is still purring, and the thought of Z's leg against my arm is taking up an awful lot of space in my brain.

Your viewers definitely think you have chemistry.

They're shipping the heck out of you guys in these comments.

And that's when I remember why I wanted to hit it off with Code in the first place. My heart stops purring and starts pounding as I click open YouTube and find my way to the video. I don't bother watching—I was there, after all—instead scrolling right down to the comments. Claire's right. It's Noog's channel, not mine or Code's, and yet probably a third of the comments are about us.

CODEWILLOW 4EVER

omg they're together they're totally dating

Who's the girl beside Code?

Youtube.com/ShadowWillow

Code + willow = <3 <3 <3 <3 <3

YESSSSSSSSSSSSSSSSS

Did you see the livestream today?!?

Yes! That wink!! OMG!!!!!!!! <3 <3 <3 <3

Claire must be reading the same comments as I am, because another message from her comes in: What wink are they talking about?

I had forgotten about the livestream, too. Man, we gave them a lot of fodder to work with today.

My thoughts of Z and of Code slip away and are replaced

with the questions I ask myself every time I try something new on my channel: Did it work? Did it do anything?

I've tried so many things to build my brand. I put in at least twelve hours a day recording video, editing, networking with other YouTubers, building my social media, doing collabs, connecting with viewers, and anything else I can think to grow my subscriber base. Nothing has worked as well as that tournament with Code.

My heart races as I tap through my different pages, looking at my stats. I've had a huge jump in subscribers on YouTube. Another jump in Twitch followers. More Twitter followers. More comments on my videos. More everything.

Yes.

Yes!

I glance through my latest video comments.

> You're so badass
>
> Are you and Code dating?
>
> I luv you so much your amazing

I have fans. Maybe tomorrow's autograph signing won't be so bad after all. Maybe people will actually show up.

Then another comment chain jumps out at me:

> If you break Code's heart, I will personally hunt you down and destroy you
>
> > omg me 2
> >
> > > me 3

Right. They aren't my fans, they're Code's fans. Which means they're here for Code, not for me. And last time, I didn't mention

Code for a few weeks, and that's all it took for the initial boost I gained to start to die off and fall away. If I'm not dating Code, if I don't even flirt with him, the same thing will happen. And if it became definitively clear that I wasn't dating Code because I was, for example, dating someone else, how much faster would they abandon me? Fans like this would probably even call for a boycott.

I swallow, slip a hand into my pajama pants pocket like I'm searching for the grin I seem to have lost.

Before I can find it, Lainey strides into the room, looking like she's walking on air.

"Good evening?" I ask her.

She smiles and nods but says nothing, as though letting the words out would cancel the magic in them. I don't press her, just roll over to stare at the wall and give her some privacy while she gets into her own PJs. Well, stare at the wall and also at my phone, where those comments stare back at me.

Is this it, then? Am I stuck with Code forever because the viewers—the sweet, sweet viewers I'm so hungry for—declare it to be so? Code, who burps beer, who brought condoms with him to LotSCON, whose comment about Confurzzle still has me unsettled.

When Lainey climbs into her own bed a couple of minutes later, I roll back over to face her. "Do you think it's possible for YouTubers to keep their relationships a secret? So viewers don't find out?"

She frowns. "Oh, I don't know. Why would they want to?"

I shrug with the one shoulder that's not pressed into the mattress. "No reason."

When I finally turn out the light to sleep a little while later, both Code's and Z's faces fill the dark, and I can't seem to think of one without the other, so I push them both away and dream of having millions of subscribers instead.

@LumberLegs: Tonight was a good night. And that's all
I'm going to say about that.

[1.4K likes]

NINETEEN

Lainey

WHEN I WALK INTO THE KITCHEN IN THE MORNING, I'M THINKING OF LEGS. MY fingers tingle at the remembrance of his fingers wrapped around mine, of his thumb tracing the outline of my thumbnail, the grooves under my knuckles, the very center of my palm.

"Coffee?" Cody's question breaks into my thoughts, and I push the image of Legs's hands away, because although part of me wants to tell someone all about it, that someone is not going to be my brother. And he's the only someone in this kitchen right now.

Cody pours me a cup without waiting for my answer. He adds half a spoonful of sugar and gives it a stir before handing it to me.

I breathe in the sweet, sweet richness before taking a sip. Cody's put in the exact right amount of sugar. "Good job remembering what I like."

He lets out a single snort-laugh. "You've been lecturing us on the right way to make coffee since you were, what, twelve? I'm surprised Mom let you drink it that young."

I take another perfect sip and push away another image of Legs sipping from his own coffee yesterday morning, peering at me over the edge with a nervous smile. "I told her that Dad let me drink it and if she didn't, that would make her the mean parent."

Cody laughs again. "Smart. Hey, remember that time Dad had that new pastor guy over, and he was talking about whether coffee is a drug and whether that makes it a sin or something like that, and then you said—what'd you say?"

The memory comes back to me in a rush. "If drinking coffee's a sin, then I guess I'm going to hell."

"Yes! So badass. Then you picked up your coffee and stalked out of the room. Perfect mic drop!"

I shake my head. "I don't think I stalked out of the room. I think I sat there wishing I could take it back, because Dad grounded me for like the next two months of weekend visits."

"No, I'm pretty sure there was an actual mic drop involved. Pure badassery." Cody grins, and I can't help but grin back at him. I'm in a good mood this morning.

"Do you have special plans with Legs today?" Cody asks with a twinkle in his eye.

I narrow my eyes at him. "To what might you be referring?"

"I knew it! I knew something was happening with you guys."

"I didn't say that!" I say, though I'm not sure why I'm keeping it a secret. He'll find out soon enough—at least, I think he will. Last night Willow said something about YouTubers needing to hide their relationships from viewers that has me the tiniest bit unsettled. What if Legs wants to keep our relationship secret because his viewers might be upset? I'm not sure I'd be okay with that. I'm nobody's secret.

"You're being safe though, right?" Cody crinkles his nose. "I mean, I don't really want to know, because gross, but I can take you to get anything you need, you know that, right?"

I won't ever be taking him up on that offer, because double gross, but somehow it's still sort of nice of him to say that. It'll be a long time before I get to that point, though, I think. I refuse to go with Mom to the massage place she loves so much because the thought of a stranger's hands on even just my shoulders or feet or whatever else makes me cringe. I like my personal space. I don't understand how people can jump right into bed together, limbs locking around each other like they're already intimately familiar, like they've known each other's hands and mouths and everythings for years, not hours. I want to take my time getting to know each body part, letting them into my bubble one by one—and judging by how long Legs took to explore my thumbnail alone last night, it seems like he's similar.

Not to mention that I still haven't decided where I stand on the whole existence-of-heaven-and-hell issue, and while I'm willing to endure the eternal fires of hell for coffee, I'm not sure I feel the same way about sex. But there's lots of time to figure that out.

"Just drop it," I say, crinkling my own nose.

"Okay, okay." Cody throws his hands up in surrender. "Did you get some good video yesterday? For the vlog?"

And that's when I remember what I decided yesterday. Oh, Cody. Why do you have to be so nice the morning after I decide to ruin your life? Though really, if you were this nice all the time, I wouldn't need to ruin anything. "I'm not sure," I say noncommittally. "I was trying to catch some candid stuff, but I don't know."

"Well, this morning we're going to check out the LotS expansions, so come along to that, and I'll actually talk to the camera and vlog for real and stuff."

"Okay," I say. And even though catching Cody's dickishness on camera proved to be a depressingly easy task, part of me wishes again that he'll prove me wrong.

Before I can even properly form the wish in my mind, though, he says, "Be sure to get some video of Willow. She's hot."

Nice one, dickhead. Yeah, I'm most definitely going through with this.

Thankfully, Z whirls into the kitchen before I can projectile vomit across the room. "Code, you've got to stop talking about girls like their only value is in their looks, man," he says as he pulls open the fridge.

Cody laughs. "Dude, I'm famous. I can say whatever I want."

He twists his mouth into a huge grin, like he's said some big joke—but his joke is built on a foundation of truth.

Which is exactly why I need to make everything he's built crumble, brother or not.

Z is rambling about all the reasons why ShadowWillow's channel is so successful—apparently she's especially badass at PvP—which I don't care about. I chug the last of my coffee and set the mug down with a thud. "I'm heading out."

Cody looks up at me, eyes narrowed like I've suggested something that doesn't fit with his boss-of-the-world plan. "You'll be there for—"

"Yes, I'll meet you guys to take video for the expansion thing. Text me when you're on your way." Then I rush out of the kitchen before Cody can protest.

My coat isn't in the front closet, which means I probably took it upstairs last night, so I duck up to my room to grab it, and sure enough, there it is on the floor by my bed.

Willow is up and in the bathroom, door open, peering at herself in the mirror as she layers on makeup. Prettying herself up for another day of flirting with my brother, probably. Ugh.

I hug my coat to my chest and march over to the bathroom, sticking my head through the door. "I don't get it."

She meets my eye in the mirror but doesn't stop wiping cream across her forehead with a sponge. "Don't get what?"

I've started it now; might as well finish it. "How you can take advantage of someone like Cody."

Her hand drops from her face, which would probably turn pure white if not for the soft beige painted across it. "I'm not trying to hurt him, Lainey." She bites her lip. "I don't know what you—"

"No, that's not what I meant. I mean, how can you *want* to use someone as terrible as Cody?"

Her mouth opens, then closes, then opens again. "He's your brother."

"Yeah, and he's a misogynistic dick. Or haven't you noticed?"

The way her skin tightens around her eyes as she sighs suggests that yes, she has indeed noticed, and she understands exactly what I'm trying to say.

But then the skin around her mouth tightens too.

"Let me get this straight," she says, crossing her arms. "I spend twenty-four hours a day in my parents' basement while my friends are out pursuing stable careers and having adventures, working my butt off to build my channel, even though half my YouTube comments are about my boob size. Even though people think being a girl means I can't possibly be any good at a game, let alone play it at a Diamond or Platinum level. Even though fans care more about my supposed relationship with Code than they do about my actual content. Even though when I get invited to conventions, it's to be on one token girl gamer panel and that's it.

"And despite all that, despite the fact that I have to put up with this crap every single day, I'm not allowed to benefit from a really big-name YouTuber noticing me, just because he might be a jerk? I get to suffer all the frustrations of sexism, but none of its benefits, is that the idea?"

I blink at her. I had no idea this pink-cheeked, purple-haired elf had all this brilliant anger inside her, and apparently she didn't either, because her shoulders drop and she sighs and says, "Sorry. I usually try not to let that stuff get to me, because what's the point, you know?"

I get where she's coming from, and I definitely get the anger—though not the way she's let it fizzle away so quickly. But there are things more important than fame. Which is why I'm willing to try to take away Cody's for the sake of making him a better person. Hopefully. "Is that really what you want, though? To be famous because you embraced all these things you hate?"

"What I want is for my hard work to pay off. For my channel to be successful. To have enough ad money coming in that I can keep doing what I love."

Which sounds like no, but is really just yes.

"Well, sounds like you two deserve each other, then," I say, my own anger flaring. Legs is sticking with his bigoted friend, but at least he's talked to the guy. At least he's planning to keep calling him out. Willow isn't planning to do any of that.

When I open my mouth to snap at her, though, a warning comes out instead. "Just a heads-up—Cody has a firestorm coming his way. And you . . . might not want to be associated with him when that happens."

I'm not sure why I warn her. Maybe it's a last-ditch effort to put a wedge between her and Cody. Maybe the words spill out because I don't know what to say. Or maybe it's that I can't attend women's marches and fight against misogyny and then not have another woman's back—even if we don't exactly agree on everything.

"Why? What'd he do?"

"What didn't he do?! You've heard the kinds of things he says!"

"And someone's angry at him?"

"Well, not yet. But they will be when a video gets posted to his channel with a dozen clips of him being a bigoted jerk." I regret the words as soon as they leave my mouth. What if she tells Cody? She won't tell Cody, will she?

"You're planning to post a video to his channel?"

"I didn't say that."

"That could do some serious damage. And he's your brother!"

I think of Cody and me in a canoe together as kids, paddling in unison. Of Cody letting me take his hand when we buried our dog, Terra.

The metallic tang of guilt fills my mouth. I swallow it away. "That's why it matters! Not that I'm doing it. I didn't say I was doing it. Just don't tell Cody, okay?"

"Hang on a minute," she says. "You were reaming me out about not caring what means I use to accomplish my goal, at the same time that you're planning to devastate your own brother's career for 'the greater good'?" She make air quotes around "the greater good."

Forget what I said about the two of us having anything in common. "At least I care about the greater good!" I snap. My phone pings, a reminder that I'm supposed to be meeting Legs soon. Which is good because I have no interest in being here any longer. "I've got to go."

I turn on my heel and head toward the door.

"When are you posting it? Today?" she calls after me.

"It's not ready yet." I stop at the door, handle on the door-knob, then look over my shoulder, meeting her eye. "Please," I say, "don't tell Cody." And then I open the door and march out.

I practically run to the coffee shop where Legs and I said we'd meet, and as a result, I get there before him. I pull out my phone to pass the time. There's another message from Janessa, probably thanking me for last night's apology.

Are you serious? You want to help me?! Yeah, right. I've spent this whole weekend crying, and so far, you've only made it worse.

Okay, so not a thank-you, then. More like a knife in my gut. I thought our apology was a good one. I reread it, my forehead crinkling. It *was* a good one. So what the heck has she been crying about?

I thought you said you were fine, I reply.

I don't know what else to say except that, so I head inside to grab pastries and coffee—because there's no trouble that another cup of coffee can't fix. And then Legs shows up as I finish paying and I'm glad my hands are full of paper cups and waxy paper bags of baked goods, because as he strides up to me, I have no idea whether I should hug him or go for our first kiss or nothing at all or what, so I thrust his coffee and cinnamon roll into his hands so neither of us can do a thing except balance our breakfast. "Hi," I say.

"Hi," he says back, his face painted with this perfect, awkward grin that kind of makes me wish I'd gone in for the kiss. I didn't think I'd be ready for that quite yet, but maybe I was wrong. As he takes a sip of coffee, I can't help but think how especially delicious his coffee-flavored lips would taste.

Which means that for one long moment, I was thinking about something other than Willow's comments about my plan. About something other than Janessa's unexpected meltdown.

The lovesickness—I've got it bad, apparently. As we sit and eat our breakfasts and talk how this is already my second coffee of the day and how Legs dreamed of Noar the Boar, the cartoon LotS wereboar created by K-Stine and the Andrees, instead of wondering whether I'm a terrible person, I can't stop thinking about how Legs's jawline is so epically perfect and how I wish his knee was touching my knee and yes, how his lips probably still taste like coffee.

Which is sort of annoying. Why hasn't anyone told me about the annoying parts of maybe kinda sorta starting to fall in love? Hollywood, you've failed me.

Still, when Legs slips away to go to the bathroom, my mind slips back to Janessa. I pull out my phone to find another reply from her:

Are you kidding? My boyfriend broke up with me, the whole school's calling me a slut, and my ex's sister keeps sending me cryptic messages. Of course I'm not fine!

I blink at the messages. The slut part makes sense, but she's also sad about my stupid idiot brother breaking up with her? That possibility didn't even occur to me. Shouldn't she be happy she dodged a bullet? Maybe, like me, she's sad to have lost the Cody he's supposed to be, not the Cody he is now. But she *said* she was fine. I'm not a mind reader.

Legs slides back into the seat across from me. "What're you looking at?" he asks.

"Message from Janessa. Apparently she's all sad about Cody."

Legs nods like it makes sense for someone to be heartbroken over my jerkface brother. "How long did they date for?"

I shrug. "I'm not sure." I think it was a few months ago that Cody winked at her in the parking lot, though I don't know if they got together right after that. Cody doesn't really talk about his love life. You know, aside from commenting on random girls' boob sizes.

"Has she had a boyfriend before?" Legs asks.

I shrug again. "I don't know. I barely know her." *And yet you sent her all these messages*, a voice in my brain says.

Well, I know now that she's sad. Maybe I can cheer her up. If it makes you feel any better, I type, I have a plan to take Cody down. It might be risky telling her that, but considering that they broke up, I'm guessing they don't talk much. Or at all.

Janessa's response comes quickly:

And what am I? Collateral damage?

Collateral damage? What the heck, Janessa? I'm trying to help you. I start to type a response, then stop myself. My fingers itch to tell her that in my defense, she did tell me she was fine. And that I was only trying to help. And that I didn't mean to hurt her. But I guess that's exactly her point. I was thinking about Cody, not her, but apparently she was the one who got hurt.

At least I won't be hurting anyone else with my plans. At least, no one else except Cody. And like Willow said, that's for the greater good—never mind that she meant that as a criticism. In my opinion, it's a good thing.

I look up from my phone. "Hey, Legs, do you think the ends always justify the means?"

"For what?"

"Anything. Everything."

"No, of course not. Do you?"

I shake my head. I don't, not as an unconditional rule. But in Cody's case, it does. Because I'm not siding with the enemy to achieve my own ends, I'm bringing him down in order to turn him into an ally. That makes it a million times better. Doesn't it?

I glance down at my phone again and type out another message.

I'm sorry is all I write. Because what can I really say aside from that?

By the time we leave the coffee shop, Janessa hasn't responded.

Still, with Legs standing beside me, it's hard to feel upset about that or about anything. "Hey, so we're dating now, right?" I ask, because apparently I can't think about anything except Legs for longer than a few seconds.

Legs smiles so broadly that the skin around his eyes crinkles adorably as he slips his hand into mine. "Yes. And it's awesome."

"You're such a dork," I say, though as his fingers braid themselves through mine, finding both familiar and new places to touch skin to skin, I decide that kinda sorta starting to fall in love isn't so annoying after all.

Also, considering that we're walking down a public street hand in hand, I don't think Legs has any interest in keeping us—*us*—a secret. Though maybe that will change when we get to LotSCON and he's surrounded by swoony fans. If Willow's willing to sacrifice her morals for the sake of her fans, maybe Legs would be willing to sacrifice me for the sake of his.

Though that doesn't really sound like Legs.

"Are you planning to hang out in the VIP room again today?" I ask.

"You know, I think maybe I could handle a few fans today." He stops to take a sip of his coffee, since he's one of those people who can't drink while walking, which means we both stop, since we're basically fused together now. He stares down at his feet. "I still feel what happened with Brian as a rock in my stomach, and I wonder again and again if I made the right choice, but after talking it out with you a few times, I also know that I couldn't have made any other choice and still be me."

"And I like you," I say, which is true even if we don't always see eye to eye. And at least he's trying to make his friend a better person in his own way.

He blushes but barrels on. "Right. So it sucks, but talking it through has helped. Plus, for some reason I can't explain, I feel weirdly happy today." He squeezes my hand to emphasize that he's joking and he knows exactly why he feels happy today, and I squeeze back, and then we keep walking. We talk for a while about all the universities I've applied to and am waiting for acceptances from, then about poor Noar the Boar, who wishes he could put people to sleep like countable sheep, but who can only ever manage to give the shadowdragons and mutant rabbits naps. And then Legs says, "So, you're still going through with the Code exposé?"

I nod. "I think so."

He raises an eyebrow. "That's less certain than last night."

I don't know why Willow and Janessa have both unsettled me so much. I may have screwed up by messaging Janessa, especially when I had—still have, really—no idea how she was feeling. But I know what I'm doing with Cody. And it's for his own good. "I mean, I'm pretty certain. But let's just see what video I get today, and take it from there."

"Okay," he says, and I think he really is okay with it. It's not what he would do, but he gets why I need to, and he doesn't think I'm reprehensible for it. "I both do and don't hope you get good video today."

"My sentiments exactly," I say. I'd really rather Cody didn't make offensive jokes at all. If only.

It's a good thing Legs thinks he can handle fans today, because at the convention center, we don't even make it to the front doors before we hear a "LumberLegs!" A pack of half a dozen tween boys comes running—literally running—down the sidewalk toward us. A scrawny Asian kid, who's clearly the leader of the group even though he hasn't gone through puberty yet and still has the voice and height of a seven-year-old, babbles away to Legs about how excited they are to see him because their parents would only get them tickets for one day, and they had to miss his panel Friday night, and he was super sad about it, but now here Legs is in front of him and it's the best day of his life.

Legs has to let go of my hand to sign all their programs—asking each kid's name as he does—and the thought occurs to me again that maybe Legs won't want his relationship with me to be public. That maybe fame poisons everyone, even big-hearted Legs.

But when Legs finishes signing and tells them all with a grin to "Be awesome!" and we continue toward the convention center, Legs slips his hand right back into mine, and we head into LotSCON hand in hand.

TWENTY

SamTheBrave

LEROY AND MARK ARE WAITING FOR ME AT THE SHADOWDRAGON, JUST LIKE we agreed. Mark is wearing another Team Meister shirt—a forest-green one this time that's not frayed along the collar, with a cartoon of the whole team fighting a mutant rabbit. Leroy's in a black T-shirt again, baggy over his sweatpants, though this one has no print. They're both grinning.

"Awesome stream last night," Mark says.

"It's cool knowing a streamer," Leroy adds, as if I'm a somebody and not just another fifteen-year-old with a mic and a Twitch account.

"I'm not much of a streamer," I say. "I've only got two hundred and nine followers."

"Not much of a streamer *yet*. But you're going to be big—I know it." And the confidence in his voice is so nice to hear that for a moment, I'm not sure I care whether it's true.

I'm not worrying about that today, though. "What's the plan for this morning?" I ask. "You guys wanted to vote on the next expansion?"

Mark bobs his head up and down. "I've heard one of the options is new rifts that spawn in the sky, full of all-new mobs— like winglings made of clouds."

"I'd rather more building supplies," Leroy chimes in. "I'm sick of making the base of my fireplaces out of coral rock. They need something black that's just as flammable."

"Well, may the best man win," Mark says.

"Indeed," Leroy says, then adds, "We should check out some of the booths before getting in line. The wait's supposed to be really long."

So that's what we do. We head up the escalator into the main hall and wind our way through the exhibitor and vendor booths. It's slower going than when I was searching for something for Code to sign yesterday, since I'm no longer a man on a mission. It's also more fun.

We win free tote bags at an indie developer booth by answering LotS trivia correctly. (It might be rare, but mutant rabbits *can* actually do more damage than wereboars in a single hit.)

At the green-screen photo booth, we grab some props and get our picture taken. We get it printed on a background that turns it into an epic scene of the three of us at arms, battling a shadowdragon—well, Mark and I are fighting the shadowdragon; Leroy's smiling for the camera like it's school picture day.

Leroy buys a new LotS shirt, and I consider trying to convince him to get it in a color other than black, but hey, if he likes black that much, who am I to stop him?

By then we're hungry, so we ride two sets of escalators down to the basement and grab a couple of slices of pizza; then I duck into the bathroom to plaster a new Band-Aid on the spot of blood I've found on my arm, and then finally we take the escalators back up and get in the long line for the expansion voting.

The line stretches along the back of the hall, the front of the line disappearing into a big tent with opaque black walls. Apparently the only way to even see what they're planning is to wait in line until you get inside.

"The idea of sky rifts sounds pretty cool," I say as we join the line. "It's going to be tough to beat that."

"No, you have to vote for the building expansion," Leroy counters. "Assuming it looks good. LotS already has good fighting mechanics. I want microblocks and the ability to paint things. And picture frames. And cactuses should be able to grow in window boxes. It makes no sense that they can't."

"I don't think that would be in a building expansion," I point out. "It's more—"

"Leroy! Sam! Look!" Mark interrupts, his voice dropping to a whisper. He's trying to point but not point, which sort of looks like he's trying to play rock-paper-scissors-lizard-Spock but can't decide what option to choose.

I look in the direction of his not-quite-point, and there, not ten feet away, are Code, Wolf, Ben, and Noog coming out of the voting tent. Wolf says something, pointing back to the tent, which makes Noog shake his head vehemently, which makes Code smack him in the arm, which makes Noog punch Code in his man-boob, which makes Ben look like he's out with his three unruly children.

"Let's ask them for a picture," Leroy suggests. The line went so quickly yesterday that there wasn't time for pictures.

"Ooh, Sam, maybe Code'll remember you from yesterday!" Mark says. "Maybe he's already looked at your channel!"

"Yeah, maybe," I say. I haven't told them about what happened yesterday with my makeshift business card—though today it doesn't feel quite so personal. Maybe he gets a hundred requests to look at people's channels every day. And just because he didn't have time to look at mine doesn't mean I don't belong here.

Judging by the fact that Mark is wearing a Team Meister shirt for the second day in a row, I bet he wants this picture more than he can admit. "Let's do it," I say. I turn to the person behind us in line and ask if they can hold our place, then start to march over to the Meisters, grateful when Leroy's long legs carry him in front of me to take the lead, because my heart is suddenly pounding.

Asking famous people for things is nerve-racking.

In only a moment, we're standing right in front of them. "Excuse me, we would like to take a picture with you," Leroy says.

"If that's okay," I add.

Code smiles. "You guys were at the signing yesterday, right?"

"We were!" Mark beams as if Code just remembered us all by name and whips out his phone so quickly that I decide not to protest that he's out of data and won't be able to send a copy to us until he gets home.

"Sure, you can take a picture," Wolf says.

"Yes, we were at your signing," Leroy says as Mark fumbles with the settings on his phone, sweat gathering in a tiny droplet above his temple, as though he's afraid if he takes too long, they'll get annoyed and disappear. "SamTheBrave here gave you—"

"I'll find someone to take the picture," I cut him off. I'm okay with the fact that my plan didn't work, but I don't need to relive it.

"Nah, it's fine," says Code. "I got this." Which for a moment makes me think he's offering to take the picture instead of being in it, but then he does a full 360, stopping partway to say, "Hey! Lainey!"

And then that girl from yesterday is wandering over from a nearby vendor booth. Today she's wearing yoga pants and a *Hamilton* T-shirt.

"Hi again," I blurt out.

To my relief, she smiles just a little. "Hi again."

"You know these guys?" Code asks her.

She bites her lip, like she's trying to figure out how to avoid telling him something. "I—uh—gave them stickers yesterday."

Code's gaze falls to Leroy's pants, which are either the same baggy gray sweatpants he wore yesterday or he's got multiples, and his grin falls off his face. "Are they the elevator—"

"Did you want me for something?" Lainey cuts him off.

Wolf jumps in to answer. "Can you snap the picture on this guy's phone? You ready, kid?"

Mark nods, hands his phone over to Lainey, and explains where to tap. Then we all huddle up in a group and grin for the camera.

"Want to check it to make sure it's okay?" Wolf asks once Lainey hands Mark's phone back, which is awfully nice, considering how much of their time we've already taken up. Mark flips through his phone, stares at the picture, and gives a big thumbs-up, so we thank them profusely and wave goodbye and they head off to do whatever superstars like them do, while we lean over Mark's phone to stare quiet and starstruck at the picture.

Which is why Code's voice reaches us as they walk away: "Great, another set of stalkers rewarded for their efforts."

"Stalkers?" Wolf echoes. "I thought you loved our fans."

"Not the nerdy ones who look like they've never left their mother's basement!" He's joking, but there's an edge to his voice, like he means it.

"Nerdy? Yeah, because you're such a jock," Wolf jokes.

My hand drops from the scab on my wrist. Opa's words from

last night come back to me: *There are bullies everywhere. Just ignore them.* "So, what should we do next?" I say loudly, hoping that Leroy and Mark didn't hear.

But clearly they have. Mark shoves his phone into his pocket and wraps his arms around his pudgy belly, shoulders sagging. His Team Meister shirt is tucked into his pants along one hip, hanging out over the other, like he's caught somewhere between wanting to listen to his mom's "Tuck your shirt in" and the world's refrain of "Don't be a dork."

Leroy slips his own hands into his sweatpants pockets. His right arm is scribbled in blue ink with player stats and schedules.

These are the guys who gave me the courage to talk to Code in the first place yesterday, the guys who made last night's livestream so much fun. These are my friends.

"So Code's a jerk, apparently," I say. "I sort of want to give him a piece of my mind."

"Don't." Mark shakes his head. "We're used to it."

There are bullies everywhere. Just ignore them.

It's the "we're used to it" that lights the fire inside me, like a dry piece of kindling thrown into a lava-filled rift. Because I'm used to it, too. Used to the taunts, the shoves, the words that tear into my flesh like my fingers. When people look at me, they see the pimples, the hair, the scabs that dot my arms and face. They see my skin and my fat and my mental illness. They don't see me.

Even Opa, who's family and is supposed to love me for me, refuses to see past it all.

There are bullies everywhere.

That part is true, I've realized. There are bullies at school; there are bullies online; there are even bullies here, in this magical world of nerd-dom.

Just ignore them.

Maybe that's good advice for home, where Opa is Opa—my family, my grandfather, who I'm never going to bring myself to talk back to. It's probably even good advice for online and at school.

But here, in this one place where I'm supposed to belong, where the same person has almost ruined the magic for me two days in a row—how can I keep silent in the face of that?

"I'll be right back," I say to Leroy and Mark. And then I whirl around and march after Code.

The four of them have been stopped for autographs just inside a corner vendor booth by a couple of girls a few years older than me. His production manager, Lainey—or whatever her role is—holds up a camera again as he freezes with his pen in hand and grins happily for a picture. Apparently it's only dorks like us who he's embarrassed to be in a picture with.

"Hey, Code!" I say, and he turns slowly, movie-star grin still on his face like he's expecting to be asked for another autograph by a hot girl. Instead, he's getting me and my hot rage, which admittedly is starting to cool into fear. I force the words out before I lose the nerve. "I heard you call us dorks who you're embarrassed to be seen in a picture with. Which sucks to hear. This is the one place

I thought I'd be safe from comments like that, but you've stolen that from me. You've made even LotSCON unsafe!"

Even though my insides have turned to jelly, the words come out loud and confident, and for one full second after they leave my mouth, I feel strong and brave, like Sam in real life is the same person as my avatar, SamTheBrave.

But then Code's eyebrows furrow together under the edge of his blue toque, and he stalks toward me, and even though he is only an inch or two taller than me, once he's within arm's length away from me, every inch feels like a foot. "You're kidding, right?" he says, his breath smelling like peppermint. "Unsafe? You think you're unsafe?" He lets out a single, breathy laugh. "I'm the one who's unsafe. I'm the one who has to worry about dorks like you who reek of BO and have zero sense of personal space, who follow me into elevators and all the way to my hotel room. Have you ever had to worry about that?"

"I—uh—no." *Dorks like me.* "I'm sorry. That sounds stressful. But I would never—"

"So don't talk to me about unsafe!" He pivots on his heel and starts walking away, leaving me standing in the corner of the vendor booth, wondering how the bully somehow turned himself into the victim. Wondering why I feel worse, not better. Wondering if Opa was right and I should have ignored him.

No, he's not right.

"I'm just saying that maybe you should be more careful with what you say!" I shout after Code.

He's already at the edge of the vendor booth, about to disappear into the river of people. "It's a free country!" he shouts back over his shoulder. "I can say what I want!" He whirls around and lowers his voice so it carries across the booth to me, but no farther. "Now get out of here, fatty!"

I stare after him, after the words that follow him.

Mark and Leroy appear on either side of me as Code disappears into the crowd. Lainey mouths a "Sorry" at me, then scurries after him, camera still in hand.

"You were awesome!" Mark says.

"I thought we weren't supposed to call people fat," Leroy says.

"I'm starting to think that Code says a lot of things we would never say," I say, thinking of Lainey's hypothetical from yesterday that's starting to feel not so hypothetical.

Before I can say anything further, Wolfmeister appears from around a wall of Funko Pop! dolls and steps toward us. "Hey, buddy, I'm so sorry about that," he says to me. "Code shoots off too much at the mouth sometimes. We were happy to have our picture taken with you guys."

"We are very photogenic," Leroy says.

Wolf's laugh is kind. "I believe it." His face is tall and thin, and when he smiles even a casual smile, it stretches all the way from one edge to the other.

"You're my favorite Meister," Mark spits out, like he's been holding it in all weekend and can't hold it any longer. "By far. I mean, I like all the Meisters, but you're the very best."

Wolf's grin practically spills off the edges of his face. "Thanks. That means a lot. I'll be bragging to the guys about that for months." Then his face grows serious again. "I really am sorry about what Code said, though. He's a good guy with a big heart who loves his fans, but who doesn't always look to see who's around before he makes his dumb jokes. But I'd like to make it up to you. Is there anything I can do?"

He looks us in the eye one by one, like he's genuinely sorry, like he genuinely wants to do something. But his words play back in my head. Apparently the main thing Code did wrong was not wait until we were gone before he talked smack about us to his friends.

Mark puts his hand on my shoulder. "Well, Sam does have a Twitch channel that—"

"That is doing fine," I say, cutting Mark off. Maybe Wolf didn't mean it that way, and his words simply aren't coming out quite right. But what I'm learning this weekend is that there are worlds within worlds. And if there are places in this big, nerdy online community where people are put down instead of built up, where a friend's hurtful comments are excused as a dumb joke, then I want nothing to do with those places—even if it means I'm giving up on promotion and maybe even all hope of fame as a result.

Wolf turns to me. "You have a channel? I'm happy to—"

"No, thank you." It's not that I suddenly don't like Wolf. Like everyone else, he's a complex human with strengths and weaknesses, and the fact that he came over to apologize to us when his friends are already long gone still means a lot. It's just that this world with LotS and Mark and Leroy and Dereck and Jones and BlastaMasta742 and my tiny but joyful streams—this is my world. And whatever world Code and Wolf and their friends are living in—I suspect it is not. "I'm pretty happy with it the way it is."

Mark narrows his eyes at me like he's trying to see into my brain, then shrugs and nods.

Leroy, on the other hand, simply says to Wolf, "Well then, do you have stickers?"

TWENTY-ONE

ShadowWillow

"THERE IT IS! YOUR SIGNING TABLE! WITH YOUR NAME!" THERE'S NO MOCKERY in Z's voice as he points to the plain wooden folding table with "ShadowWillow Autographs 1 p.m." printed on a plain white piece of paper and taped to the scaffolding above it. He is legitimately excited for me, and at this moment, I love him for it.

I'm excited too. It's my very first signing, and I'm determined to enjoy it, so I'm forcing myself to shove away all my worries from last night and my argument with Lainey from this morning.

"This is bananas. I need to take a picture." I whip out my camera and snap a shot.

"Want me to take one with you in it?" Z offers, holding out his hand for my phone.

"Can you take one once I'm actually signing?" I ask, then grab his forearm as the fear strikes me. "What if no one shows up?"

He pats my hand good-naturedly. "Then I will get in line and get your autograph fifty times."

"I don't need your pity."

"It's not pity. In a year, I'm going to sell them online for a million bucks apiece. You're going to fund my retirement."

I let go of his arm. "Your retirement? You're looking awfully good for your age, old man."

He slides a hand through his unruly mass of hair. "Thank you. It's the avocado toast I eat for breakfast every morning. But hey, look, you've already got a fan waiting." He points not at the table, but toward a nearby vendor booth.

We're in the huge vendors hall on the top floor of the convention center, and though the hall is bustling with people, the signing tables are at the far wall, where the crowds are thinner. The guy monitoring the booth has his head buried in a comic book. His only current customer, a young red-haired teen girl with her back to us, browses the wall of merchandise, which includes everything from shadowdragon mugs to an enormous plush mutant rabbit.

"The mutant rabbit? Ha ha, thanks," I say wryly.

"No, the girl."

I glance again at the red-haired girl, who's maybe fifteen and is wearing a TARDIS backpack, and who most definitely has her back to us.

I'm about to snark at Z again when the girl glances over her shoulder—not at us, but at the signing table.

"Have you noticed? She checks out your table approximately every ten seconds," Z says, and sure enough, a moment later she does it again.

"Oh my gosh, I love her." I feel a rush of mushy-heartedness for this girl who clearly—I see it now—is waiting for me to show up. "Can I go hug her? No, never mind, that's creepy. Let's go set up, so she can come wait in line instead of straining her neck muscles." I grab Z's arm again and pull him toward the table.

When we get there, Z heads a few tables down to grab chairs, since the ones for this table are missing, and I plop my shoulder bag down on the table and start unpacking the postcards I had made for the convention. They display a big-eyed, purple-haired cartoon version of my avatar, dual-wielding guns and taking down an army of all sorts of baddies from different video games. I had a cartoonist I found online design it, and it's pretty much the most badass thing I've ever seen. Boy, do I hope someone wants one.

As I study the cartoon, a tiny drop of melancholy muddies the waters of my excitement. *This* is what I wish my fans were most excited about—me being badass, not me potentially dating the Sleazemeister.

I think of Lainey's accusations from this morning, her disbelief that I'd cash in on fans' Codemeister-ShadowWillow excitement when I've learned that Code is—well, a Sleazemeister.

But I've worked hard to get here. I've put up with so much crap. Just this morning, I got another comment asking whether my boobs are real. I simply ignored it, like I ignored every other comment like that, because what else am I supposed to do?

I want this—the viewers, the panels, the signings, the fame—and if I have to put up with a few Sleazemeisters to get there, so be it.

I glance down the hall toward Z, thinking of all the Code-Willow shippers' comments from last night. Now, if only I could figure out what I want to do about all that, I'd be set.

I push all those worries out of my mind and set the postcards down on the table, where people can take them. Boy, do I hope someone wants one.

"You're doing autographs now, right?" a female voice says, and I look up, expecting to see the red-haired girl. Instead, a thin Asian woman and a curvy white woman, both in their early twenties, stand there smiling at me.

"Uh, yeah," I say. "I mean, in about fifteen minutes I will be. You can line up . . . uh, right there, I guess, if you want." Good golly, I've gone full awkward baby skunk. I wait for them to tell me that no, they're not going to waste their precious time waiting, thank you very much, and wander off to do something else and maybe or maybe not return later.

Instead, the white girl says, "Great," and then they turn to each other and start to chatter about some movie while staying put right where they are.

And in case you missed it, "right where they are" is in line. To get my autograph.

It's so many bananas that they're all going brown because they can't get used up fast enough.

And then before Z can even return from explaining to the guy a few tables down that he needs to borrow their chairs, the people start coming out of the woodwork. A small pack of young teen boys gets in line behind the women. And then the girl in a hetero couple that's passing by stops short, looks at me, then at the sign above my head, then at her oversize watch, and then grabs her boyfriend's arm and drags him over. Well, drags for the first few steps. Once he figures out where she's pulling him, he says, "Oh! Cool!" loud enough that I can hear him, and hurries toward me with her.

They make it into line just ahead of the red-haired girl, who has finally made her way over.

I kneel down and do an inventory of everything in my purse, for no reason except that I have nothing else to do and I don't want to start the signing early, because then we'd get through the line and it would all be done.

The clattering of chair legs against the concrete floor announces Z's return. I stand and he grins at me, shooting his gaze meaningfully in the direction of the growing line.

"Hey, could we get your autograph, too?" the girls in front

ask Z, and for one long moment, I worry that the whole line is confused and everyone saw Z and thought that's whose autograph they were lined up for.

But after Z happily signs a few autographs "while we wait," not a single person leaves the line as if they've already gotten what they came for. And then I overhear someone say, "Is this the line for ShadowWillow?" and someone else says, "It sure is," and my heart grows too big for my chest.

"I have to pee," I spit at Z. "Can you—?" I shove the post-cards I'm arranging in piles into his hands and then rush across the hall into the bathroom, where I hurry to a corner and turn to face the concrete brick wall. And I know, I know, it's weird and 100 percent awkward skunk that I'm staring at a brick wall, but I can't think of any better way to stop time than to stare at the ridges and lumps of a painted cream wall, and I want this moment to last forever.

This moment, when I was an invited guest at a convention for the very first time, when I had my very first autographing session and people actually showed up. This moment, when it felt like an entire lifetime of potential stretched ahead of me, and an entire mountain of work lay not behind me, because I know the work will never end, but under my feet. Something to build on, higher and higher.

Even staring at motionless, patternless walls isn't enough to stop time, though. The seconds tick past, and as they do, the hunger creeps into my stomach. This is the start, but I still want more. I want the lineups that the Meisters get, the money coming in from my channel. I want to not be surprised that people have shown up to see me.

Before the hunger fills my whole gut, I shove it away. These are dreams to dwell on another time. They're the stars, twinkling and enticing, but for now, I have the sun, and it's bright and blazing.

"People actually showed up!" I whisper at the wall. And then, with a grin, I head back out to join Z—thoughtful, huggable Z— at the table where my fans wait to meet me.

Of course, the first people in line aren't really my fans at all, but Code fans. "So, are you and Code dating?" the blond-haired girl asks as she leans in to hand me one of my own postcards to sign. "You can tell me. I won't tell anyone."

"What's he like?" the other girl asks. Her naturally tan skin is enviably smooth, and I'd ask her what type of moisturizer she uses on it if I wasn't so busy trying to keep my nose from crinkling at the thought of Code.

I want to tell them that he's actually sort of obnoxious in person and probably racist and that they should lust over someone else—someone like Z, maybe, though he's probably too young for them—but considering how starry-eyed they've gone, saying something like that would do me zero percent good. In fact, it might even do me harm. Maybe these are the girls who threatened to lynch me if I break Code's heart.

I take a deep breath and do what I have to do. "Well, there're some videos coming out this week that'll tell you more about both of us," I say with what I hope is a suggestive eyebrow wiggle. Wolf sent the bug video off to his team to edit and break into segments for each of us to upload to our own channels. "Be sure to check out the one on my channel if you want to see more of Code." I had been thinking the clip with Z making me eat that big beetle would be best, but maybe one with Code in it would be better.

"Oh, we will," perfect skin says, which is good, I guess.

As I finish signing their postcards, Z taps me on the shoulder. "I'm grabbing a water bottle. You want one?"

I hadn't been thinking about the fact that he's still sticking it out here with me when he probably has a million other things he could be doing. "Z, you don't have to stay here. You probably have people to meet and stuff."

His eyebrows knit together. "What, you don't want me here?"

"No, I—"

"I'm kidding." He smacks my arm. "Of course I'm going to stay. I'll grab us waters. Be right back."

And with that, he's off to grab water bottles. And then come back, because of course he's going to stay. *Of course.* My heart goes the tiniest bit melty in my chest.

The pack of young teen guys next in line says very little other than giving me their names so I can personalize their post-cards, and I have no idea whether they're ShadowWillow fans or Codemeister fans or kids who saw a not-terrible-looking girl and thought they'd get in line for whatever she was giving out, until the final kid in their posse says, "Thanks, Shadow," and I swear I could kiss him atop his greasy little head.

Then the couple, and then it's the girl who was espionaging my signing space from the nearby vendor's booth. She hovers for a moment, twining a strand of her red hair around her finger like she's nervous, then steps up to the table and launches in. "Hi, ShadowWillow. I'm Caitie. I'm such a big fan. I love your channel. I saw you in that tournament with Code, and you were so badass in that, taking everyone down, and I've been watching your channel ever since. I love all your silly sayings and how talented you are."

I blink rapidly, because I'm not sure this girl—Caitie—would still think I was badass if I gushed tears of gratitude all over her. "Thank you. That's really amazing to hear."

"I was wondering"—she pauses as her cheeks flush pink—"if you could by any chance give me some advice. I started my own channel recently—like, really recently—because I loved what you do with yours, and I was wondering how to make my channel successful and stuff."

"Do you want me to look at it?" I ask. I wouldn't offer that to just anyone, but this girl is making my heart seriously squishy.

Caitie turns even redder—almost as red as her hair. "Oh, no. It's so bad right now. I think my only subscribers are my friends and this boy at school. I'm still learning. But anything you could tell me . . ."

She trails off and I nod, considering her question.

I start with the advice I found most often online when I was first getting into YouTube. "For starters, invest in a good mic. It's worth it. People aren't going to bother to watch if the audio's bad. And . . ." I think through the things that have gotten me here: the hours spent in my parents' basement, recording and editing and rerecording and making thumbnails and connecting with people online and saying no to nights out with friends and romance and university (for now) because there's so much to get done.

The tournament with Code gave me a boost, but not before I had built up connections and created a solid channel with a respectable number of subscribers. Code gave me the boost, but I made something worth boosting in the first place.

"Take advantage of any and all opportunities, though you know that already, since that's what you're doing right now." I smile at her, and even her ears turn pink. "But also, work hard. Work really really really really hard. Work until your freakin' butt falls off."

She laughs. "I was worried you might say that."

I grin and shrug. "I only say that if it's what you want, though. I mean, maybe YouTube success isn't what you most want, which would be okay. I worked hard to get here, and that meant sacrificing a lot, but I feel happy because it brought me here, to this place I want to be. If you're not doing it for what you want, though, sacrifice is only going to feel like sacrifice."

Just then, Z returns with the bottles of water, and as he hands mine to me, he smiles, and I smile back.

"Isn't that right, Z?" I ask.

"Yep, definitely. She's wise. Listen to whatever she says. Unless she's telling you to sit on a porcupine. Maybe don't do that."

The girl laughs, then turns back to me. "You really are wise. That was super deep."

"I've spent a lot of time in my parents' basement; I've had a lot of time to think." And with that, I finally sign her postcard.

The rest of the line goes fairly quickly. No one else wants any down-to-the-soul advice, though they do all want my autograph. In fact, not a single person seems to be in the wrong line, or calls me by the wrong name, thinking I'm someone who's actually much more famous. They all know who I am and are there by choice. Which is banana splits with a dozen perfect maraschino cherries on top.

Afterward, Z—who, true to his word, is still there—helps me to tidy up, though there isn't much to do. "You good to go?" he asks once we've thrown away some garbage someone left and I've taken down the ShadowWillow Autographs sign and slipped it into my bag for a souvenir.

I stride up next to Z. "I'm very good to go," I say, and I am. Because I've decided what I'm going to do. I've decided what I want.

There's just one problem, and her name is Lainey.

TWENTY-TWO

Lainey

THE FIRST THING I DO WHEN I CATCH UP WITH LEGS AGAIN IN THE FOOD COURT in the basement is show him the video I've shot. I wish I could report to him that I caught nothing, and that it's because Cody has finally listened to me and fully reformed and I don't need to cause any harm to anyone at all—and especially not my own brother—for the sake of what Willow called "the greater good."

But I can't say that.

I pull out the camera and search for the videos amid the more innocuous vlog clips, playing them quietly for Legs one after the other.

Cody pointing out a girl's "excessively fat ass" to Noog.

Cody joking about how some girls are probably better at sex when they're asleep.

Cody being confronted for being a jerk by that kid from yesterday, turning it around and ranting about it being a free country, then calling the kid fat.

It's that last one that's my favorite—if you can have a favorite video of someone being a dick. Seeing a fifteen-year-old nobody stand up to twenty-one-year-old somebody fires me up to tear down dungeons and build castles in their place.

I think that one's how I'll start the video—with a short clip of Cody shouting, "It's a free country! I can say what I want!" Then moving on to show all the terrible things that Cody wants to say.

Come on, Cody. Be better.

"This guy's going to get torn apart," Legs says when the final video stops.

"Cody?"

"No, this guy that confronted him."

"What, why? He's brilliant!" We have a shared plate of fries between us; I pop one into my mouth.

"Don't you think Cody calling him a fat dork or whatever is going to cause other people to call him a fat dork?"

"No way," I say. "People are better than that." Though if that were true, I wouldn't need to make this video in the first place. "Maybe I can crop the kid out of it." Though I know that'll be hard to do. It's not like I had time to set up the perfect shot. I had to start filming from where I was taking a picture of Cody signing autographs for those girls, and the camera's pointed at Cody's side and back, with the kid in the background, their bodies slightly overlapping.

It's the perfect opening clip, though. So who cares—I'll just use it.

Except Janessa calling herself collateral damage pops into my head.

I didn't mean to hurt her. And I don't mean to hurt this kid.

But Cody hurts people constantly, I remind myself. If one more person has to get hurt in order to create a world where Cody hurts fewer people every day, that has to be a worthwhile cost.

Doesn't the end sometimes justify the means?

Except I suppose I didn't need to message Janessa in the first place. I wasn't thinking that maybe she'd be sitting there crying over Cody and over people calling her a slut and I'd only make things worse. I was only thinking about my anger and fear over Cody.

Is that all I'm thinking about now, too? I'm not, am I?

Janessa still hasn't responded, and I guess I have to accept that maybe she won't.

I steer my conversation with Legs toward other things— books, politics—as we finish our paper dish of fries, then clear the table and head toward the door. Cody and I don't fly out until tomorrow, but Legs only has a couple more hours before he needs to catch a ride to the airport. We're supposed to go upstairs so Legs can say goodbye to Z and some others. Then we thought we'd fit in one more walk by the water before Legs has to go. My heart skips a little at the thought. And then skips again when, as we step out of the food court into the busy hallway, Legs slips his hand into mine.

A group of middle-aged white guys with foam swords duels each other lazily as they pass. A three-generational family that I've seen a couple of times this weekend hangs out by the nearby bathroom, the women clearly waiting for the men to finish. The two thirty-year-old women in matching LotS shirts, who are obviously sisters even though one has curly hair and the other straight, lean over the LotSCON program as a young girl sits on the floor and another even younger boy runs circles around her and their grandmother.

I wonder if Cody would've turned out a better person if I'd been the older sibling. Maybe he'd have listened to my wisdom.

The grandmother scoops up the younger kid just as he makes a running jump toward his older sister, sweeping him away just before his boot connects with her head. "Avery! No jumping on your sister's head! We've been over this!"

Then again, maybe not. I can't help but laugh.

"Shall we go find Z and then go for that walk?" Legs asks.

"Yes, let's—wait, there he is."

"Who?"

"That kid from the video." He's in the opposite direction from the family, following his two friends toward a nearby room.

"Come on! I have an idea! I'll ask him!" I drop Legs's hand and hurry after the kid, catching up to him and tapping his arm just as they reach the door. "Hey, can I talk to you?"

He turns to me, then back to his friends. One has already disappeared into the room, which is full of people—ninety percent guys—sitting at tables with some sort of playing cards spread out in front of them. I have no idea why there are cards at a convention about a video game. Nerd culture is so confusing sometimes.

The skinny friend looks at the kid and stops.

"I'll be there in a minute, Leroy," the kid says. "Start without me." And Leroy shrugs and heads into the room. The kid turns to me. "How can I help you, Lainey?" Great, he remembers my name, while I've just been calling him "the kid."

"Well, I, uh—what's your name again?"

"Sam."

"Right, Sam. I want to talk to you about something. I took this video . . ." I trail off as Sam's gaze keeps slipping off me and onto Legs, who's caught up with me and is standing just behind me and to the right, close enough that his shoulder is touching mine. "Oh, yes, sorry, this is Caleb. Caleb, Sam. Sam, Caleb."

"It's a pleasure to meet you, Sam," Legs says, and when he sticks out his hand, Sam grins broadly and shakes it.

"I know who you are. I'm a fan." But then the joy disappears abruptly from his eyes, replaced by uncertainty and sadness—which, I realize, is Cody's fault. Cody, who Sam fanboyed over. Cody, who called Sam names in public.

If Willow were here, I'd tell her that all I'm trying to do is stop Cody from causing more hurt like this.

"Hey, Sam, I wanted to ask you if I could use a video you're in," I say quickly, before Sam can run off in fear that Legs is going to do the same thing. Poor kid. "It's video from before, from up in the vendors hall." If I have his permission to use it, then he's not collateral damage anymore.

Sam's eyes narrow as his fingers pick at a pimple on his face that's already red and inflamed. "Use it for what?"

I hesitate, unsure how much I should tell him. Surely he's not still a Codester fanboy after what happened with Cody; surely he wouldn't run and find Cody and divulge to him my whole plan. But after I stupidly spewed out the whole thing to Willow, I have to be more careful.

Before I can answer, he says, "Because I'm not a fan of being the butt of people's jokes."

I shake my head quickly. "It's not for that. Definitely not."

"Though you may end up being the butt of some people's jokes," Legs tells him, and part of me wants to hit him, while another part of me realizes that it's good that he's here with me for this. Because this kid—Sam—deserves to know that, and if I'm honest, I'm not sure I would have told him. Maybe Willow is right. Maybe I'm as bad as she is.

Maybe I'm even as bad as Cody.

Sam cocks his head and studies me, then says, "Does this have to do with what you said yesterday? About Code being a terrible person?"

"I didn't say that."

"Right. You specifically said you didn't say that. But are you saying it now? Is that what this is about?" He's stopped picking at the pimple on his face and is staring at me intently.

I'm almost certain he's not going to run to Cody with my secret, and not just because of Cody calling him names. He's a good kid. I nod. "Yeah. That's what this is about."

He takes a deep breath, his shoulders rising almost up to his ears. His fingers find that pimple on his face again. And then he says, "Okay. You can use it."

I blink at him. That was easy. "You don't want to know more?"

"Will it make some worlds better?"

It's a weird question, but I know what he means. This earth can sometimes feel like it's full of a million worlds—good ones and bad ones and kind ones and corrupt ones and complex ones and hateful ones and beautiful ones—all coexisting in the same country, the same city, the same community, the same family.

"I . . . don't know for sure," I admit. "But that's the hope."

"That's good enough for me. Go ahead and use it."

"People might make fun of you," Legs says again.

Sam looks over his shoulder into the room where his friends are playing cards. "Not in all worlds," he says with a quiet smile. "So I think I'll be okay." He turns to me as his hand finds its way back to his face. "Will you, though? I hope you have another job lined up."

"Pardon?"

"He'll fire you, won't he? When he finds out you did it?" His eyes go toward my badge like they did yesterday. It's not turned around backward this time. It says "Codemeister," just like Cody's own badge, since he's the one who got them.

This kid—Sam—has no idea that I'm Cody's sister. He thinks I'm some rogue employee. If only. That would make this all so much easier.

"I'll be okay," I say. "It was nice to meet you, Sam. Thanks for the permission to use the video." I hold out my hand, and he reaches his own out to shake it, then pulls it back abruptly like he's just remembered he's contagious.

"Sorry," he says in alarm as he stares down at his hand. I follow his gaze to see a dot of blood on his pudgy middle fingertip. His hand goes back up to his face, where there's a matching red dot blooming. His whole face flushes red. "Sorry. It's a disorder. So sorry. I know it's gross."

I mean, picking at pimples *is* sort of gross, but there's a weight to his words that makes me think there's more going on than pimple picking, and more going on than his own use of the word gross. "Who says that? Jerks at school? Just ignore them. People are idiots."

"And my opa." His fingers go to his face again, then drop immediately as he catches himself.

"Hang on, your own grandfather tells you your disorder is gross?" Legs asks.

Sam shrugs. "He's nice in other ways."

"Dude," I say, "you can't let him say that to you!"

"What am I supposed to do? He's my opa."

"Ream him out. Tell him he's a jerk."

Sam's eyes open wide like I told him he should murder the guy or something. He shakes his head. "No. I can't. He's family."

Cody is my family, too. "Being family doesn't excuse someone for being a jerk," I say.

And that's when I know for sure—for 100 percent sure—that I'm going to do it.

Once Sam disappears into the room after his friends, I turn to Legs. "I'm posting a video of Cody for sure."

Legs narrows his eyes. "I thought it was already for sure."

I shrug. "Well, now it's super for sure." If it's wrong to stand up to my bully of a brother, to try to turn him into less of a jerk, to tear him down in hopes of building him back up into a better version of himself—if that's wrong, then I don't want to be right.

I glance into the card room after Sam. Not every means is justified by the end, though. "Maybe I shouldn't post the clip with him in it."

"But he said you could."

"Yeah, but he's going to get bullied, like you said. He's the nobody in that video. I think he's badass for standing up to Cody because of it, but you're right, some people will only laugh at him. He's too nice for me to use it." I hurt Janessa. I don't have to hurt Sam, too.

"He's too brave for you not to use it," Legs counters.

I laugh. "How did we get switched around on this one?"

Legs shakes his head in amusement. "Apparently we have opposite reactions to both bad people and good."

"Apparently," I agree with a smile. Sam is clearly good people. I think of the slip of paper he gave me yesterday, of the way I immediately dismissed it as something that'd turn to dryer lint in the pocket of my other pants. I should have at least watched one video. "But we'll keep each other honest because of it, right?"

"Right."

We grin at each other.

And that's when another idea pops into my head. "Hey, Legs, remember how we were going to go say bye to people, then go for a walk? What if we went for a walk first?"

Legs recognizes, somehow, that I'm not suggesting a casual stroll by the water, that I have something else in mind. "You have an idea?" he asks.

"I have an idea," I confirm. "And this one I think you're actually going to like."

TWENTY-THREE

SamTheBrave

I SLIDE INTO THE TABLE WHERE MARK AND LEROY ARE PLAYING LOTS: THE Card Game.

"What was that about?" Mark asks.

"It turns out Code actually is a . . . what'd she say yesterday? Bigoted jerk? Misogynistic douche?"

Mark laughs. "You think?"

I laugh too. It feels nice to know that Code's just a jerk to everyone, and that his comments say more about him than about us.

"Take your turn," Leroy says to Mark. "You're being too slow."

Mark rolls his eyes but takes his turn.

I grin at them both. I thought this weekend was going to be all about winning over Code and promoting my channel, but it's ended up being about something else entirely.

I watch them play for a while, until Mark says, "Hey, when you're doing that, do you want me to say anything or just leave it?" He gestures to the back of my left wrist, where my right hand has made a bloody mess of what used to be a small scab.

My face flushes hot. As Mark waits for my answer, though, he doesn't crinkle his nose or show any other signs of disgust. His eyebrows are raised and his eyes curious, like he genuinely wants to know what he can do to help.

"I'm not sure," I admit. "I can't always control it. If something starts to bleed, my mom usually hands me a Kleenex, which usually helps."

"I can do that," Mark says. He pats his pockets. "Oh, uh, I don't think I have any Kleenex, though. Shoot, sorry."

"No worries. I'm set." I reach into my bag and pull out a little pouch of Kleenexes, taking one out and setting the package down on the table.

As I press the one Kleenex to my unintentionally self-inflicted wound, Mark reaches and grabs the Kleenex pack. "Great, thanks," he says, then he shoves it into the pocket he was just patting. He's ready, I realize, to do just what I said should the need arise—*when* the need arises.

This whole weekend has been so much better than I could have imagined.

"Let's scrap this game and teach Sam how to play," Leroy says to Mark. "You're not even paying attention."

Mark agrees, and as Leroy heads to the games station to get a loaner deck for me, I check the notification flashing on my phone.

It's from YouTube. There's a new comment on my latest video.

> MEGAdawn: Super-hilarious videos, bro! I'm subbing and making my friend sub, too. She'll <3 them.

"Anything good?" Mark asks.

"New sub. Possibly two."

"Awesome! You're on your way to fame, SamTheBrave!"

"Sure. One slow sub at a time." Which I can live with, I guess.

"Possibly two." Mark holds up two fingers.

"Right." I laugh.

Leroy slips back into his seat. "Okay, so here's your deck." He starts to fan out the new deck in front of him to show me as my phone flashes with another notification. I ignore it. "It's a starter mage deck, so—no, hang on, they gave me the wrong one." He hops back up.

I pick up my phone again while we wait. There's another YouTube comment.

> Tacos4L1fe: LMAO SUBBED!

It's weird to get two comments back to back a couple of days after the video is posted. Normally I get a decent number of comments the day I post a video, but then they trickle off. But maybe

Tacos4L1fe is MEGAdawn's friend. That would make sense.

I set the phone back down as Leroy returns with the right deck this time. He and Mark explain the rules, and it's similar in mechanics to Hearthstone, which I play online, so it seems straightforward enough. Leroy shuffles my deck for me, hands it over, then starts to shuffle his own.

There's another notification flashing on my phone. I know I shouldn't interrupt our game, but I can't help myself. I grab it and unlock it. There are three new comments on my video.

Hlibishark: hilarious!!1!!!

Life in Italics: You're doing great, sweetie! So funny!

Dewibear: I like this

What is happening?

As if in answer to my unspoken question, my phone beeps with a message from Jones.

SAMMYBOY HAVE YOU SEEN IT?!?!? YOU DIDN'T TELL ME YOU TALKED TO HIM!!!

Seen what? I glance at my YouTube channel. My subscriber count has jumped up to 271. That's thirty new people—more than I've ever gotten in one day before.

I switch over to my chat with Jones. Seen what? I type.

The link pops up a second later, and I click on it.

Holy crap!

"What are you grinning about?" Mark asks.

"He posted about my video!"

"Who did? Code?" Mark wrinkles his nose.

"No!" I hold out my phone to him.

"Holy crap!" Mark says. He snatches the phone from me. "Dude!"

Leroy, finally intrigued by our excitement, sets down his deck and holds his hand out for the phone. "Whoa," he says once Mark hands it over. He blinks at the screen.

"How'd that happen?" Mark asks, his voice shaking with almost as much excitement as I feel.

Legs couldn't have done it alone. He didn't have my channel info. "It was that girl from yesterday."

"Who you were just talking to?"

I nod. "Legs was with her."

Mark's eyes go wide. "Hang on. Legs was with her, and you didn't call us over to get his autograph?"

"I—right, yeah, I should have done that. I'm sorry. I didn't get one either. It all happened so fast."

"Is that what they wanted to talk to you about?" Leroy asks, pointing to my phone.

I shake my head. "No, it was—" I break off. There's too much in my brain right now to explain. I'll tell them the whole story later. "No. This was a complete surprise."

A new comment comes in.

KittyKat: legs and MEGAdawn are right. you're funny.
good video.

"A pretty darn good surprise," Mark says.

"No kidding."

Dereck's finally appeared in my chat window with Jones, and the two of them are freaking out.

"What are you going to do now?" Leroy asks.

I blink a few times, trying to clear my brain. "Uh, well, tonight I guess I'll do my usual stream, edit it, put the highlights on YouTube. Keep trying to make quality content. Until then . . . play cards, I guess?" I hold up my nicely shuffled deck. My phone flashes with another notification. "Though, um, I might be a little distracted."

Leroy nods. "That is acceptable."

"You never let me be distracted during our games," Mark protests.

"If LumberLegs ever tells the world about your currently non-existent videos, you will be entitled to be as distracted as you like."

Mark and I both laugh. "Cards it is, then," Mark says.

I pick up my deck, still mind-boggled and confused and over-the-moon excited.

Later, I'll probably stare at my phone for hours. I'll spend just as long writing and rewriting a thank-you tweet to Legs—and, if I can find her online somehow, Lainey. I'll ignore any troll bullies who pop up, just like Opa said. And I'll record the best video I possibly can, to keep my new subscribers interested. And did I mention staring at my phone for hours?

For now, though, as my subscriber count continues to climb and the comments keep coming in, I'll sit here at this convention and play cards with my friends.

@LumberLegs: My new all-time favorite streamer and YouTuber: SamTheBrave. I wish I could pull off pranks like this brilliant one. Check it out!

[1.7K likes]

TWENTY-FOUR

ShadowWillow

AFTER MY SIGNING, Z AND I MEET GRAY AND MARLEY AT A CLUSTER OF FAUX-
leather chairs in the big hallway outside the main auditorium.
The chairs are full of people, so we stand grouped in the back
corner, out of the way of the passing crowds.

There's a long lineup stretching down one wall of the hallway
and back up the other, waiting to be admitted to a panel featuring
a few of LotS's original developers. I had planned to catch that
panel, and if I wanted to, I could walk up to the front of the line,
flash my badge, and get let right in—which is still absurdly cool—
but I have more important things to worry about right now.

"Do you know where Lainey's at?" I ask Z and Gray and Marley. "I need to talk to her about something." I need to get on my hands and knees and beg her not to post that video. If Code gets hit by a firestorm, how will that impact his channel? And more important, how will that impact mine? Especially if I go through with what I'm planning to do.

Gray and Marley shake their heads, while Z says, "I told Legs where to meet us, and I assume Lainey'll be with him, but I don't know how long they'll be."

Even though Lainey said she wouldn't be posting her video today, I don't trust that whatever anger's brewing inside her won't spill over and make her change her mind. I don't have time to wait to see if she does or doesn't show up with Legs. I need to talk to her now. "Do you have her number?" I ask Z, and he does. It's a US number, of course, which means it'll probably cost me an arm and a leg to text her, but it'll be worth it. Hopefully.

I'm in the middle of crafting a text asking her to meet me somewhere to talk when Gray practically shouts, "Are you guys dating? I knew it!"

For a moment, I think she means me and Z, and I shift quickly away from him as I realize our shoulders are almost touching, but when I look up, Gray's looking past us. I turn around to see Legs and Lainey ambling toward us, hand in hand.

"I called it at PAX!" Gray turns to Marley. "Didn't I call it at PAX?"

Legs and Lainey have clearly heard her, because their cheeks are matching bubble-gum pink as they join our circle. It's so ador-able that I almost forget that I want to convince Lainey not to completely undermine everything I've worked for.

"Hey, Lainey, can I talk to you?" I ask. Her unplucked eye-brows rise, but she follows me over to a couple of chairs that are now freed up a little ways away.

"So, you're planning to post some sort of video trying to con-vince people that your brother is a terrible person?" Even though we're probably out of earshot of Z and the others, I speak quietly, not much above a whisper.

"You're not going to tell Cody, are you?" Lainey half whispers back.

I shrug. Telling Code wouldn't accomplish anything—except maybe gaining his trust. Knowing a storm is coming doesn't stop the storm. But she doesn't need to know that. Maybe I can use it as a bargaining chip.

"You can't stop me from posting it," she says. "If I can't post it right on Cody's channel, I'll just post it somewhere else. And if Cody starts avoiding me, well, that's fine; I have enough video already."

"I know." My heart sinks as I study the set of her jaw, the determination in her eyes. Anger seeps through the cracks she's trying to hold together, and it's an anger I know well. It's an anger I feel every time a guy says, "Do you even know how to play this game?" Every time there are more comments on my videos about my breasts than about how many enemies I managed to kill. Every time someone DMs me a dick pic.

I've learned to push my anger away, but I can't blame her for not doing the same. I just wish I wasn't going to be the one to suffer for it.

Right now, my success is tied to Code, and if I go through with my plan, that's going to be even more true. Though it's not only shippers who like my channel—or at least, it's not only the shipping they like. That girl at my signing came to my channel because she's a Code fan, but she stayed for me, because she likes my content. And that guy who asked a question at the panel yesterday said he's watched one of my CS: GO videos dozens of times. And he was wearing a Codemeister shirt, so he probably was a Code fan first, too.

If viewers come to my channel in buttloads, I need time for them to start liking me for me, and then maybe I can keep at least a single buttload of them. I already have a plan for bringing viewers to my channel; the time part is in Lainey's hands. If she brings down Code before his fans have time to become *my* fans, she'll be bringing me down, too.

I guess what I need most is time.

"Look, I'm fine with you posting the video, and I promise I won't tell Code about it, but I need something from you in return. I need you to wait."

She taps her fingers on the arm of the chair. "How long?"

"I don't know. A few months? No more than a year."

She grimaces. "I can't let Cody keep doing this for a whole year."

"Not a year, then. Just . . . six months. Please."

She counts the months on her fingers, and I count along with her. April, May, June, July, August. "September," she says aloud, then simply sits there, thinking.

I want to jump in, to give her a hundred thousand arguments, but instead I force myself to hold my breath. To give her time to consider. Time. Except then I can't stop myself. "Please. It'll really hurt my channel if you don't wait."

She looks up at me abruptly and narrows her eyes, like she's suddenly suspicious I've been reading her emails or stealing her snacks. "How would it hurt your channel?"

The answer seems obvious to me, but perhaps she hasn't been following all the CodeShadow drama. "Right now, I only have as many subs as I do because of Code. If he loses them, I probably lose them."

"Collateral damage," she mutters under her breath, and a fist of fear wraps itself around my heart. Has she decided to go ahead and drop that bomb on Cody's channel, blowing up my own as a result?

But then she says thoughtfully, "I guess it'd be nice to have moved away for school and not have to worry about Mom kicking me out of the house when it happens."

My baby skunk heart leaps. "Yes, exactly. And you want time to do a good job with whatever you're planning to post, right? Don't let your anger make you half-ass it." I could hurt myself with this argument, I realize, since if she does a good job screwing over Code, it could screw me over, too. But I have a VIP pass around my neck, a well-used Sharpie in my purse, and fans who took time to see me, to ask me questions. I have to have faith in my channel, in myself. I have to have faith that my fate won't be entirely dependent on what happens with Code.

Lainey looks over her shoulder, and it takes me a moment to follow the direction her head is pointing, to weave my gaze through cosplayers and LotSCON tote bags and the line that's moving into the auditorium, and finally figure out what she's looking at.

There's a giant poster of Code on the wall. There's one of Legs, too, and of Wolf, and of a team of LotSCON developers, but she's definitely looking at the one of Code.

"Those are all guys," I say.

"What?" She turns back to look at me.

"The posters on the wall. Code, Legs, Wolf, all those developers—they're all guys. Have you seen one of Gray anywhere? Or Aureylian? I haven't. I mean, Gray and Aurey aren't as famous, so that explains it, sort of. But . . ." I trail off, not saying the words I want to say. That I want to be on that wall. That I just want a chance to be on that wall. That I just want time.

She must hear the words I don't speak, because she says, "And you promise you won't tell Cody? You won't tell him for those entire six months?"

I look her right in the eye, trying to convey how seriously I mean it. "I promise."

"Okay," she says. "I'll wait." She stands to her feet, then points a finger at me. "But six months, no more."

I stand, too. "I can work with that."

And I can.

We head back to the little circle of our friends, where Legs is saying his goodbyes. He gives me a hug, even though he only met me yesterday, and my heart soars and dances on a million banana splits. Maybe because my favorite YouTuber just hugged me. Or maybe because Lainey said she'd wait, and now there's nothing standing in the way between me and Plan Make Shadow Famous. Well, my half of Plan Make Shadow Famous, at least.

After Legs and Lainey leave, Z and Gray and Marley and I spend the rest of the afternoon standing in line for the LotS expansion voting. Marley and I get into an in-depth discussion about our favorite teas (mine is this loose-leaf tea my mom gets called Vanilla Cupcake that tastes like birthday cake), and then we take turns picking out our favorite cosplay in the room, and it feels nice to not think about Code or YouTube or my impending decision for a while—you know, aside from when a guy comes up and asks for my autograph, but I'm not complaining about that.

He asks for Z's and Gray's autographs too, and then he asks Marley if she's a YouTuber, and we tell him that she is, but she apparently hates lying, because she admits that she isn't. But then he asks for her autograph anyway, which sets us all grinning. There are good people in this world; that is a fact.

When we finish voting—Wolf's right, the skyrift is the best

one—Gray and Marley wave their goodbyes and head off, and Z and I head back to the VIP room to meet Code and the rest of the guys for dinner.

"Good afternoon?" Z asks as we near the VIP room.

"The best," I reply. My shoulder knocks into his. With every step, my fists tighten with anxiety over what I'm planning to do.

Why the heck am I so nervous? I'm going after what I want.

Though I suppose that's exactly why I'm so nervous.

"You leave tomorrow?" Z asks.

"Yeah. I drove here, though, so I can leave whenever."

"Oh, good. So we can go for breakfast in the morning or something. With the guys, I mean. If they're up."

"With the guys," I echo. Maybe none of them will be up in time, and Z and I can go out just the two of us and talk about our separate channels. Maybe my plan will work, and we can talk about more than that.

When we get back to the VIP room, the rest of the guys are already there. We join Ben, Wolf, and Noog at the couches and chairs in the corner. Code wanders over from the coffee station.

Code is on one side of me, Z on the other.

"Can I talk to you?" I ask. I was planning to wait until dinner, but suddenly waiting seems foolish. The sooner the better.

"Sure," Z and Code both say at once.

"She means me," Code says, because he thinks the entire world revolves around him.

"Actually, I mean both of you. *All* of you." I wave my hand at the group of them. "I want to talk to all the Meisters. Aside from Oz, of course."

"Poor Oz," Z says. Then he hops over the back of the couch and settles onto it between Noog and Wolf. "Guys, Shadow wants to talk to us."

They all turn to look at me. Wolf, Z, Noog, Ben, and Code. I have the Meisters' attention.

My palms feel clammy as I lean my baby skunk self against a chair. I'm nervous, but I have to do it. I have to.

Unless you're Jennifer Aniston or William Shakespeare, fame isn't a boulder. It doesn't stay, gradually eroding from the wind and the rain, but still lasting for thousands of years.

Fame is a grain of sand on a beach, washed away with the coming tide. It's here and then gone, sometimes in months or years, sometimes in just minutes.

How long will it take for Codemeister fans to get tired of shipping us again and move on to someone else, some other ship? Six months? Two days?

And what will happen to my channel then? Will I lose my new subscribers? Stop gaining new ones? Have no hope of doing YouTube and streaming as a career? I'm not an idiot. There are thousands of teens like me, hoping to break into the industry. There are no guarantees, only hard work, luck, and big breaks.

I've had my big break already; now I have to decide what I'm going to do with it.

I force my hands to stay still and folded and calm. This is it.

"I have a proposal for you all," I say.

Noog whistles, and Z smacks him.

"Not that," I say, crinkling my nose. Ugh, definitely not that. "My proposal is . . . I think you should make me a Meister."

Code laughs, then cuts off when I don't.

"The Meisters are guys, Willow," Noog says. "Unless you've got a penis under that skirt—"

This time Wolf reaches an arm across and smacks him.

"Would you guys stop hitting me!" Noog practically shouts.

"Stop being a doofus and we will," Wolf says.

"Hear me out," I say, holding up a hand.

I look at them each in turn, setting out the arguments I've been thinking through all afternoon. For Wolf, who's big on facts and numbers, I set out the hundred thousand subscribers I had before and the hundreds of thousands I have now, and how my channel is in a rapid climb. I look at Noog as I emphasize that a higher proportion of my subscribers are women, so I'd be bringing more female viewers on board, which makes him whistle again, which makes Z look like he wants to hit him again, though he doesn't. I make it seem like as the sole Canadian, I'd be bringing in all sorts of Canadian viewers, too, though I don't know how much that's true.

I talk about the drama factor of it, and the excitement of bringing in the very first female Meister, and how epic and exciting it would be for viewers. "Look how obsessed viewers have become with shipping me and Code," I point out. "It makes good content."

"It's going to be awkward if you start dating Code," Wolf speaks up. "What if you guys break up? What happens then?" He's all business, weighing the pros and cons.

He's right. A breakup could be not just the end of a relationship, but the end of my career. They'd boot me back out of the group without a second thought.

It's not Code who I'd be interested in dating, though. Out of the corner of my eye, I can see Z, with his mess of hair and arms that seem too long for his body, his adorable grin, his ridiculous toaster fights and friendship with absolutely everyone. And I'll admit it: I want to kiss him. And I'm pretty sure he wants to kiss me, too.

Which means that I should risk it, right? You're supposed to risk everything for love, and trust that it will all work out.

But I don't believe in soul mates. I don't believe love is the only force in the world that makes life feel like a delicious banana split. There will be other people I want to kiss. There will be other chances.

Joining Team Meister, on the other hand, is a genuine once-in-a-lifetime chance. It's the opportunity that I've been dreaming of, that I've been working so hard toward.

"Let me make this clear," I say, raising my hand for emphasis. "I will not be dating any of you. Not Code, not anyone, not even Ben." Everyone laughs at that, because he's so old that absolutely no one pictures us together. "People can ship any of us they want, and you don't need to burst their bubble by telling them this, but so we're all on the same page, I will not be dating any of you under any circumstances." I meet Z's eyes for only a moment, and something passes between us—regret? Sadness? I let the feeling sit in my stomach only briefly before pushing past it. I have my whole life to fall in love; I only have right now to turn this little bit of fame into a whole lot more. "So? Am I in?"

"We'll have to vote on it," Code says. "We can let you know."

I nod. I expected that. It's why I asked Lainey for six months instead of only a couple. Even if it takes them a while to decide, I'll still have time to make my hordes of new Team Meister viewers fall enough in love with my channel that they'll stick around even if the most famous Meister goes down in flames.

Will the other Meisters support him? Disown him? If I've made enough of a name for myself by then, not dependent on shippers or anything else, it won't matter. I'll be able to make my own choices. You might say I'm foolish for joining them when I know what's coming, but given the choice between fame with complications or no fame at all, I choose the former.

They've all grown quiet as they consider my words or maybe just think about what they want for supper, but then Z almost shouts, "I vote yes!" He grins at me, and it's the type of grin that lifelong friendships are built on. I grin back.

Wolf nods. "Me too."

My heart skips in my chest. I had thought the worst-case scenario would be a month, the best maybe tonight after dinner. I didn't expect it to happen right here, right now.

"Don't you want to discuss it?" Ben asks. "Think it through?"

Wolf shakes his head. "I have thought it through. I think it'd be good for the brand. Not my problem if my brain works faster than yours, dude."

Ben laughs. "Well, if this guy's on board, that's good enough for me. He's the brains of this operation."

"I thought I was the brains of this operation," Code says, which makes everyone laugh, though judging by the delay before Code joins in the laughter, I don't think he meant it as a joke. Code turns to Noog. "What about you, man?"

"Dude, girls!" Noog says.

"That's a yes, right?" Wolf asks.

"Hell yeah it is."

"All right then," says Code.

Wolf stands. "The people have spoken. Let's go out for dinner and celebrate our new member." Which I guess means either Wolf is taking Code's "all right then" as a yes or Code has no voice here.

"Oz'll need to vote, too," Code says as he stands, but we all know it's a formality. I'm in. I'm part of Team Meister.

Holy bananas.

Holy banana bread with chocolate chips.

Holy banana Nutella smoothie with whipped cream on top.

I did it.

As we walk to a restaurant, Wolf walks on one side of me, rambling about how we shouldn't go public with it yet, because we can do some kind of video series ramping up to it, and as Z chimes in with ideas on the other side of me, his shoulder bumps mine, and there's the tiniest flash of melancholy in my stomach.

Just as quickly, it's gone, replaced by pure joy. I am working my butt off to become someone, to make a name for myself, and it's actually happening.

I bump Z's shoulder right back.

Then I turn to face them all, walking backward. "One more thing," I announce. "Just so we're clear, my name's going to be Shadowmeister, not Willowmeister."

I don't wait to see if there's agreement, because agreement's not required. I walk to the restaurant with my baby skunk tail high and proud. This is my life, and I'm making it happen.

EPILOGUE

Lainey

I POST THE VIDEO TO CODY'S CHANNEL AT 7:10 A.M. ON THE SECOND WEDNES-day of September. Cody normally sleeps until noon, but someone must call him and tell him, because by 8:43 a.m., the video is down. It's too late, though; the world has seen it, has downloaded it, has sent it flying around the internet.

I expect an immediate swell of outrage, a plunge in subscribers, the beginning of Cody's hard lesson learned, but it's more complicated than that.

Cody loses a crap-ton of subscribers, but he gains subscribers, too—people who've never met him, never even watched his channel before, but who come out of the woodwork to defend him because they're sick of "these witch hunts."

And if Cody learns something from it, I can't tell from the insults he screams at me over the phone. I stop taking his calls, and Mom's too, though I don't stop hoping that someday, when the dust clears and the immediacy of his hurt has passed, I'll see a change in him. The good kind.

Legs never comments publicly on it all, but three days after the video goes live, he posts a video of his own, highlighting his top ten female and POC gamers worth watching. It's so very Legsian, his way of lifting up where others tear down, and I love him for it—even as I know that if I had to do it all over again, I would.

Noog and Ben can't stop themselves from jumping to Cody's defense, and they face mini firestorms of their own—Noog more than Ben, since every word he says only digs himself deeper into a hole.

Wolf, Z, and Oz are all silent at first, but then they start taking a page out of Legs's book and, when forced to comment on Cody's misogynistic comments, simply remind people to lift up female gamers "like our own Shadowmeister."

When I ask Shadow if she engineered that bit of marketing brilliance, she shrugs and smiles, and I'm not sure how I feel about that, but we still talk sometimes.

Shadow, for her part, makes a single comment in a single video about how she's used to sexist comments in the gaming world, but that she chooses to focus instead on the people who support her and love her and who have, in her words, "big and beautiful hearts." That same day, she posts a video of herself, Z, Wolf, Ben, and Oz doing a rift run together and taking out a shadowdragon in impressively quick time, and it all goes too fast for me to really know what's going on, but Legs tells me that Shadow's the one calling the shots, the general over her cheering, happy troop. And the meaning seems clear to me and to anyone else who's reading between the lines.

They don't kick Cody out of the Meisters. When I ask Z why, he simply says, "It's complicated," and as I read another comment featuring one of Cody's subscribers blindly defending him, I guess I have to admit that's true.

I hope it's worth it anyways. I hope it makes a difference.

One evening in October, when the leaves are vivid yellows and oranges, I'm hanging out at Legs's place, studying for a history exam at one end of his kitchen table while he answers fan mail at the other.

For a break, I decide to watch a video Legs sent me earlier, and when I click on it, there's SamTheBrave's face—a surprise since, according to Legs, he never shows his face in videos or on streams. Even the Cody video didn't feature his face, because in the end, despite Legs's arguments, I couldn't bring myself to put his clip in. Six months of working on the video gave me more than enough clips, and even though Legs has posted about

SamTheBrave's videos multiple times, the kid still only has ten thousand subscribers—which he seems thrilled about, but which still makes him a complete nobody compared to Cody. And if the clip had caused him more harm than good, I'd never have forgiven myself.

I wish I could tell Janessa about this bit of good that came from my messages to her, but she never responded to my final apology, so I've just left her alone, because that's all I can think to do.

I press Play now on Sam's video, and instead of a gaming video, it's a heart-wrenchingly honest vlog about his skin-picking disorder and the ways it does and doesn't control his life, and even though he's only a couple of years younger than me, I want to lift him up like a child and hug him to my heart and never let him go. There's so much in the video that I didn't know—I barely even knew it was a mental disorder; I'm going to have to watch it a few times and maybe do some research to inform myself better.

When the video finishes, I scroll through its comments, and I wish I could say that they're a nonstop stream of love, without a single "your ugly" or "that's grooooooosssssssss," but I can't. What I can say is that for every "your ugly"—and there aren't many—there are ten people telling the commenter they're out of line—sometimes through friendly reminder, sometimes through angry, curse-filled threats.

I wonder if any of those comments, whether aggressive or kind, will change even one person.

I wonder if my video of Cody will change even one person. I hope so.

Across the room, Legs is scrawling "Be Awesome" across a postcard to mail to a fan.

"Good video of Sam's," I say to him. "I hope he feels encouraged by the response and doesn't let the haters get him down."

He nods and reaches for another postcard. "I hope the video reaches people who need to see it."

"That too. You going to post about it?"

"I already did."

I laugh. "Of course you did." I start to push the laptop away, reaching for my history texts again, ready to memorize the facts and dates of the world's biggest accomplishments—and its biggest mistakes. But then another video catches my eye. I click on it, and my big brother's face appears on my screen.

"So, I got this email out of the blue," Cody tells his viewers. "It was responding to my apparent inquiry about a dog at the pound. I almost tossed it into my junk mail, but then a picture caught my eye, and Codesters, just look at this beauty." He leans down toward his offscreen feet, then lifts a fluffy brown bundle into his lap. "Guys, meet Lola."

The four-year-old schnoodle in his lap looks up and licks his chin, and Cody laughs and wraps his arms around her. "As most of you know, it's been a rough month. But Miss Lola here, she makes life so much better. So thank you. Whichever of you Codesters sent that first email, I'm forever in your debt."

I stop the video and swallow back the lump in my throat. Stare at my brother's happy face looking back at me.

"Do you think he knows it was you?" Legs asks from across the room.

I think of my last phone call with Cody, where he threw every swear word in existence at me before I finally gave up and hung up on him. "No," I say. "He probably thinks I only want him to suffer. But I don't want him to be miserable. I only want him to learn something." I only want him to be better.

Legs uncaps his Sharpie and starts writing "Be Awesome" for the ten thousandth time. "We're changing this broken world one day at a time," he says.

And I nod. Because at the very least, no one can ever say we didn't try.

AUTHOR'S NOTE

IN 2013, WHEN I LEARNED THAT SKIN-PICKING DISORDER HAD BEEN CLASSI-
fied as its own mental disorder related to OCD, I wept. I had
spent over a decade overwhelmingly frustrated by the "bad habit"
that I couldn't seem to quit. I had literally hit myself, yelled at
myself, and tried dozens of habit-breaking strategies. All I had
to show for it were the hundreds of scars that litter my shoulders
and back.

Now, with the help of cognitive behavioral therapy, fidget
toys, and more knowledge, things are better. And by better, I
don't mean cured. I still pick at my skin, but less often, and I don't
feel as out of control. And more important, I'm kinder to myself
now, and more understanding.

Skin-picking disorder is not well known as a disorder. If in reading this book you've realized that it's something you might do or struggle with, I recommend that you check out bfrb.org, which is the website for the TLC Foundation for Body-Focused Repetitive Behaviors and a tremendous resource for skin pickers, hair pullers, and their families. They have information, webinars, and a community of people like us.

And finally: please be kind to yourself. And know that you're not alone.

ACKNOWLEDGMENTS

I WROTE AND REVISED THIS BOOK DURING ONE OF THE HARDEST YEARS OF MY life. That makes these acknowledgments difficult to write—not because of the hardship, but because I feel such an overwhelming outpouring of gratitude toward those who were there for me and my husband that words feel so inadequate. Of course, I could just focus these acknowledgments on those who did concrete work on this book, but let's be real: I'd never have finished this book without the support of those in my day-to-day life.

There is a reason I write books about friendship and family. Because they are such powerful forces that I feel lucky to have in my life. Because friends and family brought and ordered us meals, sat with me and rubbed my back while I cried, went to the hospital, cleaned the house, listened when I needed to talk, talked when

I needed to listen, and sent emails and notes and love.

And so I'm beyond grateful to Mom, Dad, Will and Anyu, and Em and Dan and my darling Dewi and Avery. I'm grateful to the Moses family and the Slofstra family. To Lance Priemaza, Laura Geddes, Erin Dawson, and Caitie Flum. To Craig, Lee, Matthieu, Josh, Devin and Alana and Oakley, Ben and Heather, Pat and Daniela, Lillian and Paul, Chris, Ivan, Brad, Angus, Alex, Sean, Colin, Stephen, Kevin and Cara, Seyi and Bukola, Chuba and Joy, Murray and Pat, everyone at McCuaig, and the rest of our friends and family.

I'm grateful for and so lucky to have my writer family, which helps get me through each day: Katelyn, Kristine (K), Marley, Rachel, Jo, Chelsea, Josh, Greg, Leann, Morgan, Tasha, Katie, Jess, Phillip, and Annie.

I'm thankful for the support and friendship of other authors, especially Emily Bain Murphy, Jilly Gagnon, Bree Barton, Isabel Van Wyk, Kayla Olson, Tanaz Bhathena, Carlie Sorosiak, Lianne Oelke, Faith Boughan, Gareth Wronski, Kristen Ciccarelli, Kate Watson, Stephanie Elliot, Keira Drake, Kristen Orlando, Heather Kaczynski, Amy Giles, and so many others.

And I'm beyond thankful to have Lorne Priemaza beside me as a supportive and loving partner and husband through it all.

And then, of course, there are those who've worked on this book specifically.

Thank you to Morgan Messing, who invented the Legends of the Stone logo and made it come alive for me. I am so grateful to all my early readers. To Mom, whose excitement to read always makes me more excited to write. To Katelyn Larson, whose name might have been cut from a draft of this book, but whose hand exists in every scene, especially the nerdiest ones. To Cale Dietrich, who reminded me that characters being siblings makes everything more complicated, especially revenge. To Greg Andree and Josh Hlibichuk, who helped me figure out the right number of times for Sam to refer to his own dick. To Marley Teter, who hates reading about dicks but who helped me turn Cody into more of one. To Emily Bain Murphy, who gave Cody a dog and gives me so much more. And to Chelsea Sedoti, whose kind feedback was a light whenever I felt the darkness of doubt.

I'm thankful for the valuable insight of my editor, Stephanie Stein, who always gives me the time I need to get things done. And for the rest of the awesome team at HarperTeen, including editorial assistant Louisa Currigan; Michelle Taormina in design; Renée Cafiero and Megan Gendell in copy editing, who always help save me from making a fool of myself; Bess Braswell and Shannon Cox in marketing; Kadeen Griffiths in publicity; and Erin Wallace and Kristen Eckhardt in production. I feel very lucky to be a Canadian and to have the support of Maeve O'Regan and Ashley Posluns at HarperCollins Canada, whose promotion and help I'm eternally grateful for.

I'm grateful to my stellar agent, Lauren Abramo, who I compulsively brag about to everyone, because she's just that great. And to the rest of the team at Dystel, Goderich and Bourret, especially including Mike Hoogland, Kemi Faderin, and Sharon Pelletier.

And of course, I'm so unbelievably grateful to readers, who bring so much light to my life with their emails and reviews and tweets and bookstagrams and love. You, dear reader, are the very best. Thank you!